图书在版编目（CIP）数据

绿野仙踪：中英对照全译本 / （美）鲍姆（Baum, L. F.）著；盛世教育西方名著翻译委员会译.—上海：上海世界图书出版公司，2010.4

ISBN 978-7-5100-1862-6

Ⅰ. 绿… Ⅱ. ①鲍… ②盛… Ⅲ.①英语－汉语－对照读物 ②童话－美国－近代 Ⅳ.H319.4：I

中国版本图书馆 CIP 数据核字（2010）第 034061 号

绿野仙踪

[美]莱曼·弗兰克·鲍姆 著

盛世教育西方名著翻译委员会 译

上海世界图书出版公司 出版发行

上海市广中路 88 号

邮政编码 200083

北京中科印刷有限公司印刷

如发现印刷质量问题，请与印刷厂联系

（质检科电话：010-84897777）

各地新华书店经销

开本：787×1092　1/32　印张：10.25　字数：266 000

2010 年 4 月第 1 版　2010 年 4 月第 1 次印刷

ISBN 978-7-5100-1862-6/H·977

定价：15.80 元

http://www.wpcsh.com.cn

http://www.wpcsh.com

THE
WONDERFUL WIZARD OF OZ

绿野仙踪

（美）莱曼·弗兰克·鲍姆
Layman Frank Baum

盛世教育西方名著翻译委员会
主　　任：黎小说　高民芳　杜　毅
本册委员：章　杰　李红育　李　梨

世界图书出版公司
上海·西安·北京·广州

前　言

通过阅读文学名著学语言，是掌握外语的绝佳方法。既可接触原汁原味的外语，又能享受文学之美，一举两得，何乐不为？

对于喜欢阅读名著的读者，这是一个最好的时代，因为有成千上万的书可以选择；这又是一个不好的时代，因为在浩繁的卷帙中，很难找到适合自己的好书。

然而，你手中的这套丛书，值得你来信赖。

这套精选的中英对照名著全译丛书，未改编改写、未删节削减，书中配有精美手绘插图，图文并茂，值得珍藏。

要学语言、读好书，当读名著原文。如习武者切磋交流，同高手过招能渐明其间奥妙，若一味在低端徘徊，终难登堂入室。积年流传的名著，就是书中"高手"。然而这个"高手"，却有真假之分。初读书时，常遇到一些挂了名著名家之名改写改编的版本，虽有助于了解基本情节，然而所得只是皮毛，你何曾真的就读过了那名著呢？一边是窖藏了50年的女儿红，一边是贴了女儿红标签的薄酒，那滋味，怎能一样？"朝闻道，夕死可矣。"人生短如朝露，当努力追求真正的美。

本套丛书的外文版本，是根据原版书精心挑选而来；对应的中文译文以直译为主，以方便对照学习，译文经反复推敲，对忠实理解原著极有助益。

读过本套丛书的原文全译，相信你会得书之真意、语言之精髓。

送君"开卷有益"之书，愿成文采斐然之人。

CONTENTS
目 录

I

The Wonderful Wizard of Oz

绿野仙踪

1. The Cyclone

Dorothy lived in the midst of the great Kansas prairies, with Uncle Henry, who was a farmer, and Aunt Em, who was the farmer's wife. Their house was small, for the lumber to build it had to be carried by wagon many miles. There were four walls, a floor and a roof, which made one room; and this room contained a rusty-looking cooking stove, a cupboard for the dishes, a table, three or four chairs, and the beds. Uncle Henry and Aunt Em had a big bed in one corner, and Dorothy a little bed in another corner. There was no upstairs at all, and no cellar – except a small hole dug in the ground, called a cyclone cellar, where the family could go in case one of those great whirlwinds arose, mighty enough to crush any building in its path. It was reached by a trap door in the middle of the floor, from which a ladder led down into the small, dark hole.

When Dorothy stood in the doorway and looked around, she could see nothing but the great gray prairie on every side. Not a tree nor a house broke the broad sweep of flat country that reached to the edge of the sky in all directions. The sun had baked the plowed land into a gray mass, with little cracks running through it. Even the grass was not green, for the sun had burned the tops of the long blades until they were the same gray color to be seen everywhere. Once the house had been painted, but the sun blistered the paint and the rains washed it away, and now the house was as dull and gray as everything else.

一.飓风来了

多萝茜由亨利叔叔和他的妻子艾姆婶婶带着住在广阔的堪萨斯草原中部。亨利叔叔是个农民,他用手推车从好几英里以外的地方运来木材建房子,所以房子很小,可算是家徒四壁。这间小屋子里只有一个生锈的灶头,一个橱柜,一张桌子,三四把椅子和散布在不同角落的大小两张床:一张是亨利叔叔和艾姆婶婶的,一张是多萝茜的。屋子没有阁楼,但在地板中央有一个算不上地下室的小洞,这洞从地底挖掘出来,被叫做"避风窖"。一旦横扫一切的大飓风刮来,全家人都可以顺着一架梯子躲进去。

多萝茜站在门口四处眺望,极目之处只有灰色的大草原,其他的什么也看不到。没有一棵树,也没有一座房子阻碍这乡野的平坦,它向各处延伸到天边。太阳炙烤着耕犁过的土地,将它变成灰色的一片,一条条裂缝蜿蜒在上面。草也不是绿色的了,太阳将它们的长叶炙烤成与土地一样的颜色。即使那曾经粉刷过的房子也在日晒雨淋之下消退了它的颜色,如今油漆已经剥离,房子也如它周围一切那般只是暗淡的灰色。

艾姆婶婶初来这里住下的时候,还是个年轻漂亮的少妇,而如今饱经风吹日晒的她已是另一番模样。曾经闪烁在眼里的光芒不见了,留下的只是沉重的灰色;面颊和嘴唇的粉红也不在了,留下的也是灰色。她面容憔悴,形容枯槁,笑容也不再浮现在脸

3

1. The Cyclone

When Aunt Em came there to live she was a young, pretty wife. The sun and wind had changed her, too. They had taken the sparkle from her eyes and left them a sober gray; they had taken the red from her cheeks and lips, and they were gray also. She was thin and gaunt, and never smiled now. When Dorothy, who was an orphan, first came to her, Aunt Em had been so startled by the child's laughter that she would scream and press her hand upon her heart whenever Dorothy's merry voice reached her ears; and she still looked at the little girl with wonder that she could find anything to laugh at.

Uncle Henry never laughed. He worked hard from morning till night and did not know what joy was. He was gray also, from his long beard to his rough boots, and he looked stern and solemn, and rarely spoke.

It was Toto that made Dorothy laugh, and saved her from growing as gray as her other surroundings. Toto was not gray; he was a little black dog, with long silky hair and small black eyes that twinkled merrily on either side of his funny, wee nose. Toto played all day long, and Dorothy played with him, and loved him dearly.

Today, however, they were not playing. Uncle Henry sat upon the doorstep and looked anxiously at the sky, which was even grayer than usual. Dorothy stood in the door with Toto in her arms, and looked at the sky too. Aunt Em was washing the dishes.

From the far north they heard a low wail of the wind, and Uncle Henry and Dorothy could see where the long grass bowed in waves before the coming storm. There now came a sharp whistling in the air

上。当多萝茜这个孤儿第一次来到艾姆婶婶身边时，这小女孩的笑声传到她耳朵里，便着实吓了她一跳，她甚至尖叫一声将手按在自己的胸口。她看着这小女孩，很惊讶到底有什么事物可以让多萝茜觉得快乐和好笑的。

亨利叔叔也从来没有开怀大笑过。他只顾起早贪黑地辛勤劳作，仿佛根本不知道还有快乐这回事。他也是灰色的，有灰色的胡须和灰色而粗糙的长靴，他看起来庄严肃穆，极少言谈。

带给多萝茜欢笑的是托托，也正是托托，让多萝茜没有成长为如她周围一切事物那般灰色。托托不是灰色的，它是一只小黑狗，有着如丝般柔滑的长毛，一双黑色的小眼睛在它那滑稽有趣的小鼻子之间快乐地眨着。托托整天都在玩，多萝茜陪着它一起玩，她可是非常喜欢它！

然而，今天她们却没有玩。亨利叔叔坐在门阶上，焦虑不安地看着仿佛比平日更加灰色的天空。多萝茜抱着托托站在门口，也看着那天空。而艾姆婶婶正在洗碗。

从遥远的北方传来风的哀号，亨利叔叔和多萝茜看到在野草如波浪般起伏的地方风暴正在来临。而南方的天空中，则传来了一阵急剧的呼啸声。一转眼，只见在那里的草也掀起了波浪，不断前涌。

亨利叔叔突然站了起来。

"艾姆，飓风来了！"他向他妻子喊道，"我去牛马圈看看。"

from the south, and as they turned their eyes that way they saw ripples in the grass coming from that direction also.

Suddenly Uncle Henry stood up.

"There's a cyclone coming, Em," he called to his wife. "I'll go look after the stock." Then he ran toward the sheds where the cows and horses were kept.

Aunt Em dropped her work and came to the door. One glance told her of the danger close at hand.

"Quick, Dorothy!" she screamed. "Run for the cellar!"

Toto jumped out of Dorothy's arms and hid under the bed, and the girl started to get him. Aunt Em, badly frightened, threw open the trap door in the floor and climbed down the ladder into the small, dark hole. Dorothy caught Toto at last and started to follow her aunt. When she was halfway across the room there came a great shriek from the wind, and the house shook so hard that she lost her footing and sat down suddenly upon the floor.

A strange thing then happened.

The house whirled around two or three times and rose slowly through the air. Dorothy felt as if she were going up in a balloon.

The north and south winds met where the house stood, and made it the exact center of the cyclone. In the middle of a cyclone the air is generally still, but the great pressure of the wind on every side of the house raised it up higher and higher, until it was at the very top of the cyclone; and there it remained and was carried miles and miles away as easily as you could carry a feather.

于是他跑到那些关着牛和马的小圈棚里。

艾姆婶婶放下手头的活计，跑到门口，不过是瞥了一眼，她即知危险临近了。

"多萝茜，快！"她尖叫道，"快到地窖去！"

托托从多萝茜的怀里一跃而出，躲到了床底下，这小女孩儿跑去要抓住它。

艾姆婶婶害怕极了，打开地窖的门，顺着梯子爬下去，躲到那狭小又黑暗的地洞里。

多萝茜终于抓住了托托，正要跟着她的婶婶躲到地窖去，才跑到屋子中间，房子便伴随着一阵尖锐的呼啸声剧烈地晃动起来，多萝茜难以站稳，一下子坐在了地板上。

这时，一件奇异的事情发生了！

屋子旋转了两三圈，便穿透空气慢慢升上天空，多萝茜感觉自己如同坐在氢气球上。

南北方的风暴在房子所在的地方会合，让这里成为飓风的中心。飓风的中心是平静的，但屋子四周的强大气压使它缓缓地上升，直到飓风的顶部，在那里先停下来又被飓风带往几英里以外，如同拿起一根羽毛一般轻而易举。

这时，天沉了下来，多萝茜四周的风怒吼着，她发现自己仿佛在乘风飞行，如此轻飘。在旋转了几圈之后，屋子严重倾斜，她感觉自己仿佛被放置在摇篮里一样，被温柔地摇动着。

1. The Cyclone

It was very dark, and the wind howled horribly around her, but Dorothy found she was riding quite easily. After the first few whirls around, and one other time when the house tipped badly, she felt as if she were being rocked gently, like a baby in a cradle.

Toto did not like it. He ran about the room, now here, now there, barking loudly; but Dorothy sat quite still on the floor and waited to see what would happen.

Once Toto got too near the open trap door, and fell in; and at first the little girl thought she had lost him. But soon she saw one of his ears sticking up through the hole, for the strong pressure of the air was keeping him up so that he could not fall. She crept to the hole, caught Toto by the ear, and dragged him into the room again, afterward closing the trap door so that no more accidents could happen.

Hour after hour passed away, and slowly Dorothy got over her fright; but she felt quite lonely, and the wind shrieked so loudly all about her that she nearly became deaf. At first she had wondered if she would be dashed to pieces when the house fell again; but as the hours passed and nothing terrible happened, she stopped worrying and resolved to wait calmly and see what the future would bring. At last she crawled over the swaying floor to her bed, and lay down upon it; and Toto followed and lay down beside her.

In spite of the swaying of the house and the wailing of the wind, Dorothy soon closed her eyes and fell fast asleep.

托托不喜欢那样，它狂吠着在屋子里乱窜，一会儿到这儿，一会儿到那儿；但多萝茜只是静静地坐在地板上，等待着即将发生的一切。

有一次，托托离地窖的门太近而掉了进去，起初多萝茜还以为它不见了，但很快，她便看到了托托的一只耳朵从地窖里伸出来，因为巨大的气压使它难以落进去。她爬到地窖口，抓住托托的耳朵，又把它拉进屋子里来，然后关上地窖的活动门，免得再出什么事故。

时间慢慢地过去了，多萝茜渐渐不再害怕，但她又觉得很寂寞，风的呼啸声震耳欲聋。起初她还担心如果房子倒塌下来，她会不会被压碎了，不过几个小时都过去了，还没有什么可怕的事情发生，于是她不再有什么担忧，开始静下心来等待将要发生的事情。最后，她从摇摇晃晃的地板上爬到床上，托托跟着过去，躺在她旁边。

不管房子怎样摇晃个不停，也不管风发出怎样哀泣的声音，多萝茜闭上眼睛，很快进入了梦乡。

2. The Council with the Munchkins

She was awakened by a shock, so sudden and severe that if Dorothy had not been lying on the soft bed she might have been hurt. As it was, the jar made her catch her breath and wonder what had happened; and Toto put his cold little nose into her face and whined dismally. Dorothy sat up and noticed that the house was not moving; nor was it dark, for the bright sunshine came in at the window, flooding the little room. She sprang from her bed and with Toto at her heels ran and opened the door.

The little girl gave a cry of amazement and looked about her, her eyes growing bigger and bigger at the wonderful sights she saw.

The cyclone had set the house down very gently – for a cyclone – in the midst of a country of marvelous beauty. There were lovely patches of greensward all about, with stately trees bearing rich and luscious fruits. Banks of gorgeous flowers were on every hand, and birds with rare and brilliant plumage sang and fluttered in the trees and bushes. A little way off was a small brook, rushing and sparkling along between green banks, and murmuring in a voice very grateful to a little girl who had lived so long on the dry, gray prairies.

While she stood looking eagerly at the strange and beautiful sights, she noticed coming towards her a group of the queerest people she

二．偶遇芒奇金人

一个突如其来的剧烈震动惊醒了多萝茜，如果不是躺在柔软的床上，她或许就受伤了。事实上，这个震动让她屏住了呼吸，心里纳闷着究竟发生了什么事情。托托用它那冰冷的小鼻子，触碰着她的脸颊，低沉地哀号着。多萝茜坐了起来，发现房子已经不再移动了，天色也不再昏暗，因为明亮的阳光透过窗户照了进来，洒满了整间屋子。她从床上跳了下来，打开了门，托托则跟在她的后面。

小女孩看着自己的周围，发出了一声惊讶的叫声，面对着眼前奇妙的景色，她的那双眼睛睁得越来越大。

一阵龙卷风把房子轻轻地——因为一阵龙卷风——吹到了这片令人不可思议的美景之中。那里到处都点缀着可爱的草地，还有雄伟的大树，上面结满了甘甜的果实。每一边的斜坡上都长满了耀眼夺目的花朵，鸟儿们披着非常灿烂美丽的羽毛，吟唱着歌曲，在树林里、灌木丛中鼓翼飞舞。不远处有一条小溪，沿着绿色的堤岸，湍急地流动着，闪闪发亮地冒着泡，发出潺潺的流水声，让这个生活在干燥、灰暗的草原上太久太久的小女孩欢快不已。

正当她站在那里，热切地望着这片陌生而美丽的景色时，她发现有一群她生平见过的最最古怪的人正朝她走来。他们不像她

11

had ever seen. They were not as big as the grown folk she had always been used to; but neither were they very small. In fact, they seemed about as tall as Dorothy, who was a well-grown child for her age, although they were, so far as looks go, many years older.

Three were men and one a woman, and all were oddly dressed. They wore round hats that rose to a small point a foot above their heads, with little bells around the brims that tinkled sweetly as they moved. The hats of the men were blue; the little woman's hat was white, and she wore a white gown that hung in pleats from her shoulders. Over it were sprinkled little stars that glistened in the sun like diamonds. The men were dressed in blue, of the same shade as their hats, and wore well-polished boots with a deep roll of blue at the tops. The men, Dorothy thought, were about as old as Uncle Henry, for two of them had beards. But the little woman was doubtless much older. Her face was covered with wrinkles, her hair was nearly white, and she walked rather stiffly.

When these people drew near the house where Dorothy was standing in the doorway, they paused and whispered among themselves, as if afraid to come farther. But the little old woman walked up to Dorothy, made a low bow and said, in a sweet voice:

"You are welcome, most noble Sorceress, to the land of the Munchkins. We are so grateful to you for having killed the Wicked Witch of the East, and for setting our people free from bondage."

过去见惯了的大人那么高大，但是也不算矮小。事实上，他们看起来跟多萝茜一样高（在同龄人中，多萝茜算是比较高挑的），尽管从外表上看来，他们要比多萝茜大好几岁。

他们总共3男1女，都穿着稀奇古怪的衣服。他们的头上都戴着圆形的帽子，顶端变成了一个小尖角，帽檐上系着小铃铛，在他们走动时，会发出甜美动听的叮当声。3个男人的帽子是蓝色的，小个子女人的帽子是白色的，身上穿着一件白袍，褶边从肩上垂下来，上面点缀着一颗颗小星星，在阳光下就像钻石一样闪闪发亮。3个男人穿着蓝色的衣裳，和他们戴的帽子颜色一样，脚上穿着擦得锃亮的靴子，靴子的口上有一圈深蓝色。多萝茜心想，这些男人跟亨利叔叔差不多年纪，因为其中两个留着胡子。不过那个小个子女人明显更老一些：她的脸上长满了皱纹，头发几乎全白，走路的姿态也有几分僵硬。

多萝茜站在门口，当这几个人靠近这所房子的时候，他们停了下来，相互耳语着，好像不敢再靠近一步。不过那个小个子女人走到了多萝茜面前，深深地鞠了个躬，亲切和蔼地说道：

"最最高贵的女魔法师，欢迎您来到芒奇金国。非常感谢您杀死了东方的邪恶女巫，把我们从奴役之中解放了出来。"

多萝茜惊讶地听她说着这番话。为什么这个小个子女人要称呼她为"女魔法师"，而且还说她杀死了东方的邪恶女巫？多萝茜是个天真无邪而又善良的小女孩，一阵龙卷风把她带到了远离

2. The Council with the Munchkins

Dorothy listened to this speech with wonder. What could the little woman possibly mean by calling her a sorceress, and saying she had killed the Wicked Witch of the East? Dorothy was an innocent, harmless little girl, who had been carried by a cyclone many miles from home; and she had never killed anything in all her life.

But the little woman evidently expected her to answer; so Dorothy said, with hesitation, "You are very kind, but there must be some mistake. I have not killed anything."

"Your house did, anyway," replied the little old woman, with a laugh, "and that is the same thing. See!" she continued, pointing to the corner of the house. "There are her two toes, still sticking out from under a block of wood."

Dorothy looked, and gave a little cry of fright. There, indeed, just under the corner of the great beam the house rested on, two feet were sticking out, shod in silver shoes with pointed toes.

"Oh, dear! Oh, dear!" cried Dorothy, clasping her hands together in dismay. "The house must have fallen on her. Whatever shall we do?"

"There is nothing to be done," said the little woman calmly.

"But who was she?" asked Dorothy.

"She was the Wicked Witch of the East, as I said," answered the little woman. "She has held all the Munchkins in bondage for many years, making them slave for her night and day. Now they are all set free, and are grateful to you for the favor."

"Who are the Munchkins?" inquired Dorothy.

故乡好几里路之外的地方，她这一生中从来都没有杀过任何人。

但是那个小个子女人显然在热切地等待着她回话，因此多萝茜支支吾吾地说道："谢谢你，不过肯定有什么地方搞错了，我并没有杀过什么人啊。"

"但是，你的屋子杀了人，"那个小个子女人笑着回答她说，"你看！结果都是一样的。"她指了指房子的一个角落，接着说道，"她那两个脚尖还从那块木板底下伸出来了呢。"

多萝茜看了一眼，惊慌失措地轻轻叫了一声。在那房子底下的大横梁下面果真压着两只脚，伸直了的脚尖上穿着一双银鞋。

"哦，天哪！天哪！"多萝茜叫道，慌张地紧握着双手，"肯定是房子压到她了。我们该怎么办？"

"什么都不用做。"小个子女人平静地说道。

"可她是谁呢？"多萝茜问道。

"她就是我说的东方的邪恶女巫。"小个子女人回答道，"多少年来，她一直都奴役着芒奇金人，驱使他们夜以继日地为她工作。如今，他们全都自由了，并且要感谢您的救命之恩。"

"芒奇金人是谁？"多萝茜问。

"他们是居住在这片被邪恶女巫统治着的东方领土中的百姓。"

"那你是芒奇金人吗？"多萝茜问道。

"不，但是我是他们的朋友，尽管我住在北方。芒奇金人看

15

2. The Council with the Munchkins

"They are the people who live in this land of the East where the Wicked Witch ruled."

"Are you a Munchkin?" asked Dorothy.

"No, but I am their friend, although I live in the land of the North. When they saw the Witch of the East was dead the Munchkins sent a swift messenger to me, and I came at once. I am the Witch of the North."

"Oh, gracious!" cried Dorothy. "Are you a real witch?"

"Yes, indeed," answered the little woman. "But I am a good witch, and the people love me. I am not as powerful as the Wicked Witch was who ruled here, or I should have set the people free myself."

"But I thought all witches were wicked," said the girl, who was half frightened at facing a real witch.

"Oh, no, that is a great mistake. There were only four witches in all the Land of Oz, and two of them, those who live in the North and the South, are good witches. I know this is true, for I am one of them myself, and cannot be mistaken. Those who dwelt in the East and the West were, indeed, wicked witches; but now that you have killed one of them, there is but one Wicked Witch in all the Land of Oz – the one who lives in the West."

"But," said Dorothy, after a moment's thought, "Aunt Em has told me that the witches were all dead – years and years ago."

"Who is Aunt Em?" inquired the little old woman.

"She is my aunt who lives in Kansas, where I came from."

见东方女巫死了之后，他们就迅速地给我报了信，我立刻赶到了这里。我是北方女巫。"

"哦，天哪！"多萝茜叫道，"你真的是女巫吗？"

"是啊，是真的，"小个子女人回答说，"但我是个善良的女巫，人们都喜欢我，我不像统治这里的邪恶女巫那么强势，要不然，我早就让这里的人们重获自由了。"

"可是，我原本以为所有的女巫都是恶毒的。"小女孩说道，面对这样一个真正的女巫，她不免有些害怕。

"哦，不，这么认为可就大错特错了，整个奥兹国里只有 4个女巫。其中两个分别住在北方和南方，她们都是善良的女巫。我知道这是千真万确的，因为我就是其中一个，肯定不会错的。另外两个分别住在东方和西方，她们的确凶险恶毒。但现在，其中一个已经被你杀死了，整个奥兹国就只剩下一个恶女巫了——就是住在西方的那个。"

多萝茜沉思了片刻之后，说道："可是，艾姆婶婶跟我说过，很久很久以前女巫们就已经全都死光了。"

"艾姆婶婶是谁？"小个子女人询问着。

"她是我的婶婶，住在堪萨斯州，我就是从那里来的。"

北方女巫低下了头，看着地面，似乎在思考着什么，之后她抬起头来说道："我不知道堪萨斯州在哪里，因为我从来都没有听说过这个地方。但是请你告诉我，那个地方文明化了吗？"

2. The Council with the Munchkins

The Witch of the North seemed to think for a time, with her head bowed and her eyes upon the ground. Then she looked up and said, "I do not know where Kansas is, for I have never heard that country mentioned before. But tell me, is it a civilized country?"

"Oh, yes," replied Dorothy.

"Then that accounts for it. In the civilized countries I believe there are no witches left, nor wizards, nor sorceresses, nor magicians. But, you see, the Land of Oz has never been civilized, for we are cut off from all the rest of the world. Therefore we still have witches and wizards amongst us."

"Who are the wizards?" asked Dorothy.

"Oz himself is the Great Wizard," answered the Witch, sinking her voice to a whisper. "He is more powerful than all the rest of us together. He lives in the City of Emeralds."

Dorothy was going to ask another question, but just then the Munchkins, who had been standing silently by, gave a loud shout and pointed to the corner of the house where the Wicked Witch had been lying.

"What is it?" asked the little old woman, and looked, and began to laugh. The feet of the dead Witch had disappeared entirely, and nothing was left but the silver shoes.

"She was so old," explained the Witch of the North, "that she dried up quickly in the sun. That is the end of her. But the silver shoes are yours, and you shall have them to wear." She reached down and

多萝茜回答说："哦，是的。"

"那这就说得通了。我相信，在文明化的地方确实没有女巫，也没有男巫，没有女魔法师，也没有男魔法师。但是，你看，奥兹国一直都没有文明化，因为我们与世界上的其他地方相互隔绝了。所以在我们中间还有巫婆和术士的存在。"

"术士是什么样的人？"多萝茜问。

"奥兹自己就是个大魔法师，"女巫压低了声音，耳语着回答道，"我们所有人联合起来都不及他厉害。他就住在翡翠城里。"

多萝茜正想问其他问题，但是就在这时候，一直默默站在一旁的芒奇金人大声呼喊起来，同时指着那个恶毒女巫躺着的角落。

"怎么了？"小个子女人问道。她往那边一看，就笑了起来。原来那个死了的女巫的脚已经消失得无影无踪，除了一双银鞋之外，什么都没有留下。

"她都已经一把年纪了，"北方女巫解释道，"太阳一晒就很快灰飞烟灭了。这就是她的下场。不过那双银鞋已经是你的了，穿上它吧。"她走到那边，捡起那双鞋子，拂去上面的灰尘，然后递给多萝茜。

"这双银鞋可是东方女巫的骄傲，"其中一个芒奇金人说，"这双鞋有某种魔力，但是我们一直都不知道是什么魔力。"

多萝茜把这双鞋拿进房子里，放在桌子上，然后又跑出来走

picked up the shoes, and after shaking the dust out of them, handed them to Dorothy.

"The Witch of the East was proud of those silver shoes," said one of the Munchkins, "and there is some charm connected with them; but what it is we never knew."

Dorothy carried the shoes into the house and placed them on the table. Then she came out again to the Munchkins and said:

"I am anxious to get back to my aunt and uncle, for I am sure they will worry about me. Can you help me find my way?"

The Munchkins and the Witch first looked at one another, and then at Dorothy, and then shook their heads.

"At the East, not far from here," said one, "there is a great desert, and none could live to cross it."

"It is the same at the South," said another, "for I have been there and seen it. The South is the country of the Quadlings."

"I am told," said the third man, "that it is the same at the West. And that country, where the Winkies live, is ruled by the Wicked Witch of the West, who would make you her slave if you passed her way."

"The North is my home," said the old lady, "and at its edge is the same great desert that surrounds this Land of Oz. I'm afraid, my dear, you will have to live with us."

Dorothy began to sob at this, for she felt lonely among all these strange people. Her tears seemed to grieve the kind-hearted

到芒奇金人的面前，说道：

"我想要回到我叔叔婶婶身边，因为我知道他们肯定会为我担心的。你们能帮我找到回去的路吗？"

芒奇金人和女巫先是面面相觑，然后又看了看多萝茜，最后摇了摇头。

"在距离这里不远的东方，"一个芒奇金人说道，"有一个大沙漠，没有人能活着穿越它。"

"南方也是如此，"另一个芒奇金人说，"因为我就住在那里，亲眼看到过。南方是奎特林人的地盘。"

第三个芒奇金人说："我听说，西方也一样有个大沙漠。那里住着温基人，被西方的恶女巫统治着，如果你从她那边经过她，她就会把你抓去当奴隶。"

"北方是我的家，"小个子女人说道，"在它的边界上也是一个围绕着奥兹国的沙漠。亲爱的，我想，你得跟我们住在一起了。"

听到这番话，多萝茜哭了起来，因为在这群奇怪的人中间，她感到了寂寞。她的眼泪似乎让热心的芒奇金人感到了悲伤，他们立刻拿出了手帕，开始擦起眼泪来。至于那个小个子的老妇人，她摘下了自己的帽子，把帽尖顶在自己的鼻尖上，同时一本正经地数着："1、2、3"，刹那间，这顶帽子就变成一块石板，上面写着一行大大的粉笔字：

Munchkins, for they immediately took out their handkerchiefs and began to weep also. As for the little old woman, she took off her cap and balanced the point on the end of her nose, while she counted "One, two, three" in a solemn voice. At once the cap changed to a slate, on which was written in big, white chalk marks:

"LET DOROTHY GO TO THE CITY OF EMERALDS"

The little old woman took the slate from her nose, and having read the words on it, asked, "Is your name Dorothy, my dear?"

"Yes," answered the child, looking up and drying her tears.

"Then you must go to the City of Emeralds. Perhaps Oz will help you."

"Where is this city?" asked Dorothy.

"It is exactly in the center of the country, and is ruled by Oz, the Great Wizard I told you of."

"Is he a good man?" inquired the girl anxiously.

"He is a good Wizard. Whether he is a man or not I cannot tell, for I have never seen him."

"How can I get there?" asked Dorothy.

"You must walk. It is a long journey, through a country that is sometimes pleasant and sometimes dark and terrible. However, I will use all the magic arts I know of to keep you from harm."

"让多萝茜去翡翠城"。

小个子老妇人把这块石板从她的鼻子上拿了下来，念着上面的这些字，问道："亲爱的，你的名字是叫多萝茜吗？"

"是的。"小女孩抬起了头，擦干了眼泪，回答道。

"那么，你必须得去翡翠城，奥兹可能会帮助你的。"

"翡翠城在哪里呢？"多萝茜问道。

"就在这个国家的中心，奥兹统治着那里，就是我跟你提起的那个大魔法师。"

小女孩忧心忡忡地问道："那他是好人吗？"

"他是个善良的魔法师。但我并不知道他是不是一个人，因为我从来都没有见过他。"

多萝茜问："我该怎么去他那里呢？"

"你必须得步行过去。这是一段漫长的路程，要经过一个时而让人愉悦，时而黑暗而让人恐怖的地方。不过，我会使出自己所有的魔法来帮助你，让你免遭伤害的。"

"你能跟我一起去吗？"小女孩望着小个子老妇人，祈求着她，此时这个人已经是她唯一的朋友了。

"不，我不能这么做，"她回答道，"但是我会给你一个吻，只要是被北方女巫吻过的人，就没人敢去伤害他了。"

2. The Council with the Munchkins

"Won't you go with me?" pleaded the girl, who had begun to look upon the little old woman as her only friend.

"No, I cannot do that," she replied, "but I will give you my kiss, and no one will dare injure a person who has been kissed by the Witch of the North."

She came close to Dorothy and kissed her gently on the forehead. Where her lips touched the girl they left a round, shining mark, as Dorothy found out soon after.

"The road to the City of Emeralds is paved with yellow brick," said the Witch, "so you cannot miss it. When you get to Oz do not be afraid of him, but tell your story and ask him to help you. Good-bye, my dear."

The three Munchkins bowed low to her and wished her a pleasant journey, after which they walked away through the trees. The Witch gave Dorothy a friendly little nod, whirled around on her left heel three times, and straightway disappeared, much to the surprise of little Toto, who barked after her loudly enough when she had gone, because he had been afraid even to growl while she stood by.

But Dorothy, knowing her to be a witch, had expected her to disappear in just that way, and was not surprised in the least.

她走近多萝茜，在她的额头上轻轻地吻了一下。很快，多萝茜就发现，被她的嘴唇吻过的地方留下了一个又圆又亮的印记。

"去翡翠城的路全都是用黄砖铺砌而成的，"女巫说，"因此你绝对不会迷路。当你找到奥兹的时候，不用怕他，只要把你的故事告诉他，求他帮助你就行了。再见了，亲爱的孩子。"

3个芒奇金人也深深地向她鞠了个躬，并祝福她一路顺风，之后他们就穿过树林走了。女巫友好地、微微地向多萝茜点了点头，用左脚跟转了3圈，立刻就不见了。小托托大吃了一惊，当女巫消失不见的时候，它还在后面大声地吠着，因为刚才女巫站在旁边的时候，它吓得根本不敢吭声。

不过多萝茜知道她是一个女巫，早就已经料到她会用这种方式离开，因此丝毫没有觉得惊讶。

3. How Dorothy Saved the Scarecrow

When Dorothy was left alone she began to feel hungry. So she went to the cupboard and cut herself some bread, which she spread with butter. She gave some to Toto, and taking a pail from the shelf she carried it down to the little brook and filled it with clear, sparkling water. Toto ran over to the trees and began to bark at the birds sitting there. Dorothy went to get him, and saw such delicious fruit hanging from the branches that she gathered some of it, finding it just what she wanted to help out her breakfast.

Then she went back to the house, and having helped herself and Toto to a good drink of the cool, clear water, she set about making ready for the journey to the City of Emeralds.

Dorothy had only one other dress, but that happened to be clean and was hanging on a peg beside her bed. It was gingham, with checks of white and blue; and although the blue was somewhat faded with many washings, it was still a pretty frock. The girl washed herself carefully, dressed herself in the clean gingham, and tied her pink sunbonnet on her head. She took a little basket and filled it with bread from the cupboard, laying a white cloth over the top. Then she looked down at her feet and noticed how old and worn her shoes were.

三.拯救稻草人

就只剩下多萝茜独自一人了，她觉得肚子有点饿，于是就走到橱柜旁，给自己切了几片面包，抹了一点奶酪。她还分给托托吃了一些，又从架子上拿下一只木桶，来到小河边，舀了些清澈发亮的溪水。托托跑进了树林，对着那些蹲在树上的鸟儿吠着。多萝茜跑过去抓住托托，她发现树上结满了美味芳香的果实，于是就摘了一些下来，正好可以用来当早餐。

然后她又回到房子里，和托托一起喝了许多清凉的溪水之后，就准备动身前往翡翠城。

多萝茜只有一件可更换的衣服，碰巧洗干净了，挂在床边的衣帽钩上。这是一件蓝白格子的棉布衣服，因为洗了好多次，蓝色已经褪得差不多了，但这件衣服仍旧非常漂亮。小女孩仔细地洗了把脸，穿上这件干净的格子衣服，戴上粉红色的遮阳帽。她拿起一只小篮子，里面装满了从橱柜里拿来的面包，又在上面盖了一块白布。随后她低头看了看自己的脚，发现自己穿的这双鞋又旧又破。

她说："托托，这双鞋子肯定走不了多少路。"托托抬起头来，那双黑色的小眼睛望着她的脸，摇晃着尾巴，说明它听懂了她说的话。

这时候，多萝茜看到了那双放在桌子上的银鞋，那原本是东

"They surely will never do for a long journey, Toto," she said. And Toto looked up into her face with his little black eyes and wagged his tail to show he knew what she meant.

At that moment Dorothy saw lying on the table the silver shoes that had belonged to the Witch of the East.

"I wonder if they will fit me," she said to Toto. "They would be just the thing to take a long walk in, for they could not wear out."

She took off her old leather shoes and tried on the silver ones, which fitted her as well as if they had been made for her.

Finally she picked up her basket.

"Come along, Toto," she said. "We will go to the Emerald City and ask the Great Oz how to get back to Kansas again."

She closed the door, locked it, and put the key carefully in the pocket of her dress. And so, with Toto trotting along soberly behind her, she started on her journey.

There were several roads nearby, but it did not take her long to find the one paved with yellow bricks. Within a short time she was walking briskly toward the Emerald City, her silver shoes tinkling merrily on the hard, yellow road-bed. The sun shone bright and the birds sang sweetly, and Dorothy did not feel nearly so bad as you might think a little girl would who had been suddenly whisked away from her own country and set down in the midst of a strange land.

She was surprised, as she walked along, to see how pretty the country was about her. There were neat fences at the sides of the road,

方女巫的鞋子。

"不知道这双鞋子合不合我的脚，"她对托托说道，"如果要走很长一段路的话，这双鞋正好派得上用处，这种鞋子不容易磨破。"

她脱下旧皮鞋，穿上了那双银鞋，大小正合适，就像是为她定做的一般。

最后她提起了篮子。

"托托，走吧，"她说，"我们要去翡翠城，求助伟大的奥兹，让他告诉我们该如何回到堪萨斯州。"

她关上门，上了锁，小心翼翼地把钥匙放进衣服口袋里。她就这样开始了自己的旅程，托托则认认真真地跟在她的后面。

在这附近有好几条路，不过很快她就找到了那条用黄砖铺砌而成的路。没花多少时间她就轻轻松松地踏上了通往翡翠城的路，她的银鞋走在坚硬的黄色路面上，发出叮叮当当悦耳动听的声音。阳光明媚，鸟儿欢唱，一个小女孩突然被一阵龙卷风从自己的故乡吹到了一片陌生的土地上，但是多萝茜似乎并不像你们想象的那样感到伤心难过。

在这一路上，她惊讶地发现周围的景色都那么漂亮。道路两旁竖着整齐的围墙，漆着精致的蓝色，围墙外面是大片大片丰收的谷物和蔬菜。很明显，芒奇金人都是种地的能手，才能有这么好的收成。在她偶尔经过一所房子的时候，人们就会跑出来看她，

painted a dainty blue color, and beyond them were fields of grain and vegetables in abundance. Evidently the Munchkins were good farmers and able to raise large crops. Once in a while she would pass a house, and the people came out to look at her and bow low as she went by; for everyone knew she had been the means of destroying the Wicked Witch and setting them free from bondage. The houses of the Munchkins were odd-looking dwellings, for each was round, with a big dome for a roof. All were painted blue, for in this country of the East blue was the favorite color.

Towards evening, when Dorothy was tired with her long walk and began to wonder where she should pass the night, she came to a house rather larger than the rest. On the green lawn before it many men and women were dancing. Five little fiddlers played as loudly as possible, and the people were laughing and singing, while a big table near by was loaded with delicious fruits and nuts, pies and cakes, and many other good things to eat.

The people greeted Dorothy kindly, and invited her to supper and to pass the night with them; for this was the home of one of the richest Munchkins in the land, and his friends were gathered with him to celebrate their freedom from the bondage of the Wicked Witch.

Dorothy ate a hearty supper and was waited upon by the rich Munchkin himself, whose name was Boq. Then she sat upon a settee and watched the people dance.

对她深深地鞠躬，目送她离开。因为每个人都知道是她杀死了邪恶女巫，是她解放了他们，让他们不再受人奴役。芒奇金人住的房子，都非常稀奇古怪，一幢幢都是圆的，上面都有一个大圆屋顶。所有房子都被漆成了蓝色，因为在这片东方国度上，大家最喜爱的就是蓝色了。

夜幕降临时，多萝茜走了很长一段路，已经疲惫不堪，这时候她开始担心起自己该在哪里过夜了。她来到一所比较大点的房子前，在房子前面的绿草地上，有许多男男女女在跳舞。5 个小提琴手尽情地、大声地拉奏着曲子，人们笑着，唱着。旁边的一张大桌子上摆着美味的水果和糕点，还有许许多多其他好吃的东西。

人们亲切地向多萝茜问好，还邀请她跟他们一起吃晚饭，在这里过夜。这户人家是芒奇金这片区域中最富有的，他的朋友们聚集在他家，一起庆祝他们从邪恶女巫的统治中重获自由。

多萝茜吃了一顿丰盛的晚餐，这家的男主人亲自招待她，这个人的名字叫波奎。晚饭之后，多萝茜就坐在一把靠背长椅上，看大家跳舞。

当波奎看见她那双银鞋的时候，他说："你肯定是个大魔法师吧！"

"为什么这么说？"小女孩问道。

"因为你穿着一双银鞋，而且还杀死了邪恶女巫。还有，你

When Boq saw her silver shoes he said, "You must be a great sorceress."

"Why?" asked the girl.

"Because you wear silver shoes and have killed the Wicked Witch. Besides, you have white in your frock, and only witches and sorceresses wear white."

"My dress is blue and white checked," said Dorothy, smoothing out the wrinkles in it.

"It is kind of you to wear that," said Boq. "Blue is the color of the Munchkins, and white is the witch color. So we know you are a friendly witch."

Dorothy did not know what to say to this, for all the people seemed to think her a witch, and she knew very well she was only an ordinary little girl who had come by the chance of a cyclone into a strange land.

When she had tired watching the dancing, Boq led her into the house, where he gave her a room with a pretty bed in it. The sheets were made of blue cloth, and Dorothy slept soundly in them till morning, with Toto curled up on the blue rug beside her.

She ate a hearty breakfast, and watched a wee Munchkin baby, who played with Toto and pulled his tail and crowed and laughed in a way that greatly amused Dorothy. Toto was a fine curiosity to all the people, for they had never seen a dog before.

"How far is it to the Emerald City?" the girl asked.

穿着白色的长袍,只有女巫和魔法师才穿白色的衣服。"

"我的衣服是蓝白格子的,"多萝茜一边说着,一边抚平了衣服上的皱褶。

"你穿那种衣服很好看,"波奎说,"蓝色是芒奇金人的颜色,白色是女巫的颜色,因此我们知道你是一个友好的女巫。"

对于这一点,多萝茜不知道该如何回答才好,因为所有人似乎都以为她是女巫,她自己非常清楚,她不过是个普普通通的小女孩,被一阵龙卷风吹到了这个奇怪的地方。

当她看跳舞看累了的时候,波奎就带着她走进房子,给她安排了一个房间,里面放着一张漂亮的床,床单是用蓝布做成的,多萝茜就躺在上面,托托则蜷缩在她旁边的蓝色小毯子上,一直酣睡到天亮。

她吃了一顿丰盛的早餐,看着一个芒奇金的小婴儿跟托托一起玩耍,拉着托托的尾巴,欢叫着,嬉笑着,把多萝茜逗得开心极了。在所有人眼中,托托都是那么令人好奇,因为他们从来都没有见过小狗。

小女孩问:"到翡翠城还有多远?"

"我不知道,"波奎一本正经地回答道,"因为我从没有去过那里。如果没什么事情,大伙儿都尽量离奥兹远远的。不过这里距离翡翠城还有很长很长的一段路程呢,得花好几天时间。我们这个地方富饶而又快乐,但是你必须经过一些贫瘠而又危险的

33

"I do not know," answered the Boq gravely, "for I have never been there. It is better for people to keep away from Oz, unless they have business with him. But it is a long way to the Emerald City, and it will take you many days. The country here is rich and pleasant, but you must pass through rough and dangerous places before you reach the end of your journey."

This worried Dorothy a little, but she knew that only the Great Oz could help her get to Kansas again, so she bravely resolved not to turn back.

She bade her friends good-bye, and again started along the road of yellow brick. When she had gone several miles she thought she would stop to rest, and so climbed to the top of the fence beside the road and sat down. There was a great cornfield beyond the fence, and not far away she saw a Scarecrow, placed high on a pole to keep the birds from the ripe corn.

Dorothy leaned her chin upon her hand and gazed thoughtfully at the Scarecrow. Its head was a small sack stuffed with straw, with eyes, nose, and mouth painted on it to represent a face. An old, pointed blue hat, that had belonged to some Munchkin, was perched on his head, and the rest of the figure was a blue suit of clothes, worn and faded, which had also been stuffed with straw. On the feet were some old boots with blue tops, such as every man wore in this country, and the figure was raised above the stalks of corn by means of the pole stuck up its back.

地方，才能到达旅程的目的地。"

这番话让多萝茜增添了几分忧愁，但是她知道，只有伟大的奥兹才能帮助她回到堪萨斯州，因此她勇敢地下定了决心，绝不回头。

她跟她的朋友们告了别，然后再次沿着黄砖路动身了。赶了好几里路之后，她心想该停下来休息一下了，于是就爬到路边的围墙上坐了下来。围墙之外是一大片稻田，在不远处，她看见了一个稻草人，被高高地插在竹竿上，防止那些鸦雀靠近已经成熟的稻子。

多萝茜用手托着下巴，若有所思地凝视着稻草人。他的头是一只塞满了稻草的小口袋，上面画着眼睛、鼻子和嘴巴，就当是他的脸。他的头上戴着一顶破旧的、蓝色的尖顶帽子，这顶帽子原本是属于某个芒奇金人的。他的身上穿着一件蓝色的衣服，破破烂烂的，颜色也已经褪掉了，衣服里面也塞满了稻草。脚上套着一双蓝布面的旧靴子。这里的每一个人穿的都是这种鞋。他的身子被高高地挂在稻草秆上，一根竹竿支撑在他的背后。

正当多萝茜认真地注视着稻草人那张画出来的奇怪面孔时，她惊讶地发现稻草人的一只眼睛正慢慢地对她眨动着。刚开始，她还以为是自己弄错了，因为在堪萨斯州，稻草人从来都不会眨眼睛。但是这时候，这个家伙却友好地向她点了点头。于是她爬下了围墙，向他走了过去，与此同时托托绕着竹竿跑着，吠着。

3. How Dorothy Saved the Scarecrow

While Dorothy was looking earnestly into the queer, painted face of the Scarecrow, she was surprised to see one of the eyes slowly wink at her. She thought she must have been mistaken at first, for none of the scarecrows in Kansas ever wink; but presently the figure nodded its head to her in a friendly way. Then she climbed down from the fence and walked up to it, while Toto ran around the pole and barked.

"Good day," said the Scarecrow, in a rather husky voice.

"Did you speak?" asked the girl, in wonder.

"Certainly," answered the Scarecrow. "How do you do?"

"I'm pretty well, thank you," replied Dorothy politely. "How do you do?"

"I'm not feeling well," said the Scarecrow, with a smile, "for it is very tedious being perched up here night and day to scare away crows."

"Can't you get down?" asked Dorothy.

"No, for this pole is stuck up my back. If you will please take away the pole I shall be greatly obliged to you."

Dorothy reached up both arms and lifted the figure off the pole, for, being stuffed with straw, it was quite light.

"Thank you very much," said the Scarecrow, when he had been set down on the ground. "I feel like a new man."

Dorothy was puzzled at this, for it sounded queer to hear a stuffed man speak, and to see him bow and walk along beside her.

"你好啊。"稻草人声音沙哑地说道。

"是你在说话吗？"小女孩惊讶地问道。

"当然喽，"稻草人回答道，"你好吗？"

"我很好，谢谢你"。多萝茜礼貌地回答说，"你好吗？"

"我觉得不舒服，"稻草人笑着说，"整天整夜被插在这里吓走乌鸦，太让人厌倦了。"

多萝茜问："你不能从那上面下来吗？"

"不能，因为有一根竹竿插在我的背里。如果你愿意帮我拔掉它，我会非常感谢你的。"

多萝茜伸出双手，把稻草人从竹竿上拔了下来，因为里面塞的都是稻草，所以稻草人非常轻。

"真谢谢你，"当稻草人坐在地上的时候，他说，"我觉得自己就像得到了新生。"

对此，多萝茜感到了一脸困惑，因为听一个稻草人说话，看着他鞠躬，还在自己的身旁走动，这一切都让她觉得十分诡异。

"你是谁？"稻草人一边伸着懒腰，打着哈欠，一边问道，"要去什么地方？"

"我叫多萝茜，"小女孩说，"要去翡翠城，请求伟大的奥兹送我回堪萨斯州。"

"翡翠城在哪儿？"他又问道，"奥兹又是什么人？"

"什么，连你也不知道吗？"她惊讶地回答说。

"Who are you?" asked the Scarecrow when he had stretched himself and yawned. "And where are you going?"

"My name is Dorothy," said the girl, "and I am going to the Emerald City, to ask the Great Oz to send me back to Kansas."

"Where is the Emerald City?" he inquired. "And who is Oz?"

"Why, don't you know?" she returned, in surprise.

"No, indeed. I don't know anything. You see, I am stuffed, so I have no brains at all," he answered sadly.

"Oh," said Dorothy, "I'm awfully sorry for you."

"Do you think," he asked, "if I go to the Emerald City with you, that Oz would give me some brains?"

"I cannot tell," she returned, "but you may come with me, if you like. If Oz will not give you any brains you will be no worse off than you are now."

"That is true," said the Scarecrow. "You see," he continued confidentially, "I don't mind my legs and arms and body being stuffed, because I cannot get hurt. If anyone treads on my toes or sticks a pin into me, it doesn't matter, for I can't feel it. But I do not want people to call me a fool, and if my head stays stuffed with straw instead of with brains, as yours is, how am I ever to know anything?"

"I understand how you feel," said the little girl, who was truly sorry for him. "If you will come with me I'll ask Oz to do all he can for you."

"Thank you," he answered gratefully.

"不知道，真的，我什么都不知道。你看，我是用稻草做成的，因此我根本没有脑子。"他伤心地回答道。

"哦，"多萝茜说，"我真替你感到难过。"

他问："那你觉得如果我和你一起去翡翠城的话，奥兹会给我一个脑子吗？"

"我不敢肯定，"她回答道，"但是如果你愿意的话，可以跟我一块儿去。即使奥兹没有给你脑子，你也不会比现在这样还要糟糕啊"。

"那倒是，"稻草人说，"你看，"他对多萝茜倍感信任，接着说道，"我的双手双脚和身体都是用稻草填塞而成的，对此我并不介意，因为这样我并不会受伤。如果有人踩了我的脚，或是用针扎我，没关系，因为我感觉不到痛。但是我不愿被人叫做傻瓜，如果我的脑袋里塞的是稻草，而不是像你这样是一个脑子的话，我又怎么能知道事情呢？"

"我理解你的心情，"小女孩说，她真心替他感到难过，"如果你跟我一块儿去，我会求奥兹尽力帮助你的。"

"谢谢你！"他感激地回答道。

他们回到了路上，多萝茜帮助他翻过围墙，然后顺着去翡翠城的黄砖路继续向前走着。

刚开始，托托并不喜欢和这个新朋友一起。它把稻草人嗅了个遍，好像怀疑这稻草里面有一窝的老鼠，而且还经常很不友好

3. How Dorothy Saved the Scarecrow

They walked back to the road. Dorothy helped him over the fence, and they started along the path of yellow brick for the Emerald City.

Toto did not like this addition to the party at first. He smelled around the stuffed man as if he suspected there might be a nest of rats in the straw, and he often growled in an unfriendly way at the Scarecrow.

"Don't mind Toto," said Dorothy to her new friend. "He never bites."

"Oh, I'm not afraid," replied the Scarecrow. "He can't hurt the straw. Do let me carry that basket for you. I shall not mind it, for I can't get tired. I'll tell you a secret," he continued, as he walked along. "There is only one thing in the world I am afraid of."

"What is that?" asked Dorothy; "the Munchkin farmer who made you?"

"No," answered the Scarecrow; "it's a lighted match."

地对着稻草人乱吠。

"别理托托，"多萝茜对她的新朋友说道，"它不会咬人的。"

"哦，我不害怕，"稻草人回答说，"它不会咬伤稻草的。让我来帮你提那只篮子吧。我不在乎，因为我不会觉得疲累。我跟你说个秘密，"他一边向前走，一边继续说道，"在这个世界上，我只害怕一样东西。"

"是什么？"多萝茜问，"是那个做出你的芒奇金农夫吗？"

"不，"稻草人回答说，"是燃烧着的火柴。"

4. The Road Through the Forest

After a few hours the road began to be rough, and the walking grew so difficult that the Scarecrow often stumbled over the yellow bricks, which were here very uneven. Sometimes, indeed, they were broken or missing altogether, leaving holes that Toto jumped across and Dorothy walked around. As for the Scarecrow, having no brains, he walked straight ahead, and so stepped into the holes and fell at full length on the hard bricks. It never hurt him, however, and Dorothy would pick him up and set him upon his feet again, while he joined her in laughing merrily at his own mishap.

The farms were not nearly so well cared for here as they were farther back. There were fewer houses and fewer fruit trees, and the farther they went the more dismal and lonesome the country became.

At noon they sat down by the roadside, near a little brook, and Dorothy opened her basket and got out some bread. She offered a piece to the Scarecrow, but he refused.

"I am never hungry," he said, "and it is a lucky thing I am not, for my mouth is only painted, and if I should cut a hole in it so I could eat, the straw I am stuffed with would come out, and that would spoil the shape of my head."

Dorothy saw at once that this was true, so she only nodded and went on eating her bread.

㈣.穿过森林的路

几个小时之后，道路开始变得崎岖不平，越来越难走了，稻草人时常被黄砖绊倒。有的地方黄砖已经碎了，或是不见了，留下一个个洞穴，托托跳了过去，多萝茜绕了过去。至于稻草人，因为他没有脑子，就笔直地向前走去，结果就踩进了洞里，整个身子摔倒在坚硬的砖头上。不过他从来都不会受伤，多萝茜把他扶了起来，然后让他重新站直，而他则为自己的小事故感到好笑，继续跟多萝茜赶着路。

这里的农田并不像远在后面的农田那样得到了细心的耕种。这里的房子很少，果树也是寥寥无几。他们越往前走，乡村就变得越阴沉，人迹罕至。

中午时分，他们在一条靠近小溪的路旁边坐了下来，多萝茜打开篮子，拿出一些面包，分了一片给稻草人，不过被他谢绝了。

"我永远都不会感到饥饿，"他说，"这是一件让我觉得幸运的事，因为我的嘴巴只是画出来的，如果在上面挖出个洞来，我就能吃东西了，但是这么一来，那些塞在里面的稻草就会跑出来，会破坏我脑袋的形状。"

多萝茜立刻就发现他说得没错，因此她只是点了点头，继续吃她的面包。

"跟我说说你自己的事情吧，还有你的故乡。"当多萝茜吃

"Tell me something about yourself and the country you came from," said the Scarecrow, when she had finished her dinner. So she told him all about Kansas, and how gray everything was there, and how the cyclone had carried her to this queer Land of Oz.

The Scarecrow listened carefully, and said, "I cannot understand why you should wish to leave this beautiful country and go back to the dry, gray place you call Kansas."

"That is because you have no brains" answered the girl. "No matter how dreary and gray our homes are, we people of flesh and blood would rather live there than in any other country, be it ever so beautiful. There is no place like home."

The Scarecrow sighed.

"Of course I cannot understand it," he said. "If your heads were stuffed with straw, like mine, you would probably all live in the beautiful places, and then Kansas would have no people at all. It is fortunate for Kansas that you have brains."

"Won't you tell me a story, while we are resting?" asked the child.

The Scarecrow looked at her reproachfully, and answered:

"My life has been so short that I really know nothing whatever. I was only made day before yesterday. What happened in the world before that time is all unknown to me. Luckily, when the farmer made my head, one of the first things he did was to paint my ears, so that I heard what was going on. There was another Munchkin with him, and

完午饭，稻草人说道。于是她就把关于堪萨斯州的事全都跟他说了一遍，告诉他那里的每样东西有多么灰暗，龙卷风又是如何把她带到了这个奇异的奥兹国度。

稻草人仔细地听着，然后说："我不明白你为什么想要离开这个美丽的地方，回到那个干燥而又灰暗的堪萨斯州。"

"因为你没有脑子啊，"小女孩回答说，"不管我们的家乡有多么凄凉灰暗，我们这些血肉做成的人都喜欢住在那里，而不是其他地方，尽管它非常漂亮。任何地方都不如自己的家乡好。"

稻草人叹了一口气。

"我当然理解不了了，"他说，"如果你们的脑袋里也像我这样塞满了稻草，你们或许就都住在这个美丽的地方了，到时候堪萨斯州就完全没人住喽。你们有脑子，对堪萨斯州来说，这是它的福气。"

"我们休息的时候，你能给我讲个故事吗？"小女孩问道。

稻草人用责备的目光看着她，回答说：

"我的生命如此短暂，我实在不知道有什么故事可说。我还是前天才被做出来的。在那之前，我完全不知道这个世界上发生了些什么。幸运的是，在农夫做出我的头之后，他做的第一件事就是给我画了耳朵，因此我听到了接下来发生的事情。当时，他边上还有另一个芒奇金人，我听到的第一句话就是这个农夫说：
'你觉得这两只耳朵画得怎么样？'

the first thing I heard was the farmer saying, 'How do you like those ears?'

" 'They aren't straight,' answered the other.

" 'Never mind,' said the farmer. 'They are ears just the same,' which was true enough.

" 'Now I'll make the eyes,' said the farmer. So he painted my right eye, and as soon as it was finished I found myself looking at him and at everything around me with a great deal of curiosity, for this was my first glimpse of the world.

" 'That's a rather pretty eye,' remarked the Munchkin who was watching the farmer. 'Blue paint is just the color for eyes.'

" 'I think I'll make the other a little bigger,' said the farmer. And when the second eye was done I could see much better than before. Then he made my nose and my mouth. But I did not speak, because at that time I didn't know what a mouth was for. I had the fun of watching them make my body and my arms and legs; and when they fastened on my head, at last, I felt very proud, for I thought I was just as good a man as anyone.

" 'This fellow will scare the crows fast enough,' said the farmer. 'He looks just like a man.'

" 'Why, he is a man,' said the other, and I quite agreed with him. The farmer carried me under his arm to the cornfield, and set me up on a tall stick, where you found me. He and his friend soon after walked away and left me alone.

"另一个回答道：'画得不够直。'

"'不要紧，'农夫说，'反正都是耳朵。'这话说得倒是没错。

"'现在我要画眼睛了。'农夫说。于是他给我画了右眼，不一会儿他就画完了，我发现自己正带着十足的好奇心打量着他，看着在我周围的每一样东西，因为这是我看到这个世界的第一眼。

"'那只眼睛真是漂亮啊，'另一个芒奇金人看着农夫，说道，'蓝颜色正适合用来画眼睛。'

"'我想我应该把另一只眼睛画得更大些。'农夫说。当第二只眼睛画完之后，我就看得比刚才更清楚了。接着，他又给我画了鼻子和嘴巴。但是我没办法说话，因为那时候我还不知道嘴巴能干什么。我兴致盎然地看着他们做出我的身体、双手跟双脚。最后，当他们装上我的脑袋的时候，我觉得非常骄傲，因为我以为我已经是个健健康康的人了。

"'这家伙肯定能一下子就吓退乌鸦的，'农夫说，'它看起来就像个真人一样。'

"'哎呀，它本来就是个人嘛。'另外一个说。我非常认同他的话。农夫把我挟在他的手臂下，带到稻田里，把我插在一根很高的竹竿上，就是你遇见我的那个地方。很快，农夫和他的朋友就离开了，把我独自一个人丢在那里。

"我不喜欢就这样被处置了，因此我试着走在他们后面，但

47

4. The Road Through the Forest

"I did not like to be deserted this way. So I tried to walk after them. But my feet would not touch the ground, and I was forced to stay on that pole. It was a lonely life to lead, for I had nothing to think of, having been made such a little while before. Many crows and other birds flew into the cornfield, but as soon as they saw me they flew away again, thinking I was a Munchkin; and this pleased me and made me feel that I was quite an important person. By and by an old crow flew near me, and after looking at me carefully he perched upon my shoulder and said:

" 'I wonder if that farmer thought to fool me in this clumsy manner. Any crow of sense could see that you are only stuffed with straw.' Then he hopped down at my feet and ate all the corn he wanted. The other birds, seeing he was not harmed by me, came to eat the corn too, so in a short time there was a great flock of them about me.

"I felt sad at this, for it showed I was not such a good Scarecrow after all; but the old crow comforted me, saying, 'If you only had brains in your head you would be as good a man as any of them, and a better man than some of them. Brains are the only things worth having in this world, no matter whether one is a crow or a man.'

"After the crows had gone I thought this over, and decided I would try hard to get some brains. By good luck you came along and pulled me off the stake, and from what you say I am sure the Great Oz will give me brains as soon as we get to the Emerald City."

是我的脚根本够不着地，我就被迫插在那根竹竿上。这种生活可真孤单啊，因为我才刚刚被做出来，也没什么事情可想的。许多乌鸦和其他鸟类飞到稻田里，但是它们一看见我就立刻飞走了，以为我是一个芒奇金人，这倒让我挺高兴的，我觉得自己是一个非常重要的人物。不久之后，一只老乌鸦飞近了我，在仔细地打量了我一番之后，它站在我的肩头，说道：

"'真是奇怪，那个农夫竟然想用这种笨拙的方法愚弄我。不管是哪只有见识的乌鸦，都可以看出你不过是用稻草做成的。'说完，它就跳到我的脚上，尽情地吃起谷粒来。其他的鸟儿发现我并没有伤害它，也都飞过来吃谷粒，因此不一会儿，在我的身边就围满了一大群鸟。

"这就让我犯了愁，因为这毕竟说明了我不是一个称职的稻草人，不过那只老乌鸦安慰我说：'如果你的脑袋里装的是脑子，你就会跟他们一样称职了，甚至会比他们更有能耐。不管是乌鸦还是人，只有脑子是这世上唯一有价值的东西。'

"乌鸦飞走之后，我想了又想，决定要努力找一个脑子过来。很幸运，你跑了过来，把我从竹竿上拔了下来，而根据你说的那番话，等我们到了翡翠城之后，我想伟大的奥兹一定会给我一个脑子的。"

"但愿如此，"多萝茜真诚地说道，"你似乎很渴望得到它。"

4. The Road Through the Forest

"I hope so," said Dorothy earnestly, "since you seem anxious to have them."

"Oh, yes; I am anxious," returned the Scarecrow. "It is such an uncomfortable feeling to know one is a fool."

"Well," said the girl, "let us go." And she handed the basket to the Scarecrow.

There were no fences at all by the roadside now, and the land was rough and untilled. Toward evening they came to a great forest, where the trees grew so big and close together that their branches met over the road of yellow brick. It was almost dark under the trees, for the branches shut out the daylight; but the travelers did not stop, and went on into the forest.

"If this road goes in, it must come out," said the Scarecrow, "and as the Emerald City is at the other end of the road, we must go wherever it leads us."

"Anyone would know that," said Dorothy.

"Certainly; that is why I know it," returned the Scarecrow. "If it required brains to figure it out, I never should have said it."

After an hour or so the light faded away, and they found themselves stumbling along in the darkness. Dorothy could not see at all, but Toto could, for some dogs see very well in the dark; and the Scarecrow declared he could see as well as by day. So she took hold of his arm and managed to get along fairly well.

"哦,是啊,我渴望极了,"稻草人回答道,"如果知道自己是个笨蛋,那心里是多么不舒服啊!"

小女孩说:"好了,我们走吧。"她把篮子交给了稻草人。

这时候,路边已经没有了围墙,土地也没有开垦。临近黄昏时,他们来到了一片大森林之中,那里的树木都非常高大,相互紧挨着,树枝交错着掩盖了黄砖铺砌的道路。在树底下几乎一片黑暗,因为树枝掩盖了阳光,但是这两位旅人并没有停下脚步,径直走进了森林中。

"如果这条路通向树林,那它也一定可以带我们走出森林,"稻草人说,"既然翡翠城就在路的另一端,那么不管这条路带我们去哪儿,我们都必须一直走下去。"

多萝茜说:"谁都知道这个道理。"

"当然,所以我也知道,"稻草人回答说,"如果这需要动脑子才能想得到,那我永远都说不出来。"

大概一小时之后,太阳下山了,他们在黑暗中磕磕绊绊地向前走着。多萝茜完全看不见东西,但是托托可以,某些狗可以在黑暗中看得非常清楚。稻草人说他自己也能像白天一样看得清清楚楚。因此她就拉着稻草人的手,结果倒也走得很稳当。

"如果你看见了房子,或是任何可以过夜的地方,"她说,"你一定得告诉我,因为在黑暗中走路让人很不舒服。"

不一会儿,稻草人就停住了脚步。

4. The Road Through the Forest

"If you see any house, or any place where we can pass the night," she said, "you must tell me; for it is very uncomfortable walking in the dark."

Soon after the Scarecrow stopped.

"I see a little cottage at the right of us," he said, "built of logs and branches. Shall we go there?"

"Yes, indeed," answered the child. "I am all tired out."

So the Scarecrow led her through the trees until they reached the cottage, and Dorothy entered and found a bed of dried leaves in one corner. She lay down at once, and with Toto beside her soon fell into a sound sleep. The Scarecrow, who was never tired, stood up in another corner and waited patiently until morning came.

"我看见在我们的左边有一间小房子，"他说，"是用木头和树枝造成的。我们要过去吗？"

"要，当然要了，"女孩子回答道，"我已经累死了。"

于是稻草人带着她穿过了树林，一直来到那间小木屋前面，多萝茜走了进去，在角落里找到了一张用干树叶铺成的床。她立刻躺了上去，不一会儿就睡着了，托托躺在她的身旁。稻草人永远都不会觉得疲倦，他站在另一个角落，耐心地等待着黎明的到来。

5. The Rescue of the Tin Woodman

When Dorothy awoke the sun was shining through the trees and Toto had long been out chasing birds around him and squirrels. She sat up and looked around her. There was the Scarecrow, still standing patiently in his corner, waiting for her.

"We must go and search for water," she said to him.

"Why do you want water?" he asked.

"To wash my face clean after the dust of the road, and to drink, so the dry bread will not stick in my throat."

"It must be inconvenient to be made of flesh," said the Scarecrow thoughtfully, "for you must sleep, and eat and drink. However, you have brains, and it is worth a lot of bother to be able to think properly."

They left the cottage and walked through the trees until they found a little spring of clear water, where Dorothy drank and bathed and ate her breakfast. She saw there was not much bread left in the basket, and the girl was thankful the Scarecrow did not have to eat anything, for there was scarcely enough for herself and Toto for the day.

When she had finished her meal, and was about to go back to the road of yellow brick, she was startled to hear a deep groan near by.

"What was that?" she asked timidly.

五.营救铁皮人

当多萝茜醒来时，阳光透过树丛照射下来，托托早就已经跑到了外面，追逐着围绕着它的鸟儿和那些松鼠。多萝茜坐了起来，打量着四周，发现稻草人仍旧耐心地站在那个角落里，等候着她。

"我们该走了，去找水。"她对稻草人说道。

"找水干吗？"他问。

"可以用来洗掉这一路上的灰尘，还可以拿来喝，这样，干面包就不会卡在我的喉咙里了。"

"血肉之躯肯定很不方便，"稻草人关切地说道，"你们必须得睡觉、吃饭、喝水。但是无论如何，你们有脑子，可以正确地思考问题，就算有再多的烦恼也是值得的。"

他们离开了小屋，穿过了树林，最后找到了一小眼清澈的泉水，多萝茜就在那里喝了点水，洗了把脸，吃了点面包。她发现篮子里所剩的面包已经不多了，几乎只够给自己和托托坚持一天。因此，小女孩子非常感谢稻草人，因为他什么都不用吃。

当她吃完了早饭，正准备走回到黄砖路上的时候，忽然从附近传来了一声低沉的呻吟，把她吓了一跳。

她胆怯地问道："那是什么声音？"

"不知道，"稻草人回答说，"不过我们可以过去看看。"

就在这时候，又传来了一声呻吟，这个声音似乎是从他们背

"I cannot imagine," replied the Scarecrow; "but we can go and see."

Just then another groan reached their ears, and the sound seemed to come from behind them. They turned and walked through the forest a few steps, when Dorothy discovered something shining in a ray of sunshine that fell between the trees. She ran to the place and then stopped short, with a little cry of surprise.

One of the big trees had been partly chopped through, and standing beside it, with an uplifted axe in his hands, was a man made entirely of tin. His head and arms and legs were jointed upon his body, but he stood perfectly motionless, as if he could not stir at all.

Dorothy looked at him in amazement, and so did the Scarecrow, while Toto barked sharply and made a snap at the tin legs, which hurt his teeth.

"Did you groan?" asked Dorothy.

"Yes," answered the tin man, "I did. I've been groaning for more than a year, and no one has ever heard me before or come to help me."

"What can I do for you?" she inquired softly, for she was moved by the sad voice in which the man spoke.

"Get an oil-can and oil my joints," he answered. "They are rusted so badly that I cannot move them at all; if I am well oiled I shall soon be all right again. You will find an oil-can on a shelf in my cottage."

后传来的。他们转过身来，往树林里走了几步，这时候多萝茜发现树丛中有样东西在阳光的照耀下闪闪发亮。她跑到那个地方，突然又停住了脚步，惊叫了起来。

原来有一棵大树被砍掉了一半，而在这棵树的旁边站着一个完全用铁皮做成的人，手中还高举着一把斧头。他的头、手和脚全都连接在他的身上，但是他却站在那里一动不动，好像根本就不能动弹了一样。

多萝茜惊异地注视着他，稻草人也是一脸的惊讶，而托托则激烈地吠着，在铁皮人的腿上咬了一口，可是却咬疼了自己的牙齿。

"是你在呻吟吗？"多萝茜问道。

"是的，"铁皮人回答说，"就是我，我都已经在这里叫唤一年多了，可就是没人听得到我，或是过来帮我。"

"我有什么可以帮你的呢？"多萝茜已经被铁皮人那忧愁的声音感动了，温柔地询问道。

"去拿一个油罐，然后在我身体的各个关节上添点油。"他回答说，"这些地方都已经严重生锈了，害得我根本没法动弹。只要给我添了油，我就能立刻活动了。你可以在我小屋的架子上找到一个油罐。"

多萝茜立刻跑回小屋，找到了那个油罐，然后跑回来，焦急地问道："你的关节在哪里？"

Dorothy at once ran back to the cottage and found the oil-can, and then she returned and asked anxiously, "Where are your joints?"

"Oil my neck, first," replied the Tin Woodman. So she oiled it, and as it was quite badly rusted the Scarecrow took hold of the tin head and moved it gently from side to side until it worked freely, and then the man could turn it himself.

"Now oil the joints in my arms," he said. And Dorothy oiled them and the Scarecrow bent them carefully until they were quite free from rust and as good as new.

The Tin Woodman gave a sigh of satisfaction and lowered his axe, which he leaned against the tree.

"This is a great comfort," he said. "I have been holding that axe in the air ever since I rusted, and I'm glad to be able to put it down at last. Now, if you will oil the joints of my legs, I shall be all right once more."

So they oiled his legs until he could move them freely; and he thanked them again and again for his release, for he seemed a very polite creature, and very grateful.

"I might have stood there always if you had not come along," he said; "so you have certainly saved my life. How did you happen to be here?"

"We are on our way to the Emerald City to see the Great Oz," she answered, "and we stopped at your cottage to pass the night."

"Why do you wish to see Oz?" he asked.

"先给我的脖子添上点油。"铁皮人回答道。于是多萝茜就在他脖子上添了点油，因为那里锈得实在太厉害了，稻草人扶着铁皮人的头，轻轻地左右摆动着，直到这个头可以自由活动，然后，铁皮人也可以自己转动脑袋了。

"现在，给我手臂上的那些关节添点油。"他说。于是，多萝茜又在那些关节上添了些油。稻草人则小心翼翼地弯曲着手臂，直到生了锈的手臂可以灵活运动，像新生的手一样才停了下来。

这个铁皮人心满意足地叹了口气，放下那把斧头。

"真是舒服极了，"他说，"自从我生锈之后，我就一直把这斧头高举在空中。我终于把它放下来了，真是开心。现在，只要你再给我腿上的关节添上油，我就可以恢复正常了。"

于是他们给他的腿添上了油，直到他可以自由自在地走动为止。铁皮人再三地对他们的救命之恩表示感谢，他似乎是个很有礼貌的人，懂得感恩戴德。

"如果你们没有出现，那我可能就要一直站在这里了，"他说，"你们确实是救了我一条命。你们怎么会来这里呢？"

"我们要去翡翠城，拜访伟大的奥兹，"多萝茜回答说，"我们在你的小屋里过了一夜。"

"你们为什么要去拜访奥兹？"他问。

"我想让他送我回堪萨斯州，稻草人想求奥兹给他一个脑子。"她回答道。

"I want him to send me back to Kansas, and the Scarecrow wants him to put a few brains into his head," she replied.

The Tin Woodman appeared to think deeply for a moment. Then he said:

"Do you suppose Oz could give me a heart?"

"Why, I guess so," Dorothy answered. "It would be as easy as to give the Scarecrow brains."

"True," the Tin Woodman returned. "So, if you will allow me to join your party, I will also go to the Emerald City and ask Oz to help me."

"Come along," said the Scarecrow heartily, and Dorothy added that she would be pleased to have his company. So the Tin Woodman shouldered his axe and they all passed through the forest until they came to the road that was paved with yellow brick.

The Tin Woodman had asked Dorothy to put the oil-can in her basket. "For," he said, "if I should get caught in the rain, and rust again, I would need the oil-can badly."

It was a bit of good luck to have their new comrade join the party, for soon after they had begun their journey again they came to a place where the trees and branches grew so thick over the road that the travelers could not pass. But the Tin Woodman set to work with his axe and chopped so well that soon he cleared a passage for the entire party.

铁皮人似乎沉思了一会儿，然后说道："你觉得奥兹会给我一颗心吗？"

"这个，我想应该会吧，"多萝茜回答说，"这就像给稻草人一个脑子一样轻而易举。"

"这倒是没错，"铁皮人回答说，"这样的话，如果你们能同意我加入你们的队伍，那我也想去翡翠城，请求奥兹帮帮我。"

"那就走吧。"稻草人热心地说道。多萝茜也表示她很乐意有他的陪伴。于是铁皮人就扛起他的斧头，他们一起穿过了树林，踏上了黄砖路。

铁皮人求多萝茜把油罐放在她的篮子里。他说："如果淋到了雨，我就又会生锈，因此这个油罐是必不可少的。"

有了这个新伙伴的加入，还真是他们的运气。因为在他们再次起程之后没多久，就来到了一个树木和枝叶浓密丛生的地方，那里的路已经完全被树枝挡住了，行人根本就过不去。不过铁皮人熟练地挥舞着斧头，开始砍起树枝来，不一会儿就给他们清出了一条道路。

多萝茜一边走路，一边全神贯注地思考着，以至于没有注意到稻草人跌进了坑里，滚到了路边。他不得不叫喊着，让她过去扶他起来。

"你为什么不绕过坑走过来呢？"铁皮人问道。

"我不知道呀，"稻草人高兴地回答说，"你看，我的脑袋

5. The Rescue of the Tin Woodman

Dorothy was thinking so earnestly as they walked along that she did not notice when the Scarecrow stumbled into a hole and rolled over to the side of the road. Indeed he was obliged to call to her to help him up again.

"Why didn't you walk around the hole?" asked the Tin Woodman.

"I don't know enough," replied the Scarecrow cheerfully. "My head is stuffed with straw, you know, and that is why I am going to Oz to ask him for some brains."

"Oh, I see," said the Tin Woodman. "But, after all, brains are not the best things in the world."

"Have you any?" inquired the Scarecrow.

"No, my head is quite empty," answered the Woodman. "But once I had brains, and a heart also; so, having tried them both, I should much rather have a heart."

"And why is that?" asked the Scarecrow.

"I will tell you my story, and then you will know."

So, while they were walking through the forest, the Tin Woodman told the following story:

"I was born the son of a woodman who chopped down trees in the forest and sold the wood for a living. When I grew up, I too became a woodchopper, and after my father died I took care of my old mother as long as she lived. Then I made up my mind that instead of living alone I would marry, so that I might not become lonely.

里装的都是稻草，所以我才要去奥兹那里，请他给我一个脑子。"

"哦，我明白了，"铁皮人说，"但是，脑子毕竟不是这个世界上最美妙的东西。"

"那你有脑子吗？"稻草人问。

"没有，我的脑袋里也是空空的，"铁皮人回答说，"但是从前我有脑子，也有心，但是用过这两个之后，我宁愿只要一颗心。"

"那又是为什么呢？"稻草人问道。

"等我把我的故事告诉你之后，你就会明白了。"

于是，当他们穿行在这片树林的时候，铁皮人就讲起了这个故事：

"我是一个樵夫的儿子，父亲在树林砍伐树木，然后以卖木柴为生。当我长大成人之后，也成了一个樵夫。后来我父亲去世了，就由我照顾着年迈的母亲，直到她也去世了。之后，我下定决心准备结婚，不再独自一人生活，这样我就不会寂寞孤独了。

"有一个芒奇金姑娘，她长得非常漂亮，很快我就真心地爱上了她。至于她，她也答应了等到我赚到足够的钱为她造一所更好的房子以后，就嫁给我，因此我比以往更加辛勤地工作着。但是这个姑娘跟一个老太婆住在一起，这个老太婆不愿把这个姑娘嫁给任何人，因为她非常懒惰，想让这个姑娘一直跟她住在一起，给她烧饭、做家务。于是这个老太婆就去找东方恶女巫帮忙，并

5. The Rescue of the Tin Woodman

"There was one of the Munchkin girls who was so beautiful that I soon grew to love her with all my heart. She, on her part, promised to marry me as soon as I could earn enough money to build a better house for her; so I set to work harder than ever. But the girl lived with an old woman who did not want her to marry anyone, for she was so lazy she wished the girl to remain with her and do the cooking and the housework. So the old woman went to the Wicked Witch of the East, and promised her two sheep and a cow if she would prevent the marriage. Thereupon the Wicked Witch enchanted my axe, and when I was chopping away at my best one day, for I was anxious to get the new house and my wife as soon as possible, the axe slipped all at once and cut off my left leg.

"This at first seemed a great misfortune, for I knew a one-legged man could not do very well as a wood-chopper. So I went to a tinsmith and had him make me a new leg out of tin. The leg worked very well, once I was used to it. But my action angered the Wicked Witch of the East, for she had promised the old woman I should not marry the pretty Munchkin girl. When I began chopping again, my axe slipped and cut off my right leg. Again I went to the tinsmith, and again he made me a leg out of tin. After this the enchanted axe cut off my arms, one after the other; but, nothing daunted, I had them replaced with tin ones. The Wicked Witch then made the axe slip and cut off my head, and at first I thought that was the end of me. But the

且答应她，如果她能阻止这门婚事，就给她两只羊和一头牛。因此恶女巫就在我的斧头上施了魔法。有一天，当我使劲全力砍树的时候——因为我急切地想要造好新房，尽快迎娶那位姑娘——那把斧头突然就滑了出去，砍断了我的左腿。

"刚开始，这件事似乎是个天大的不幸，因为我知道，一条腿的人是没办法成为一个好樵夫的。所以我去铁皮匠那里，请他用铁皮给我做了一条新腿。等我习惯了这条腿之后，我就可以熟练地工作了。但是我的行为惹怒了东方恶女巫，因为她答应了那个老太婆，要阻止我娶那位漂亮的芒奇金姑娘。当我重新开始砍树的时候，斧头又滑了出去，砍断了我的右腿。我又去找那个铁皮匠，他又用铁皮给我做了一条腿。在那之后，这把被施了魔法的斧头又相继砍断了我的手臂，但是我并没有心灰意冷，用铁皮做成的双手代替了它们。这时候，恶女巫就让那斧头滑出去，砍掉了我的脑袋，起初我还以为自己完蛋了。但是那个铁皮匠碰巧路过这里，他又用铁皮给我做了一个新头。

"当时我以为自己已经打败了那个恶女巫，而且比以往更加辛勤地工作着，但是我根本没想到我的仇敌竟会如此残忍，她想出了一个新方法来毁灭我对美丽的芒奇金姑娘的爱。她让我的斧头再次滑了出去，刚好划过我的身体，把我砍成了两半。那个铁皮匠又一次过来帮助了我，替我做了一副铁皮身躯，用一个个关节把我那铁皮的双手双脚以及脑袋连接在一起，因此我又能像从

tinsmith happened to come along, and he made me a new head out of tin.

"I thought I had beaten the Wicked Witch then, and I worked harder than ever; but I little knew how cruel my enemy could be. She thought of a new way to kill my love for the beautiful Munchkin maiden, and made my axe slip again, so that it cut right through my body, splitting me into two halves. Once more the tinsmith came to my help and made me a body of tin, fastening my tin arms and legs and head to it, by means of joints, so that I could move around as well as ever. But, alas! I had now no heart, so that I lost all my love for the Munchkin girl, and did not care whether I married her or not. I suppose she is still living with the old woman, waiting for me to come after her.

"My body shone so brightly in the sun that I felt very proud of it and it did not matter now if my axe slipped, for it could not cut me. There was only one danger – that my joints would rust; but I kept an oil-can in my cottage and took care to oil myself whenever I needed it. However, there came a day when I forgot to do this, and, being caught in a rainstorm, before I thought of the danger my joints had rusted, and I was left to stand in the woods until you came to help me. It was a terrible thing to undergo, but during the year I stood there I had time to think that the greatest loss I had known was the loss of my heart. While I was in love I was the happiest man on earth; but no one can love who has not a heart, and so I am resolved to ask Oz to

前那样活动自如了。但是，唉！如今我却没有了心，因此失去了所有对那个芒奇金姑娘的爱，根本不在乎自己能不能娶到她，我想她应该仍然和那个老太婆住在一起，等着我去娶她吧。

"在阳光下，我的身子闪闪发光，对此我感到了无比的自豪，现在我再也不担心斧头是否会从手中滑落，因为它已经伤害不到我了。现在就只剩下一个危险了——那就是我的关节会生锈。不过我在自己的小屋里藏了一个油罐，不管什么时候，只要有需要，我就给自己添点油。可是，有那么一天，我忘记给自己添油了，而且还被暴风雨淋了个透，在我想到这个危险之前，我的关节已经生锈了，然后就一直等到你们来帮助我。经历这样的事情着实让人觉得害怕，但是，在这一年里，我站在这里，让我有时间去思考，让我认识到自己最大的损失就是失去了自己的心。当我沉浸在恋爱中时，我是这世界上最幸福的人；但是没有人会喜欢一个没有心的人，因此我下定决心求奥兹给我一颗心。如果他给了，我就回到那位芒奇金姑娘的身边，娶她为妻。"

铁皮人的这个故事让多萝茜和稻草人听得津津有味，这时候，他们才知道铁皮人为什么如此急切地想要得到一颗崭新的心。

"尽管如此，"稻草人说，"我还是想要脑子，而不是一颗心，因为一个笨蛋即使有了心，也不知道该用它干什么。"

"我还是想要一颗心，"铁皮人回应道，"因为有了脑子并不会让人觉得幸福，而幸福是这世上最美好的事物。"

give me one. If he does, I will go back to the Munchkin maiden and marry her."

Both Dorothy and the Scarecrow had been greatly interested in the story of the Tin Woodman, and now they knew why he was so anxious to get a new heart.

"All the same," said the Scarecrow, "I shall ask for brains instead of a heart; for a fool would not know what to do with a heart if he had one."

"I shall take the heart," returned the Tin Woodman; "for brains do not make one happy, and happiness is the best thing in the world."

Dorothy did not say anything, for she was puzzled to know which of her two friends was right, and she decided if she could only get back to Kansas and Aunt Em, it did not matter so much whether the Woodman had no brains and the Scarecrow no heart, or each got what he wanted.

What worried her most was that the bread was nearly gone, and another meal for herself and Toto would empty the basket. To be sure neither the Woodman nor the Scarecrow ever ate anything, but she was not made of tin nor straw, and could not live unless she was fed.

多萝茜什么也没有说，因为她不知道这两位朋友谁说得对。她心想着，只要能够回到堪萨斯州，回到艾姆婶婶的身边，不管铁皮人有没有心，不管稻草人有没有脑子，又或是他们每个人都得到了自己想要的东西，这些都不关她的事。

最最令她担心的是面包已经快要吃完了，她和托托再吃上一顿，这个篮子就要空了。当然，铁皮人和稻草人肯定什么都不用吃，但是她既不是铁皮做的，也不是稻草做的，只有吃饱了，她才能活下去。

6. The Cowardly Lion

All this time Dorothy and her companions had been walking through the thick woods. The road was still paved with yellow brick, but these were much covered by dried branches and dead leaves from the trees, and the walking was not at all good.

There were few birds in this part of the forest, for birds love the open country where there is plenty of sunshine. But now and then there came a deep growl from some wild animal hidden among the trees. These sounds made the little girl's heart beat fast, for she did not know what made them; but Toto knew, and he walked close to Dorothy's side, and did not even bark in return.

"How long will it be," the child asked of the Tin Woodman, "before we are out of the forest?"

"I cannot tell," was the answer, "for I have never been to the Emerald City. But my father went there once, when I was a boy, and he said it was a long journey through a dangerous country, although nearer to the city where Oz dwells the country is beautiful. But I am not afraid so long as I have my oil-can, and nothing can hurt the Scarecrow, while you bear upon your forehead the mark of the Good Witch's kiss, and that will protect you from harm."

"But Toto!" said the girl anxiously. "What will protect him?"

六.一只胆小的狮子

多萝茜和她的同伴们一直都穿行在这片浓密的树林之中。虽然这条路依旧铺砌着黄砖，但是地上却覆盖着许多树上掉下来的枯枝败叶，走在上面非常之不方便。

在这一带的树林中，几乎见不到小鸟，因为它们喜欢阳光明媚的空旷田野；但是一些藏匿于树林之中的野兽会时不时地发出低沉的嚎叫声。这些声音吓得小女孩的心怦怦直跳，因为她不知道这是什么东西。不过托托知道，它紧紧地靠在多萝茜的身边，甚至没有吠叫回应。

小女孩问铁皮人说："我们还要走多长时间才能走出这片森林呢？"

"我也不是很清楚，"他回答道，"因为我从没有去过翡翠城。不过，在我还小的时候，我父亲去过那里。他说那是一段漫长的旅程，要经过一个非常危险的地方，尽管在奥兹居住的城市附近，那些地方都非常美丽。不过只要我有油罐，就什么都不怕了，而且任何东西都无法伤害稻草人，你的额头上还留有善良女巫吻过的印记，它也会保护你不受任何伤害的。"

"但是托托呢！"小女孩子忧心忡忡地说道，"什么东西能保护它呢？"

"如果它遇到了危险，我们就必须亲自去保护它。"铁皮人

71

"We must protect him ourselves if he is in danger," replied the Tin Woodman.

Just as he spoke there came from the forest a terrible roar, and the next moment a great Lion bounded into the road. With one blow of his paw he sent the Scarecrow spinning over and over to the edge of the road, and then he struck at the Tin Woodman with his sharp claws. But, to the Lion's surprise, he could make no impression on the tin, although the Woodman fell over in the road and lay still.

Little Toto, now that he had an enemy to face, ran barking toward the Lion, and the great beast had opened his mouth to bite the dog, when Dorothy, fearing Toto would be killed, and heedless to danger, rushed forward and slapped the Lion upon his nose as hard as she could, while she cried out:

"Don't you dare to bite Toto! You ought to be ashamed of yourself, a big beast like you, to bite a poor little dog!"

"I didn't bite him," said the Lion, as he rubbed his nose with his paw where Dorothy had hit it.

"No, but you tried to," she retorted. "You are nothing but a big coward."

"I know it," said the Lion, hanging his head in shame. "I've always known it. But how can I help it?"

"I don't know, I'm sure. To think of your striking a stuffed man, like the poor Scarecrow!"

回答道。

正当他说出这句话的时候，从森林里传来了一个可怕的怒吼声。紧接着，一只大狮子跳到了路中间。它那爪子一挥，稻草人就打着转儿滚到了路边上；随后它用尖锐的爪子袭击铁皮人，但是让它惊讶的是尽管铁皮人摔倒在路上，一动不动地躺在那儿，但是他的身上却没有任何伤痕。

这时候，小托托面对着这个敌人，吠了起来，而这只大狮子张开了它那血盆大口想要去咬这只小狗。此时，多萝茜担心托托会被咬死，于是就奋不顾身地贸然冲上前去，用尽全力拍打着狮子的鼻子，同时大声呼喊道：

"你怎么敢咬托托！你应该为你自己感到羞愧，像你这么大的一只野兽，却还要咬一只这么可怜的小狗！"

"我没有咬它。"狮子一边说着话，一边用爪子擦着被多萝茜打过的鼻子。

"是，可你想要咬它，"多萝茜反驳道，"你只是个胆小怕事的大怪物而已。"

"我知道，"狮子说着，羞愧地低下了头，"我一直都知道这个缺点。但是我又能怎么办呢？"

"我当然不知道怎么办。可你自己想想看，你竟然袭击一个用稻草填塞而成的可怜的稻草人！"

"他是个稻草人吗？"狮子吃惊地问道，他看着多萝茜扶起

"Is he stuffed?" asked the Lion in surprise, as he watched her pick up the Scarecrow and set him upon his feet, while she patted him into shape again.

"Of course he's stuffed," replied Dorothy, who was still angry.

"That's why he went over so easily," remarked the Lion. "It astonished me to see him whirl around so. Is the other one stuffed also?"

"No," said Dorothy, "he's made of tin." And she helped the Woodman up again.

"That's why he nearly blunted my claws," said the Lion. "When they scratched against the tin it made a cold shiver run down my back. What is that little animal you are so tender with?"

"He is my dog, Toto," answered Dorothy.

"Is he made of tin, or stuffed?" asked the Lion.

"Neither. He's a – a – a meat dog," said the girl.

"Oh! He's a curious animal and seems remarkably small, now that I look at him. No one would think of biting such a little thing, except a coward like me," continued the Lion sadly.

"What makes you a coward?" asked Dorothy, looking at the great beast in wonder, for he was as big as a small horse.

"It's a mystery," replied the Lion. "I suppose I was born that way. All the other animals in the forest naturally expect me to be brave, for the Lion is everywhere thought to be the King of Beasts. I learned that if I roared very loudly every living thing was frightened and got

稻草人，让他站直，然后又轻轻地拍打着他，让他恢复了原貌。

"他当然是稻草人了。"多萝茜回答道，她仍旧非常愤怒。

"难怪他这么轻易就摔了出去，"狮子说道，"看着他打转的样子着实令我惊讶。另外一个也是用稻草做成的吗？"

"不，"多萝茜说，"他是铁皮做的。"说着，她又过去扶起了铁皮人。

"所以他几乎磨钝了我的爪子，"狮子说，"当我的爪子抓住铁皮的时候，感觉到我的背上一阵寒战。那只小家伙又是谁，你为什么待它这么温柔？"

"它是我的狗狗，叫托托。"多萝茜回答说。

"那它是用铁皮做的，还是用稻草扎的？"狮子问道。

"都不是。它是一只有血有肉的狗。"小女孩说道。

"啊！它长得可真稀奇，现在看起来还真是非常小呢。除了像我这样的胆小鬼，谁都不会想去咬这样一个小东西的。"狮子又伤心地说了起来。

"你为什么会变成胆小鬼呢？"多萝茜惊讶地注视着这头大野兽问道，因为它都有一匹小马驹那么大了。

"这是一个谜，"狮子回答说，"我想我出生的时候就是这样的吧。树林中的所有野兽都自然而然地觉得我非常勇敢，因为不管在什么地方，狮子都被奉为百兽之王。我得知只要自己非常响亮地咆哮一声，所有的动物都会受到惊吓，避开我所走的路。

out of my way. Whenever I've met a man I've been awfully scared; but I just roared at him, and he has always run away as fast as he could go. If the elephants and the tigers and the bears had ever tried to fight me, I should have run myself – I'm such a coward; but just as soon as they hear me roar they all try to get away from me, and of course I let them go."

"But that isn't right. The King of Beasts shouldn't be a coward," said the Scarecrow.

"I know it," returned the Lion, wiping a tear from his eye with the tip of his tail. "It is my great sorrow, and makes my life very unhappy. But whenever there is danger, my heart begins to beat fast."

"Perhaps you have heart disease," said the Tin Woodman.

"It may be," said the Lion.

"If you have," continued the Tin Woodman, "you ought to be glad, for it proves you have a heart. For my part, I have no heart; so I cannot have heart disease."

"Perhaps," said the Lion thoughtfully, "if I had no heart I should not be a coward."

"Have you brains?" asked the Scarecrow.

"I suppose so. I've never looked to see," replied the Lion.

"I am going to the Great Oz to ask him to give me some," remarked the Scarecrow, "for my head is stuffed with straw."

"And I am going to ask him to give me a heart," said the Woodman.

每次，我遇到人的时候，就会非常害怕，但是只要我对着人吼叫一声，他就会拼了命地逃跑。如果有大象、老虎或熊来跟我一比高下，我就会自己逃跑——我就是这样一个胆小鬼。但是只要一听到我的吼声，它们就会尽快逃离，当然，我也会放它们一马的。"

"但是这样是不对的。百兽之王不应该是个胆小鬼。"稻草人说。

"我知道，"狮子一边回答着，一边用尾巴尖擦去眼睛中的泪水，"这是我最大的悲哀，让我的生活非常不开心。因为每次我遇到危险，我的心就会跳得飞快。"

"可能是你有心脏病吧。"铁皮人说。

"或许是吧。"狮子说。

"如果你真有心脏病，"铁皮人接着说道，"那你应该开心才对，因为那就说明你有心。至于我，我没有心，所以我不会有心脏病。"

"可能是吧，"狮子若有所思地说道，"如果我没有心，那我就不会是胆小鬼了。"

"那你有脑子吗？"稻草人问道。

"我想应该有的。我从来都没有见过它。"狮子回答说。

"我要去伟大的奥兹那里，求他给我一个脑子，"稻草人说，"因为我的脑袋里面塞的都是稻草。"

"我去求他给我一颗心。"铁皮人说。

6. The Cowardly Lion

"And I am going to ask him to send Toto and me back to Kansas," added Dorothy.

"Do you think Oz could give me courage?" asked the Cowardly Lion.

"Just as easily as he could give me brains," said the Scarecrow.

"Or give me a heart," said the Tin Woodman.

"Or send me back to Kansas," said Dorothy.

"Then, if you don't mind, I'll go with you," said the Lion, "for my life is simply unbearable without a bit of courage."

"You will be very welcome," answered Dorothy, "for you will help to keep away the other wild beasts. It seems to me they must be more cowardly than you are if they allow you to scare them so easily."

"They really are," said the Lion, "but that doesn't make me any braver, and as long as I know myself to be a coward I shall be unhappy."

So once more the little company set off upon the journey, the Lion walking with stately strides at Dorothy's side. Toto did not approve of this new comrade at first, for he could not forget how nearly he had been crushed between the Lion's great jaws. But after a time he became more at ease, and presently Toto and the Cowardly Lion had grown to be good friends.

During the rest of that day there was no other adventure to mar the peace of their journey. Once, indeed, the Tin Woodman stepped upon a beetle that was crawling along the road, and killed the poor little thing. This made the Tin Woodman very unhappy, for he was always

"我去求他送我和托托回堪萨斯州。"多萝茜跟着说道。

"你们觉得奥兹会给我勇气吗？"胆小的狮子说道。

"就像给我脑子一样简单。"稻草人说。

"或者像给我心一样容易。"铁皮人说。

"或者像送我回堪萨斯州一样轻而易举。"多萝茜说。

"那么，如果你们不介意的话，我想跟你们一块儿去，"狮子说，"因为没有一丁点儿胆量，我的生活简直令人无法容忍。"

"热烈欢迎呢，"多萝茜回答说，"因为你可以帮我们吓走其他野兽。我看，如果它们这么轻易就被你吓走了，那么它们肯定比你更胆小。"

"它们的确很胆小，"狮子说，"但是那并不会让我变得更勇敢。只要我知道自己是个胆小鬼，我就开心不起来了。"

于是这一小群伙伴又开始了他们的旅程，狮子雄赳赳气昂昂地走在多萝茜的身边。刚开始，托托并不喜欢这个新同伴，因为它无法忘记自己差点被这只狮子的血盆大口咬得粉碎的情景，但是过了一会儿之后，托托就变得自在多了，此时，它已经和这只胆小的狮子变成了好朋友。

在这一天接下来的时间里，没有发生别的危险，一路上都相安无事。不过，有一次，铁皮人踩到了一只在路上爬的甲虫，杀死了这个可怜的小生命。这让铁皮人感到非常伤心，因为他总是小心翼翼地不去伤害任何生命。因此在他继续向前赶路的时候，

careful not to hurt any living creature; and as he walked along he wept several tears of sorrow and regret. These tears ran slowly down his face and over the hinges of his jaw, and there they rusted. When Dorothy presently asked him a question the Tin Woodman could not open his mouth, for his jaws were tightly rusted together. He became greatly frightened at this and made many motions to Dorothy to relieve him, but she could not understand. The Lion was also puzzled to know what was wrong. But the Scarecrow seized the oil-can from Dorothy's basket and oiled the Woodman's jaws, so that after a few moments he could talk as well as before.

"This will serve me a lesson," said he, "to look where I step. For if I should kill another bug or beetle I should surely cry again, and crying rusts my jaws so that I cannot speak."

Thereafter he walked very carefully, with his eyes on the road, and when he saw a tiny ant toiling by he would step over it, so as not to harm it. The Tin Woodman knew very well he had no heart, and therefore he took great care never to be cruel or unkind to anything.

"You people with hearts," he said, "have something to guide you, and need never do wrong; but I have no heart, and so I must be very careful. When Oz gives me a heart of course I needn't mind so much."

他流下了几滴伤心后悔的泪水。这些眼泪慢慢地从他的脸上流下来，流到了他下巴的连接处，那个地方就生了锈。过了一会儿，当多萝茜问他问题的时候，铁皮人连嘴都张不开了，因为他的上下腭已经紧紧地锈在了一起。这让铁皮人惊慌失措，对着多萝茜指手画脚地做着手势，想让她救救自己，可是多萝茜根本不知道这是什么意思，狮子也是一脸困惑，不知道发生了什么事情。不过稻草人从多萝茜的篮子里拿出了油罐，给铁皮人的下巴加了些油，片刻之后，铁皮人又能像从前一样说话了。

"这真是给了我一个教训，"他说，"走路的时候要先看清楚了再踏出脚步。因为如果我再踏死一只小虫子，我肯定又会哭的，我一哭下巴就会生锈，到时候就说不了话了。"

因此他看着路面，小心翼翼地走着。他看见一只小蚂蚁艰难地爬过，为了不伤害它，铁皮人就跨了过去。铁皮人非常明白，他没有心，因此他就要特别留心，绝不会残忍或无情地对待任何东西。

"你们都有心。"他说，"可以指引着你们行动，永远都不会犯错。但是我却没有，所以就必须非常谨慎。等到奥兹给我心之后，我当然就用不着这么担心了。"

7. The Journey to the Great Oz

They were obliged to camp out that night under a large tree in the forest, for there were no houses near. The tree made a good, thick covering to protect them from the dew, and the Tin Woodman chopped a great pile of wood with his axe and Dorothy built a splendid fire that warmed her and made her feel less lonely. She and Toto ate the last of their bread, and now she did not know what they would do for breakfast.

"If you wish," said the Lion, "I will go into the forest and kill a deer for you. You can roast it by the fire, since your tastes are so peculiar that you prefer cooked food, and then you will have a very good breakfast."

"Don't! Please don't," begged the Tin Woodman. "I should certainly weep if you killed a poor deer, and then my jaws would rust again."

But the Lion went away into the forest and found his own supper, and no one ever knew what it was, for he didn't mention it. And the Scarecrow found a tree full of nuts and filled Dorothy's basket with them, so that she would not be hungry for a long time. She thought this was very kind and thoughtful of the Scarecrow, but she laughed heartily at the awkward way in which the poor creature picked up the nuts. His padded hands were so clumsy and the nuts were so small

七.惊险的旅程

那天夜里，他们不得不露宿在森林中的一棵大树底下，因为附近没有一户人家。那棵树非常高大，枝繁叶茂，可以帮他们挡住露水。铁皮人用他的斧头，砍来了一大堆木柴，多萝茜点起了一堆旺火，温暖着她，同时驱散了她的寂寞感。她和托托吃着最后那一点面包，现在她都不知道明天的早餐该吃什么了。

狮子说："如果你愿意的话，我这就去森林里给你抓一只鹿过来。你可以用火把它烤了，因为你们的口味那么特别，喜欢吃煮熟的食物，烤完之后，你们就可以吃上一顿非常美味的早餐了。"

"别！求你别这么做！"铁皮人恳求道，"如果你杀死了一只可怜的鹿，我肯定会哭的，到时候，我的下巴又要生锈了。"

不过狮子还是跑进了森林中，给自己找晚餐去了，谁也不知道它吃了什么，因为它什么都没有提起过。稻草人找到了一棵长满坚果的果树。他用多萝茜的篮子装了满满一篮的坚果，那样，在之后的一段时间里，多萝茜就不会饿到了。她心里想着稻草人真是体贴周到，但是看见这可怜的家伙摘坚果时那笨拙的样子后，她又不由哈哈大笑起来。他那稻草填塞而成的手如此笨拙，而坚果又那么小，因此那些他掉在地上的坚果都已经跟篮子里的一样多了。可是稻草人并不在乎自己要花多少时间才能装满这个篮子，

that he dropped almost as many as he put in the basket. But the Scarecrow did not mind how long it took him to fill the basket, for it enabled him to keep away from the fire, as he feared a spark might get into his straw and burn him up. So he kept a good distance away from the flames, and only came near to cover Dorothy with dry leaves when she lay down to sleep. These kept her very snug and warm, and she slept soundly until morning.

When it was daylight, the girl bathed her face in a little rippling brook, and soon after they all started toward the Emerald City.

This was to be an eventful day for the travelers. They had hardly been walking an hour when they saw before them a great ditch that crossed the road and divided the forest as far as they could see on either side. It was a very wide ditch, and when they crept up to the edge and looked into it they could see it was also very deep, and there were many big, jagged rocks at the bottom. The sides were so steep that none of them could climb down, and for a moment it seemed that their journey must end.

"What shall we do?" asked Dorothy despairingly.

"I haven't the faintest idea," said the Tin Woodman, and the Lion shook his shaggy mane and looked thoughtful.

But the Scarecrow said, "We cannot fly, that is certain. Neither can we climb down into this great ditch. Therefore, if we cannot jump over it, we must stop where we are."

因为这可以让他离那堆火远远的，他担心有火钻进他的稻草里，把自己烧了个精光。所以他远远地离开那堆火，只是在多萝茜躺下睡觉的时候，他才走过去在她的身上盖了些干树叶。这些树叶让她感到了舒适和温暖，一直酣睡到了天亮。

天亮之后，小女孩在一条潺潺流动的小河边洗了把脸，过后，他们一伙人就又开始向翡翠城进发了。

对于这几个旅行者来说，这一天真是个多事的日子。他们刚刚走了不到一个钟头，就看见前面有一条非常宽阔的壕沟横在路上，把他们眼前的森林分成了两半。这是一条极其宽阔的壕沟。当他们蹑手蹑脚地爬到沟边向下望时，发现这条沟非常之深，而且在沟的下面还有许多嶙峋的巨大石块。沟的两边非常陡峭，没有人可以爬得下去，一时间看来，他们的旅程似乎必须要到此为止了。

"我们该怎么办呢？"多萝茜失望地问道。

"我什么办法也想不出来。"铁皮人说。而狮子抖动着蓬松的鬃毛，似乎在思考着什么。

不过稻草人说："我们肯定是飞不过去的，也没办法爬到壕沟的下面，因此，如果我们跳不过去，那就必须得停在这里了。"

"我想我可以跳得过去。"在仔细地估量完壕沟的宽度之后，胆小的狮子这么说道。

"那我们就没问题了，"稻草人回答道，"你可以一个个地

"I think I could jump over it," said the Cowardly Lion, after measuring the distance carefully in his mind.

"Then we are all right," answered the Scarecrow, "for you can carry us all over on your back, one at a time."

"Well, I'll try it," said the Lion. "Who will go first?"

"I will," declared the Scarecrow, "for, if you found that you could not jump over the gulf, Dorothy would be killed, or the Tin Woodman badly dented on the rocks below. But if I am on your back it will not matter so much, for the fall would not hurt me at all."

"I am terribly afraid of falling, myself," said the Cowardly Lion, "but I suppose there is nothing to do but try it. So get on my back and we will make the attempt."

The Scarecrow sat upon the Lion's back, and the big beast walked to the edge of the gulf and crouched down.

"Why don't you run and jump?" asked the Scarecrow.

"Because that isn't the way we Lions do these things," he replied. Then giving a great spring, he shot through the air and landed safely on the other side. They were all greatly pleased to see how easily he did it, and after the Scarecrow had got down from his back the Lion sprang across the ditch again.

Dorothy thought she would go next; so she took Toto in her arms and climbed on the Lion's back, holding tightly to his mane with one hand. The next moment it seemed as if she were flying through the air; and then, before she had time to think about it, she was safe on the

把我们全都背过去。"

"行，那我试试看，"狮子说，"谁愿意先来呢？"

"我，"稻草人郑重地说道，"因为，如果你觉得自己跳不过这条壕沟的时候，多萝茜可能就会摔死，而铁皮人可能会摔在下面的石头上，造成严重的凹痕。但是如果我坐在你背上，就用不着担心那些问题了，因为即使摔下去了，也完全不会伤害到我。"

"我自己都非常害怕会掉下去，"胆小的狮子说道，"但是我想除了尝试一下之外，也别无他法了，所以你就骑上我的背，让我们来试试看吧。"

于是稻草人跨上了狮子的后背，这只大狮子走到壕沟的旁边，蹲了下来。

"你为什么不先助跑，然后再跳过去呢？"稻草人问道。

"因为我们狮子不会这么跳。"它回答说，之后就纵身一跳，飞向空中，平平安安地落到了对面。看着狮子这么轻而易举就跳了过去，大家伙儿全都非常高兴。稻草人从它背上下来之后，狮子又跳回到壕沟的这边。

多萝茜心想着下一个应该是她了，于是她抱着托托，爬上狮子的后背，一只手紧紧地抓住它的鬃毛，紧接着就像飞在空中一样，她还没有来得及回想，就已经平安到达了对面。狮子又跳了回去，把铁皮人背了过来。然后他们全都坐了下来，让狮子可以

other side. The Lion went back a third time and got the Tin Woodman, and then they all sat down for a few moments to give the beast a chance to rest, for his great leaps had made his breath short, and he panted like a big dog that has been running too long.

They found the forest very thick on this side, and it looked dark and gloomy. After the Lion had rested they started along the road of yellow brick, silently wondering, each in his own mind, if ever they would come to the end of the woods and reach the bright sunshine again. To add to their discomfort, they soon heard strange noises in the depths of the forest, and the Lion whispered to them that it was in this part of the country that the Kalidahs lived.

"What are the Kalidahs?" asked the girl.

"They are monstrous beasts with bodies like bears and heads like tigers," replied the Lion, "and with claws so long and sharp that they could tear me in two as easily as I could kill Toto. I'm terribly afraid of the Kalidahs."

"I'm not surprised that you are," returned Dorothy. "They must be dreadful beasts."

The Lion was about to reply when suddenly they came to another gulf across the road. But this one was so broad and deep that the Lion knew at once he could not leap across it.

So they sat down to consider what they should do, and after serious thought the Scarecrow said:

好好休息一下，这几次剧烈的跳动已经让它气喘吁吁，就像一只跑了很长一段路的狗似的喘着气。

他们发现这一边的森林非常浓密，看上去阴森而黑暗。待狮子休息完之后，他们又沿着黄砖路出发了，每个人心中都默默地发出一个疑问：他们到底能不能走出这片森林，再度见到明媚的阳光？没过多久，他们听到从树林深处传来了一种奇怪的声音，这又增添了他们心中的不安。狮子悄悄地对他们说卡利达斯就住在这片区域。

"卡利达斯是什么东西？"小女孩问。

"它们是一种恐怖的怪兽：身子像熊，头像老虎，"狮子回答说，"它们的爪子大而锋利，可以毫不费劲地把我撕成两半，就像我杀死托托那么简单。我非常害怕它们。"

"这并不会让我觉得奇怪，"多萝茜回答说，"它们肯定是非常可怕的野兽。"

正当狮子想要回话的时候，他们眼前突然又出现了一道壕沟。不过这道壕沟很深很宽阔，狮子立刻就知道自己跳不过去了。

于是他们坐下来商量该怎么办，经过认真思考之后，稻草人说：

"壕沟的旁边有一棵大树。如果铁皮人能够砍倒这棵树，让它横倒在壕沟的另一边，那么我们就能方便地走过去了。"

"这可是个最棒的办法了，"狮子说，"我们几乎都要怀疑

"Here is a great tree, standing close to the ditch. If the Tin Woodman can chop it down, so that it will fall to the other side, we can walk across it easily."

"That is a first-rate idea," said the Lion. "One would almost suspect you had brains in your head, instead of straw."

The Woodman set to work at once, and so sharp was his axe that the tree was soon chopped nearly through. Then the Lion put his strong front legs against the tree and pushed with all his might, and slowly the big tree tipped and fell with a crash across the ditch, with its top branches on the other side.

They had just started to cross this queer bridge when a sharp growl made them all look up, and to their horror they saw running towards them two great beasts with bodies like bears and heads like tigers.

"They are the Kalidahs!" said the Cowardly Lion, beginning to tremble.

"Quick!" cried the Scarecrow. "Let us cross over."

So Dorothy went first, holding Toto in her arms, the Tin Woodman followed, and the Scarecrow came next. The Lion, although he was certainly afraid, turned to face the Kalidahs, and then he gave so loud and terrible a roar that Dorothy screamed and the Scarecrow fell over backward, while even the fierce beasts stopped short and looked at him in surprise.

But, seeing they were bigger than the Lion, and remembering that there were two of them and only one of him, the Kalidahs again

你的脑袋里装的不是稻草，而是真正的脑子了。"

铁皮人立刻就动起手来，他的斧头非常锋利，很快那棵树就几乎要被砍倒了。然后狮子用它那强而有力的前腿顶住树干，用尽全力推着这棵树。大树慢慢地倾斜了，砰的一声倒躺在壕沟之上，树梢上的枝干落在了壕沟的另一边。

正当他们出发走过这座怪异的树桥时，一声尖锐的咆哮使得所有人都抬起头来张望，只见两头巨大的长着熊身虎头的野兽向他们跑了过来，他们惊恐万分。

"它们就是卡利达斯！"胆小的狮子说着开始颤抖起来。

"快跑！"稻草人大声叫道，"我们快点过去。"

于是多萝茜抱着托托跑在最前面，铁皮人紧随其后，稻草人也跟在后面。狮子虽然非常害怕，但是仍旧转过身来，面对着卡利达斯，然后发出一声洪亮而又可怕的怒吼。多萝茜被吓得尖叫起来，稻草人向后退了一步，甚至连那凶猛的野兽也停了一会儿，惊讶地看着狮子。

可是当它们发现自己比狮子还要高大，而且想到它们有两个，可狮子却只有一个时，它们又继续向前冲去。狮子穿过了这棵树，转过身去看看它们想要干什么。那两头凶猛的野兽毫不迟疑也同样跨上了这棵树。狮子对多萝茜说：

"我们完了，它们肯定会用尖利的爪子把我们撕成碎片的。但是，你就躲我后面吧，只要我还活着，我就会跟它们搏斗到底。"

rushed forward, and the Lion crossed over the tree and turned to see what they would do next. Without stopping an instant the fierce beasts also began to cross the tree. And the Lion said to Dorothy:

"We are lost, for they will surely tear us to pieces with their sharp claws. But stand close behind me, and I will fight them as long as I am alive."

"Wait a minute!" called the Scarecrow. He had been thinking what was best to be done, and now he asked the Woodman to chop away the end of the tree that rested on their side of the ditch. The Tin Woodman began to use his axe at once, and, just as the two Kalidahs were nearly across, the tree fell with a crash into the gulf, carrying the ugly, snarling brutes with it, and both were dashed to pieces on the sharp rocks at the bottom.

"Well," said the Cowardly Lion, drawing a long breath of relief, "I see we are going to live a little while longer, and I am glad of it, for it must be a very uncomfortable thing not to be alive. Those creatures frightened me so badly that my heart is beating yet."

"Ah," said the Tin Woodman sadly, "I wish I had a heart to beat."

This adventure made the travelers more anxious than ever to get out of the forest, and they walked so fast that Dorothy became tired, and had to ride on the Lion's back. To their great joy the trees became thinner the farther they advanced, and in the afternoon they suddenly came upon a broad river, flowing swiftly just before them. On the other side of the water they could see the road of yellow brick

"等一等！"稻草人叫道，刚才他一直在想最佳的解决之道，这时候，他让铁皮人砍断靠在他们这一边的树梢。铁皮人立刻就挥动起斧头，正当这两头卡利达斯快要冲过来的时候，这棵树轰的一声，连这两头丑陋的、咆哮着的野兽一同掉进了壕沟，落在底部那些锋利的石块上，摔了个粉身碎骨。

"好了，"胆小的狮子一边说着，一边深深地吸了口气，放下了心中的不安，"看来咱们还能再活得久一点了，真是让人开心啊，因为死亡肯定是一件非常痛苦的事情。那些野兽真是吓死我了，我的心到现在还怦怦直跳呢。"

"唉，"铁皮人却伤心地说道，"我倒希望自己能有一颗怦怦跳的心。"

这个危险使得这些旅行者更加急切地想要走出这片森林。他们走得太快，多萝茜开始感到了疲倦，只得骑在狮子的背上。让他们颇为欣喜的是，他们越往前走，树林就变得越稀疏。到了下午，他们面前突然出现了一条宽阔的河流，河水湍急地流动着。在河的另外一边，他们可以看见一条黄砖路穿过了一个美丽的地方。绿茵茵的草地上点缀着灿烂的鲜花，路的两旁全都是挂满鲜果的果树。看着面前这个美好的地方，他们甭提有多开心了。

"我们要怎么过河呢？"多萝茜问道。

"那简单得很，"稻草人回答说，"只要铁皮人给我们做出一个木筏，我们就能漂到对岸去啦。"

running through a beautiful country, with green meadows dotted with bright flowers and all the road bordered with trees hanging full of delicious fruits. They were greatly pleased to see this delightful country before them.

"How shall we cross the river?" asked Dorothy.

"That is easily done," replied the Scarecrow. "The Tin Woodman must build us a raft, so we can float to the other side."

So the Woodman took his axe and began to chop down small trees to make a raft, and while he was busy at this the Scarecrow found on the riverbank a tree full of fine fruit. This pleased Dorothy, who had eaten nothing but nuts all day, and she made a hearty meal of the ripe fruit.

But it takes time to make a raft, even when one is as industrious and untiring as the Tin Woodman, and when night came the work was not done. So they found a cozy place under the trees where they slept well until the morning; and Dorothy dreamed of the Emerald City, and of the good Wizard Oz, who would soon send her back to her own home again.

　　于是铁皮人挥动他的斧头，砍倒几棵小树，准备做出个木筏来。就在他为此而忙碌的时候，稻草人发现岸边的一棵树上结满了新鲜的水果。多萝茜开心极了，这一整天，除了坚果之外，她什么都没吃过，这时候，她大快朵颐，美美地吃了一顿红润的水果。

　　但是做木筏是件费时的工作，即使是像铁皮人这样手脚勤快、不知疲倦的人，在天黑的时候，也依旧没有完成工作。因此他们就在树下找了一个舒适的地方，一觉睡到了第二天早晨。多萝茜梦见了翡翠城，还有善良的魔法师奥兹，一下子就把她送回到自己的家中。

8. The Deadly Poppy Field

Our little party of travelers awakened the next morning refreshed and full of hope, and Dorothy breakfasted like a princess off peaches and plums from the trees beside the river. Behind them was the dark forest they had passed safely through, although they had suffered many discouragements; but before them was a lovely, sunny country that seemed to beckon them on to the Emerald City.

To be sure, the broad river now cut them off from this beautiful land. But the raft was nearly done, and after the Tin Woodman had cut a few more logs and fastened them together with wooden pins, they were ready to start. Dorothy sat down in the middle of the raft and held Toto in her arms. When the Cowardly Lion stepped upon the raft it tipped badly, for he was big and heavy; but the Scarecrow and the Tin Woodman stood upon the other end to steady it, and they had long poles in their hands to push the raft through the water.

They got along quite well at first, but when they reached the middle of the river the swift current swept the raft downstream, farther and farther away from the road of yellow brick. And the water grew so deep that the long poles would not touch the bottom.

"This is bad," said the Tin Woodman, "for if we cannot get to the land we shall be carried into the country of the Wicked Witch of the West, and she will enchant us and make us her slaves."

八.致命的罂粟园

第二天早晨，我们这一小群旅行者醒了，重新振作了精神，心中充满了希望。多萝茜像个公主似的吃着从河边的树上摘来的桃子和梅子，这些就是她的早餐。他们的身后是一片黑暗的森林，虽然他们在那里遭遇了许许多多危险，不过总算是平平安安地走出来了。而在他们眼前的，是一个可爱而又充满阳光的地方，它似乎在召唤着他们去翡翠城。

当然，眼前这条宽阔的河流仍旧把他们和这片美丽的地方分隔开来，幸亏木筏就快要完成了，铁皮人又砍来了一些木头，用木楔把它们紧紧地钉在一起，然后他们就准备出发了。多萝茜手里抱着托托，坐在木筏的中间。胆小的狮子踏上木筏时，这条木筏就严重倾斜了，因为它又大又重。不过稻草人和铁皮人站在另一边，才让木筏平稳了下来。他们各自拿着一根长长的木杆，撑着木筏穿过这条河。

刚开始，他们划得非常顺利，但是，当他们划到河中间的时候，湍急的流水却把木筏冲到了下游，使他们离黄砖路越来越远。同时，河水也变得非常之深，长木杆已经触不到河底了。

"这可糟了，"铁皮人说，"如果没办法上岸，那我们就要被带到西方邪恶女巫的地盘里了，她会对我们施展妖术，让我们成为她的奴隶。"

"And then I should get no brains," said the Scarecrow.

"And I should get no courage," said the Cowardly Lion.

"And I should get no heart," said the Tin Woodman.

"And I should never get back to Kansas," said Dorothy.

"We must certainly get to the Emerald City if we can," the Scarecrow continued, and he pushed so hard on his long pole that it stuck fast in the mud at the bottom of the river. Then, before he could pull it out again, or let go, the raft was swept away, and the poor Scarecrow left clinging to the pole in the middle of the river.

"Good-bye!" he called after them, and they were very sorry to leave him. Indeed, the Tin Woodman began to cry, but fortunately remembered that he might rust, and so dried his tears on Dorothy's apron.

Of course this was a bad thing for the Scarecrow.

"I am now worse off than when I first met Dorothy," he thought. "Then, I was stuck on a pole in a cornfield, where I could pretend to scare the crows, at any rate. But surely there is no use for a Scarecrow stuck on a pole in the middle of a river. I am afraid I shall never have any brains, after all!"

Down the stream the raft floated, and the poor Scarecrow was left far behind. Then the Lion said:

"Something must be done to save us. I think I can swim to the shore and pull the raft after me, if you will only hold fast to the tip of my tail."

"那样我就得不到脑子了。"稻草人说。

"我就得不到胆量了。"胆小的狮子说。

"我就得不到心了。"铁皮人说。

"我永远也回不到堪萨斯州了。"多萝茜说。

"如果我们努力的话，一定能到翡翠城的。"稻草人接着说道。他使劲撑着长木杆，可是木杆却牢牢地插在了河底的淤泥中，还没等他拔出木杆，或是在他丢掉木杆之前，木筏就被河水冲走了。可怜的稻草人被插在了河中间的木杆上。

"再见了！"他朝着伙伴们叫喊着。他们为失去了稻草人而感到伤心，铁皮人开始哭了起来，不过幸亏他记得自己会因此而生锈，于是就用多萝茜的围裙把眼泪擦干了。

当然，这件事对稻草人来说实在是令人遗憾。

"现在的我比起当初遇见多萝茜时更加糟糕了，"他想，"那时候，我被插在稻田里的竹竿上，不管怎么样，我还可以在那里扮成个人恐吓恐吓乌鸦，但是，一个被插在河中间的木杆上的稻草人肯定是毫无用处的。恐怕我是永远得不到脑子了！"

木筏顺着河水往下漂去，可怜的稻草人离他们越来越远。这时候，狮子说道：

"我们必须得想点办法来救救自己。我想我可以游到岸边，把木筏拖在后面，只要你们紧紧拉住我的尾巴就行。"

于是狮子跳进了水里，当他使尽全力向岸边游去的时候，铁

8. The Deadly Poppy Field

So he sprang into the water, and the Tin Woodman caught fast hold of his tail. When the Lion began to swim with all his might toward the shore. It was hard work, although he was so big; but by and by they were drawn out of the current, and then Dorothy took the Tin Woodman's long pole and helped push the raft to the land.

They were all tired out when they reached the shore at last and stepped off upon the pretty green grass, and they also knew that the stream had carried them a long way past the road of yellow brick that led to the Emerald City.

"What shall we do now?" asked the Tin Woodman, as the Lion lay down on the grass to let the sun dry him.

"We must get back to the road, in some way," said Dorothy.

"The best plan will be to walk along the riverbank until we come to the road again," remarked the Lion.

So, when they were rested, Dorothy picked up her basket and they started along the grassy bank, back to the road from which the river had carried them. It was a lovely country, with plenty of flowers and fruit trees and sunshine to cheer them, and had they not felt so sorry for the poor Scarecrow, they could have been very happy.

They walked along as fast as they could, Dorothy only stopping once to pick a beautiful flower; and after a time the Tin Woodman cried out: "Look!"

Then they all looked at the river and saw the Scarecrow perched upon his pole in the middle of the water, looking very lonely and sad.

皮人紧紧地拉着它的尾巴。虽然狮子的身体高大威猛，但这仍旧是一项艰巨的工作。不久之后，他们就被拖出了这股急流。多萝茜拿起铁皮人的长木杆，帮助木筏向岸边划去。

最终，他们到达了岸边，踏上了那片碧绿的草地，这时候，他们所有人都已经筋疲力尽，并且他们知道，那股急流已经把他们带到距离那条通往翡翠城的黄砖路很远很远的地方了。

正当狮子躺在草地上，让太阳晒干身子的时候，铁皮人问道："现在我们该怎么办？"

"我们必须想办法回到那条路上去。"多萝茜说。

"最好的办法就是沿着河岸往回走，一直到那条黄砖路为止。"狮子说。

因此，在他们休息完毕之后，多萝茜提起她的篮子，他们一伙人开始沿着绿意盎然的河岸走回到河水冲走他们的地方。这是个可爱的地方，百花齐放，果实累累，明媚的阳光让他们心旷神怡，若不是为可怜的稻草人感到伤心难过，他们一定会非常快乐的。

他们用最快的速度向前赶着路，多萝茜只停下过一次，摘了一朵漂亮的花。过了一会儿，铁皮人大声叫道："快看！"

所有人都朝河里望去，只见稻草人停留在河中间的那根木杆子上，神情非常寂寞悲伤。

"我们可以用什么办法来救他呢？"多萝茜问道。

"What can we do to save him?" asked Dorothy.

The Lion and the Woodman both shook their heads, for they did not know. So they sat down upon the bank and gazed wistfully at the Scarecrow until a Stork flew by, who, upon seeing them, stopped to rest at the water's edge.

"Who are you and where are you going?" asked the Stork.

"I am Dorothy," answered the girl, "and these are my friends, the Tin Woodman and the Cowardly Lion; and we are going to the Emerald City."

"This isn't the road," said the Stork, as she twisted her long neck and looked sharply at the queer party.

"I know it," returned Dorothy, "but we have lost the Scarecrow, and are wondering how we shall get him again."

"Where is he?" asked the Stork.

"Over there in the river," answered the little girl.

"If he wasn't so big and heavy I would get him for you," remarked the Stork.

"He isn't heavy a bit," said Dorothy eagerly, "for he is stuffed with straw; and if you will bring him back to us, we shall thank you ever and ever so much."

"Well, I'll try," said the Stork, "but if I find he is too heavy to carry I shall have to drop him in the river again."

So the big bird flew into the air and over the water till she came to where the Scarecrow was perched upon his pole. Then the Stork with

　　狮子和铁皮人全都摇了摇头，不知道该怎么办。于是，他们就坐在岸边，愁眉苦脸地望着稻草人，这时候一只鹳鸟飞了过来，看见了他们，于是就在岸边停了下来，休息休息。

　　"你们是谁？要去哪里？"鹳鸟问。

　　"我叫多萝茜，"小女孩回答道，"他们都是我的朋友，铁皮人和胆小狮；我们要去翡翠城。"

　　"你们走错路了。"鹳鸟一边说着，一边扭动着修长的脖子，敏锐地打量着这群奇怪的人。

　　"我知道，"多萝茜回答说，"只是我们少了一个稻草人，正想着该怎么把他救回来呢。"

　　"他在哪儿？"鹳鸟问道。

　　"就在这条河里。"小女孩回答说。

　　"如果他不那么庞大沉重的话，我可以替你们把他救出来。"鹳鸟说道。

　　"他一点儿都不重，"多萝茜急切地说道，"因为他是用稻草扎成的。如果你能把他救回来，我们会永远永远感谢你的。"

　　"好，那我就试试看，"鹳鸟说，"但是，如果我发现他太重而带不动的话，我就会重新把他丢回河里去的。"

　　于是这只大鹳鸟飞向空中，来到水面上，飞到了抱着木杆的稻草人那里。然后鹳鸟用它那硕大的爪子抓住稻草人的手臂，把他拖到了空中，飞回到岸边。多萝茜、狮子，以及铁皮人和托托

her great claws grabbed the Scarecrow by the arm and carried him up into the air and back to the bank, where Dorothy and the Lion and the Tin Woodman and Toto were sitting.

When the Scarecrow found himself among his friends again, he was so happy that he hugged them all, even the Lion and Toto; and as they walked along he sang "Tol-de-ri-de-oh!" at every step, he felt so gay.

"I was afraid I should have to stay in the river forever," he said, "but the kind Stork saved me, and if I ever get any brains I shall find the Stork again and do her some kindness in return."

"That's all right," said the Stork, who was flying along beside them. "I always like to help anyone in trouble. But I must go now, for my babies are waiting in the nest for me. I hope you will find the Emerald City and that Oz will help you."

"Thank you," replied Dorothy, and then the kind Stork flew into the air and was soon out of sight.

They walked along listening to the singing of the brightly colored birds and looking at the lovely flowers which now became so thick that the ground was carpeted with them. There were big yellow and white and blue and purple blossoms, besides great clusters of scarlet poppies, which were so brilliant in color they almost dazzled Dorothy's eyes.

"Aren't they beautiful?" the girl asked, as she breathed in the spicy scent of the flowers.

都坐在那里。

当稻草人发现自己又回到了朋友们的身边时，他高兴极了，和所有人拥抱了一遍，甚至还拥抱了狮子和托托。在他们向前赶路时，他每走一步，就唱一句："托—德—列—德—哦！"他感觉快活极了。

"我还担心自己要永远留在那条河当中了呢，"稻草人说，"但是那只热心的鹳鸟救了我，如果我能得到脑子，那么我会再去找那只鹳鸟，为它做些好事以示报答。"

"没什么，"鹳鸟说，它就飞在他们旁边，"我一直都很喜欢帮助那些有困难的人。不过现在我得走了，我的孩子们还在巢里等我呢。祝愿你们能找到翡翠城，希望奥兹会帮助你们。"

"谢谢你。"多萝茜回答说，然后这只善良的鹳鸟就飞到了空中，一会儿就消失不见了。

他们一边向前走，一边听着艳丽的鸟儿歌唱，看着可爱的花儿漫山遍野，争相开放。那里有黄色的、白色的、蓝色的、紫色的大花朵。除此之外，还有一大簇一大簇猩红色的罂粟花，色彩如此艳丽，几乎让多萝茜看得眼花缭乱了。

当小女孩呼吸着这些花儿的芳香时，问道："这些花是不是很漂亮？"

"我想是吧，"稻草人回答说，"等我有了脑子之后，或许会更喜欢它们的。"

"I suppose so," answered the Scarecrow. "When I have brains, I shall probably like them better."

"If I only had a heart, I should love them," added the Tin Woodman.

"I always did like flowers," said the Lion. "They seem so helpless and frail. But there are none in the forest so bright as these."

They now came upon more and more of the big scarlet poppies, and fewer and fewer of the other flowers; and soon they found themselves in the midst of a great meadow of poppies. Now it is well known that when there are many of these flowers together their odor is so powerful that anyone who breathes it falls asleep, and if the sleeper is not carried away from the scent of the flowers, he sleeps on and on forever. But Dorothy did not know this, nor could she get away from the bright red flowers that were everywhere about; so presently her eyes grew heavy and she felt she must sit down to rest and to sleep.

But the Tin Woodman would not let her do this.

"We must hurry and get back to the road of yellow brick before dark," he said; and the Scarecrow agreed with him. So they kept walking until Dorothy could stand no longer. Her eyes closed in spite of herself and she forgot where she was and fell among the poppies, fast asleep.

"What shall we do?" asked the Tin Woodman.

"如果我有了心，我应该会喜欢它们的。"铁皮人接着说道。

"我一直都非常喜欢花，"狮子说，"它们看起来虽然孱弱无力，但是在这森林之中，没有比这更加鲜艳的花朵了。"

这时候他们面前出现了越来越多猩红色的大罂粟花，而其他花朵却愈来愈少，不一会儿他们发现自己已经来到了大片罂粟地里。如今，人人都知道，当这种花大量地集中在一起时，它们的气味会变得非常浓郁，任何人闻过之后就会昏昏欲睡。如果这个沉睡的人没有远离这种花的香气，他就会永远永远地睡着了。但是多萝茜并不知道这些，也没有远离这些到处生长着的艳丽的红色花朵，因此，很快她的眼睛就变得沉重起来，她感觉自己必须坐下来休息一下，睡个觉。

不过铁皮人并没有让她睡觉。

"我们必须快点赶路，在天黑之前回到黄砖路上。"他说。稻草人也对此表示赞同，因此他们一直不停地赶路，直到多萝茜再也坚持不住了。她的眼睛不由自主地闭了起来，她忘记自己身在何处，倒在这片罂粟花丛中，一转眼就睡着了。

"我们该怎么办？"铁皮人问道。

"如果我们把她丢在这里，她就会死的，"狮子说，"这些花的气味会杀了我们所有人。我的眼睛几乎都快睁不开了，那条狗已经睡着了。"

狮子说得没错，托托已经倒在了它小主人的旁边。不过因为

"If we leave her here she will die," said the Lion. "The smell of the flowers is killing us all. I myself can scarcely keep my eyes open, and the dog is asleep already."

It was true; Toto had fallen down beside his little mistress. But the Scarecrow and the Tin Woodman, not being made of flesh, were not troubled by the scent of the flowers.

"Run fast," said the Scarecrow to the Lion, "and get out of this deadly flower bed as soon as you can. We will bring the little girl with us, but if you should fall asleep you are too big to be carried."

So the Lion aroused himself and bounded forward as fast as he could go. In a moment he was out of sight.

"Let us make a chair with our hands and carry her," said the Scarecrow. So they picked up Toto and put the dog in Dorothy's lap, and then they made a chair with their hands for the seat and their arms for the arms and carried the sleeping girl between them through the flowers.

On and on they walked, and it seemed that the great carpet of deadly flowers that surrounded them would never end. They followed the bend of the river, and at last came upon their friend the Lion, lying fast asleep among the poppies. The flowers had been too strong for the huge beast and he had given up at last, and fallen only a short distance from the end of the poppy bed, where the sweet grass spread in beautiful green fields before them.

稻草人和铁皮人并非血肉之躯，所以这些花的香气并没有让他们感到不适。

"快跑，"稻草人对狮子说道，"尽快逃离这片致命的花园。我们会带小女孩一起走的，可是如果你睡着了，你那么大，我们可抬不动。"

于是狮子振作起精神，使尽全力向前跑去，不一会儿就消失在他们眼前。

"我们用手搭成一把椅子，抬着她走。"稻草人说。于是他们就抱起托托，把它放在多萝茜的膝上，然后用手搭成一把椅子，手臂当做扶手，抬着这个熟睡的女孩，穿过这片花丛。

他们一直不停地向前走，这一大片围绕着他们的致命的罂粟花就像永无边际似的没有尽头。他们沿着弯曲的河流向前走着，最后遇到了他们的朋友——狮子，它躺在罂粟丛中，睡得正酣。这些花的香气如此强烈，最终这只庞然大物也只得放弃，在距离罂粟园尽头不过一箭之地倒下了。在他们面前，芳香的青草在美丽的绿草地上随风摆动着。

"我们什么也帮不了它，"铁皮人伤心地说道，"它实在太重，我们根本抬不动。我们只能让它永远睡在这里，最后，它或许会在梦中找到胆量。"

"真让人难过，"稻草人说，"对于一个这样胆小的狮子来说，它的确是一个很好的同伴。不过我们还是继续往前走吧。"

8. The Deadly Poppy Field

"We can do nothing for him," said the Tin Woodman, sadly; "for he is much too heavy to lift. We must leave him here to sleep on forever, and perhaps he will dream that he has found courage at last."

"I'm sorry," said the Scarecrow. "The Lion was a very good comrade for one so cowardly. But let us go on."

They carried the sleeping girl to a pretty spot beside the river, far enough from the poppy field to prevent her breathing any more of the poison of the flowers, and here they laid her gently on the soft grass and waited for the fresh breeze to waken her.

他们抬着这个睡着了的小女孩，来到河边一个美丽的地方，远离那片罂粟园，防止她再闻到那些花朵散发的毒素。他们轻轻地把她放在柔软的草地上，等待着清风把她吹醒。

9. The Queen of the Field Mice

"We cannot be far from the road of yellow brick, now," remarked the Scarecrow, as he stood beside the girl, "for we have come nearly as far as the river carried us away."

The Tin Woodman was about to reply when he heard a low growl, and turning his head (which worked beautifully on hinges) he saw a strange beast come bounding over the grass toward them. It was, indeed, a great yellow Wildcat, and the Woodman thought it must be chasing something, for its ears were lying close to its head and its mouth was wide open, showing two rows of ugly teeth, while its red eyes glowed like balls of fire. As it came nearer the Tin Woodman saw that running before the beast was a little gray field mouse, and although he had no heart he knew it was wrong for the Wildcat to try to kill such a pretty, harmless creature.

So the Woodman raised his axe, and as the Wildcat ran by he gave it a quick blow that cut the beast's head clean off from its body, and it rolled over at his feet in two pieces.

The field mouse, now that it was freed from its enemy, stopped short; and coming slowly up to the Woodman it said, in a squeaky little voice:

"Oh, thank you! Thank you ever so much for saving my life."

九.田鼠女王

"现在我们应该离那条黄砖路不远了，"稻草人正站在小女孩旁边，说道，"我们走过的路已经差不多跟被流水带走的一样多了。"

铁皮人正想要回应，却听到一声低沉的怒吼，他转过头去（他这头活动起来还是相当灵活的），看见一只奇怪的野兽跃过草地直奔他们而来。那是一只硕大的黄色野猫，铁皮人心想它一定是在追捕什么东西，因为它那双耳朵紧紧地贴在脑袋边上，嘴巴张得很大，露出两排可怕的牙齿，一双血红的眼睛像燃烧着的火球一般闪闪发光。当这只野猫跑近之后，铁皮人发现跑在它前面的是一只灰色的小田鼠。铁皮人虽然没有心，但是他仍旧知道，野猫想要杀死这样一只于人无害的小动物是不对的。

于是铁皮人举起斧头，当野猫往自己身边跑过的时候，他迅速地劈了下去，那只野猫被砍成了两半，猫头从猫身上掉了下来，滚到了铁皮人的脚边。

此刻，那只死里逃生、重获自由的田鼠停了下来，慢慢地走到铁皮人跟前，用非常短促而尖锐细小的声音说道：

"哦，谢谢你！非常感谢你救了我的命。"

"请你别这么说，"铁皮人回答道，"你知道，我没有心，因此对于那些需要帮助的朋友，我会格外留心地加以帮助，哪怕

9. The Queen of the Field Mice

"Don't speak of it, I beg of you," replied the Woodman. "I have no heart, you know, so I am careful to help all those who may need a friend, even if it happens to be only a mouse."

"Only a mouse!" cried the little animal, indignantly. "Why, I am a Queen – the Queen of all the Field Mice!"

"Oh, indeed," said the Woodman, making a bow.

"Therefore you have done a great deed, as well as a brave one, in saving my life," added the Queen.

At that moment several mice were seen running up as fast as their little legs could carry them, and when they saw their Queen they exclaimed:

"Oh, your Majesty, we thought you would be killed! How did you manage to escape the great Wildcat?" They all bowed so low to the little Queen that they almost stood upon their heads.

"This funny tin man," she answered, "killed the Wildcat and saved my life. So hereafter you must all serve him, and obey his slightest wish."

"We will!" cried all the mice, in a shrill chorus. And then they scampered in all directions, for Toto had awakened from his sleep, and seeing all these mice around him he gave one bark of delight and jumped right into the middle of the group. Toto had always loved to chase mice when he lived in Kansas, and he saw no harm in it.

只是一只小田鼠也是如此。"

"只是一只小田鼠！"这个小家伙义愤填膺地叫喊了起来，"什么！我可是女王——是这里所有田鼠的女王！"

"啊，真的吗！"铁皮人向它鞠了个躬，说道。

"你救了我的命，这不但是立了大功，而且还非常之勇敢。"田鼠女王接着说道。

这时候，有好几只田鼠摆动着小腿，用它们最快的速度跑了过来，当它们看见自己的女王之后，都叫喊着：

"啊，女王陛下，我们还以为您已经驾鹤西去了呢！您是怎么从那只大野猫手中逃脱的！"它们全都深深地向小女王鞠了个躬，那姿势几乎就像是用头站在了地上。

"是这位古怪的铁皮人杀死了野猫，救了我的性命。因此从今往后，你们必须服侍他，顺从他的意愿。"田鼠女王说道。

"遵命！"小田鼠们用尖锐的声音异口同声地回答道，接着它们向各个方向跑开了，因为这时候托托睡醒了，看见有那么多田鼠围在自己身边，便欣喜若狂地吠了起来，跳进田鼠群中。以前在堪萨斯州的时候，托托总是喜欢追赶老鼠，它觉得这没什么坏处。

但是铁皮人却捉住了这只小狗，紧紧地把它抱在怀里，与此同时，他召唤着田鼠们："回来！快回来！托托不会伤害你们的。"

听到这话，田鼠女王便从下面的草丛里探出头来，胆怯地问

But the Tin Woodman caught the dog in his arms and held him tight, while he called to the mice, "Come back! Come back! Toto shall not hurt you."

At this the Queen of the Mice stuck her head out from underneath a clump of grass and asked, in a timid voice, "Are you sure he will not bite us?"

"I will not let him," said the Woodman; "so do not be afraid."

One by one the mice came creeping back, and Toto did not bark again, although he tried to get out of the Woodman's arms, and would have bitten him had he not known very well he was made of tin. Finally one of the biggest mice spoke.

"Is there anything we can do," it asked, "to repay you for saving the life of our Queen?"

"Nothing that I know of," answered the Woodman; but the Scarecrow, who had been trying to think, but could not because his head was stuffed with straw, said, quickly, "Oh, yes; you can save our friend, the Cowardly Lion, who is asleep in the poppy bed."

"A Lion!" cried the little Queen. "Why, he would eat us all up."

"Oh, no," declared the Scarecrow; "this Lion is a coward."

"Really?" asked the Mouse.

"He says so himself," answered the Scarecrow, "and he would never hurt anyone who is our friend. If you will help us to save him I promise that he shall treat you all with kindness."

"Very well," said the Queen, "we trust you. But what shall we do?"

道："你肯定它不会咬我们吗？"

"我不会让它咬你们的，"铁皮人说，"不用担心。"

于是田鼠们又一个个地爬了回来，而托托也没再叫唤了，尽管它仍旧想从铁皮人的手臂中挣脱出来，若不是知道铁皮人是用铁皮做的，说不定还会咬他呢。最后，其中最大的那只田鼠开口了。

"我们可以做些什么来报答您对我们女王的救命之恩呢？"它问道。

"我不知道有什么事。"铁皮人回答说。

但是稻草人（他一直都想要转动脑筋，只可惜他那脑袋里装的都是稻草，动不了脑筋）立刻说道：

"啊，对了，你们可以去救我们的朋友——胆小狮，它现在正睡在罂粟园里呢。"

"狮子！"田鼠女王大声叫道，"哎呀，它会把我们大家伙儿全都吃掉的。"

"哦，不会，"稻草人郑重地说道，"这个狮子是一个胆小鬼。"

"真的吗？"一只田鼠问道。

"它自己是这么说的，"稻草人回答说，"它绝对不会伤害我们的朋友。如果你们能帮忙救它出来，我保证它会友好地对待你们的。"

9. The Queen of the Field Mice

"Are there many of these mice which call you Queen and are willing to obey you?"

"Oh, yes; there are thousands," she replied.

"Then send for them all to come here as soon as possible, and let each one bring a long piece of string."

The Queen turned to the mice that attended her and told them to go at once and get all her people. As soon as they heard her orders they ran away in every direction as fast as possible.

"Now," said the Scarecrow to the Tin Woodman, "you must go to those trees by the riverside and make a truck that will carry the Lion."

So the Woodman went at once to the trees and began to work; and he soon made a truck out of the limbs of trees, from which he chopped away all the leaves and branches. He fastened it together with wooden pegs and made the four wheels out of short pieces of a big tree trunk. So fast and so well did he work that by the time the mice began to arrive the truck was all ready for them.

They came from all directions, and there were thousands of them: big mice and little mice and middle-sized mice; and each one brought a piece of string in his mouth. It was about this time that Dorothy woke from her long sleep and opened her eyes. She was greatly astonished to find herself lying upon the grass, with thousands of mice standing around and looking at her timidly. But the Scarecrow told her about everything, and turning to the dignified little Mouse, he said:

"那就好，"女王说，"我们相信你。但是我们该怎么救它呢？"

"这里有那么多田鼠，它们全都是你的子民，并且愿意服从你的命令吗？"

"哦，是啊，有好几千呢。"女王回答说。

"那么把它们全都召集到这里，越快越好，让每只田鼠都带一根长绳过来。"

田鼠女王转过身来面对着它的侍从，吩咐它们立即把所有的子民全都召集过来。它们一听到这命令就迅速地向各个方向跑开了。

"现在，"稻草人对铁皮人说，"你得去河边，砍一些树来，然后造一辆载狮子用的车子。"

铁皮人立刻就跑到树林里，开始工作起来。没过多久，他就用树干造出了一辆木车，他削掉树干上的所有枝叶，用木钉把树干全都钉在一起，用几小段大树的树干做成车的 4 个轮子。铁皮人的工作如此迅速和熟练，在田鼠们陆续到来之前，他就已经造好了车子，等着它们了。

好几千只田鼠从四面八方赶来：有大田鼠，小田鼠，不大不小的田鼠；每一只的嘴里都衔着一根绳子。就在这个时候，多萝茜从她悠长的睡梦中醒了过来，睁开了眼睛。她发现自己躺在草地上，身边还围绕着成千上万只田鼠，胆怯地注视着她，心中充

9. The Queen of the Field Mice

"Permit me to introduce to you her Majesty, the Queen."

Dorothy nodded gravely and the Queen made a curtsy, after which she became quite friendly with the little girl.

The Scarecrow and the Woodman now began to fasten the mice to the truck, using the strings they had brought. One end of a string was tied around the neck of each mouse and the other end to the truck. Of course the truck was a thousand times bigger than any of the mice who were to draw it; but when all the mice had been harnessed, they were able to pull it quite easily. Even the Scarecrow and the Tin Woodman could sit on it, and were drawn swiftly by their queer little horses to the place where the Lion lay asleep.

After a great deal of hard work, for the Lion was heavy, they managed to get him up on the truck. Then the Queen hurriedly gave her people the order to start, for she feared if the mice stayed among the poppies too long they also would fall asleep.

At first the little creatures, many though they were, could hardly stir the heavily loaded truck; but the Woodman and the Scarecrow both pushed from behind, and they got along better. Soon they rolled the Lion out of the poppy bed to the green fields, where he could breathe the sweet, fresh air again, instead of the poisonous scent of the flowers.

Dorothy came to meet them and thanked the little mice warmly for saving her companion from death. She had grown so fond of the big Lion she was glad he had been rescued.

满了惊讶。不过铁皮人把事情的来龙去脉全都告诉了她，之后，他转向令人敬畏的田鼠女王，说道：

"请允许我向你介绍田鼠女王。"

多萝茜庄重地点了点头，女王向她行了个礼，然后，它便和小女孩成为了非常友好的朋友。

这时候，稻草人和铁皮人开始用田鼠们带来的绳子，把它们跟车子连在一起。绳子的一端绕在每一只田鼠的脖子上，另一端绑在车子上。当然，车子本身要比任何一只拉着它的田鼠大上一千倍。但是当所有的田鼠都套上绳子之后，它们就可以轻而易举地拉动这辆车了。即使稻草人和铁皮人坐在上面，这些奇特的小马也能快速地将这辆车拉到狮子熟睡的地方。

狮子的身体非常笨重，因此费尽一番工夫之后，他们才把它搬上了车。接着女王便急忙命令它的子民们开始拉车，因为它担心田鼠们在罂粟园里停留太长时间，也会昏睡过去的。

虽然这些小动物数量众多，但是刚开始它们也很难拉动这辆沉重的车子。不过有铁皮人和稻草人他们俩在后面推着，车子才顺利地拉动起来。很快，它们就把狮子拉出了罂粟园，来到绿草地上，狮子又能在那里呼吸到甜美清新的空气，而不是那些罂粟花散发出来的有毒香气了。

多萝茜上前迎接他们，真心诚意地感谢小田鼠们救出了自己的朋友。她如此喜欢这只大狮子，见到它能得救，心里别提有多

9. The Queen of the Field Mice

Then the mice were unharnessed from the truck and scampered away through the grass to their homes. The Queen of the Mice was the last to leave.

"If ever you need us again," she said, "come out into the field and call, and we shall hear you and come to your assistance. Good-bye!"

"Good-bye!" they all answered, and away the Queen ran, while Dorothy held Toto tightly lest he should run after her and frighten her.

After this they sat down beside the Lion until he should awaken; and the Scarecrow brought Dorothy some fruit from a tree near by, which she ate for her dinner.

开心了。

然后，田鼠们从车子上卸下绳子，穿过草地，回它们的老家去了。田鼠女王最后一个离开。

"如果你们要再有什么需要，"它说，"就到田里来叫唤一声，我们会听到，然后跑出来帮助你们的。再见！"

"再见！"他们齐声回答。当田鼠女王离开时，多萝茜紧紧地抱着托托，不让它去追赶田鼠女王，让女王受了惊吓。

田鼠女王离开之后，他们就坐在狮子旁边，等它醒过来。稻草人从附近的树上摘了许多水果，给多萝茜当午餐。

10. The Guardian of the Gate

It was some time before the Cowardly Lion awakened, for he had lain among the poppies a long while, breathing in their deadly fragrance; but when he did open his eyes and roll off the truck he was very glad to find himself still alive.

"I ran as fast as I could," he said, sitting down and yawning, "but the flowers were too strong for me. How did you get me out?"

Then they told him of the field mice, and how they had generously saved him from death; and the Cowardly Lion laughed, and said:

"I have always thought myself very big and terrible; yet such little things as flowers came near to killing me, and such small animals as mice have saved my life. How strange it all is! But, comrades, what shall we do now?"

"We must journey on until we find the road of yellow brick again," said Dorothy, "and then we can keep on to the Emerald City."

So, the Lion being fully refreshed, and feeling quite himself again, they all started upon the journey, greatly enjoying the walk through the soft, fresh grass; and it was not long before they reached the road of yellow brick and turned again toward the Emerald City where the great Oz dwelt.

The road was smooth and well paved, now, and the country about was beautiful, so that the travelers rejoiced in leaving the forest far

十.翡翠城的守门人

因为胆小狮睡在罂粟园中的时间太长，一直呼吸着它们的致命香气，所以过了很久它才醒过来。但是当它张开眼睛，滚下车子的时候，它发现自己还活着，真是高兴极了。

"我使尽全力向前跑，"它一边坐起来，打着哈欠，一边说道，"但是那些花的香气太强烈了，我根本抵挡不住。你们是怎么把我救出来的？"

于是他们跟它说起了田鼠，说它们是如何勇敢地把它从死亡中救出来的。胆小狮笑着说道：

"我一直以为自己是个庞然大物，令人畏惧，可是就连花这样的小东西都会要了我的命，而田鼠这样的小动物又能救了我，这可真是奇怪啊！可是，朋友们，我们现在要怎么办呢？"

"我们必须得继续往前走，重新找到那条黄砖路，"多萝茜说，"然后才能去翡翠城。"

因此，等狮子完全清醒，重新振作之后，他们一行人就又开始了旅程，十分惬意地走在柔软清新的草地上。没花多少时间，他们就来到了那条黄砖路，重新向伟大的奥兹居住的翡翠城进发。

这会儿，路又变得非常平坦整洁，周围的景色也很怡人，因此这几位旅行者都很庆幸自己能把那片森林远远地抛在身后，远离在那阴沉的树荫中所遇到的众多危险。他们再一次看到了筑在

behind, and with it the many dangers they had met in its gloomy shades. Once more they could see fences built beside the road; but these were painted green, and when they came to a small house, in which a farmer evidently lived, that also was painted green. They passed by several of these houses during the afternoon, and sometimes people came to the doors and looked at them as if they would like to ask questions; but no one came near them nor spoke to them because of the great Lion, of which they were very much afraid. The people were all dressed in clothing of a lovely emerald-green color and wore peaked hats like those of the Munchkins.

"This must be the Land of Oz," said Dorothy, "and we are surely getting near the Emerald City."

"Yes," answered the Scarecrow. "Everything is green here, while in the country of the Munchkins blue was the favorite color. But the people do not seem to be as friendly as the Munchkins, and I'm afraid we shall be unable to find a place to pass the night."

"I should like something to eat besides fruit," said the girl, "and I'm sure Toto is nearly starved. Let us stop at the next house and talk to the people."

So, when they came to a good-sized farmhouse, Dorothy walked boldly up to the door and knocked.

A woman opened it just far enough to look out, and said, "What do you want, child, and why is that great Lion with you?"

路边上的围墙，不过这些围墙都被漆成了绿色。当他们走进一间显然居住着一位农夫的小屋时，那间小屋同样被漆成了绿色。这个下午，他们经过了很多这样的房子，有时候房子里的人会跑出来，看着他们，似乎要问他们些问题。但是没有一个人敢走近他们，也没有一个人跟他们说话，因为他们都非常害怕那只大狮子。这里的居民都穿着翠绿色的漂亮衣服，头上戴着像芒奇金人那样的尖顶帽子。

"这里一定就是奥兹国了，"多萝茜说，"我们已经越来越靠近翡翠城了。"

"是啊，"稻草人回答说，"这里所有东西都是绿色的，就像在芒奇金人的国家里，他们喜爱蓝色一样。但是，这里的人似乎并不像芒奇金人那般友好，只怕我们找不到地方过夜喽。"

"我要吃点其他东西，不能总是吃水果，"小女孩说，"我想托托也差不多饿了。到了下一户人家我们就停下来，跟那里的住户商量一下吧。"

于是，当他们来到一座不大不小的农舍前面时，多萝茜鼓起勇气走上前去敲门。

一位妇人开了条门缝，刚好可以探出头来，说："孩子，你想干什么，为什么跟一只大狮子在一起？"

"如果您允许的话，我们想在这儿借宿一个晚上，"多萝茜回答道，"这只狮子是我的朋友，也是我的伙伴，它绝不会伤害

"We wish to pass the night with you, if you will allow us," answered Dorothy; "and the Lion is my friend and comrade, and would not hurt you for the world."

"Is he tame?" asked the woman, opening the door a little wider.

"Oh, yes," said the girl, "and he is a great coward, too. He will be more afraid of you than you are of him."

"Well," said the woman, after thinking it over and taking another peep at the Lion, "if that is the case you may come in, and I will give you some supper and a place to sleep."

So they all entered the house, where there were, besides the woman, two children and a man. The man had hurt his leg, and was lying on the couch in a corner. They seemed greatly surprised to see so strange a company, and while the woman was busy laying the table the man asked:

"Where are you all going?"

"To the Emerald City," said Dorothy, "to see the Great Oz."

"Oh, indeed!" exclaimed the man. "Are you sure that Oz will see you?"

"Why not?" she replied.

"Why, it is said that he never lets anyone come into his presence. I have been to the Emerald City many times, and it is a beautiful and wonderful place; but I have never been permitted to see the Great Oz, nor do I know of any living person who has seen him."

"Does he never go out?" asked the Scarecrow.

您的。"

"它很温驯吗?"妇人把门稍微开大了一点儿,问道。

"哦,是的,"小女孩说,"而且它还非常胆小,所以它更加怕你才是。"

妇人想了想,又偷看了一眼狮子,然后,她说:"那好吧,如果情况属实,你们就进来吧,我先给你们准备晚饭,然后再找个地方让你们睡一觉。"

于是他们全都走进了屋子,房间里除了妇人以外,还住着两个小孩和一个男人。那个男的腿受了伤,躺在一张安放在角落的床上。他们看见这样一群奇怪的人,都感到特别诧异,在妇人忙着摆放桌子的时候,那男人问道:

"你们这几个是要去哪里啊?"

"去翡翠城,"多萝茜说,"拜访伟大的奥兹。"

"哦,真的吗!"男人大声叫道,"你们确定奥兹会接见你们吗?"

"为什么不呢?"多萝茜回答说。

"为什么!听说他从来不让任何人接近他。我去过翡翠城很多次,那是一个美丽而奇妙的地方。但是我从来都没有得到允许去拜见伟大的奥兹,我也不知道有谁见过他。"

"他从来都没有外出过吗?"稻草人问道。

"从来没有。每天他都坐在皇宫中那宽敞的王座室里,即使

10. The Guardian of the Gate

"Never. He sits day after day in the great throne room of his Palace, and even those who wait upon him do not see him face to face."

"What is he like?" asked the girl.

"That is hard to tell," said the man thoughtfully. "You see, Oz is a Great Wizard, and can take on any form he wishes. So that some say he looks like a bird; and some say he looks like an elephant; and some say he looks like a cat. To others he appears as a beautiful fairy, or a brownie, or in any other form that pleases him. But who the real Oz is, when he is in his own form, no living person can tell."

"That is very strange," said Dorothy, "but we must try, in some way, to see him, or we shall have made our journey for nothing."

"Why do you wish to see the terrible Oz?" asked the man.

"I want him to give me some brains," said the Scarecrow eagerly.

"Oh, Oz could do that easily enough," declared the man. "He has more brains than he needs."

"And I want him to give me a heart," said the Tin Woodman.

"That will not trouble him," continued the man, "for Oz has a large collection of hearts, of all sizes and shapes."

"And I want him to give me courage," said the Cowardly Lion.

"Oz keeps a great pot of courage in his throne room," said the man, "which he has covered with a golden plate, to keep it from running over. He will be glad to give you some."

"And I want him to send me back to Kansas," said Dorothy.

"Where is Kansas?" asked the man, with surprise.

是那些侍从也都没有见过他的面。"

"那他长什么样子呢？"小女孩问。

"那可就难说了，"这个人沉思着说道，"你知道，奥兹是一个伟大的魔法师，他可以随心所欲地变成自己希望的样子。因此有人说他像一只鸟，有人说他像一头象，也有人说他像一只猫。而对于另一些人来说，他的样子就像是一个美丽的仙子，像是一个善良的精灵，又或是任何他自己喜欢的样子。但是没有一个人可以说出真正的奥兹是谁，他本来的样子又是如何。"

"那真是奇怪极了，"多萝茜说，"但是我们必须得看到他，不管什么方法都要尝试一下，要不然，我们就白走这一趟了。"

"你们为什么想要去拜见那可怕的奥兹呢？"这个人问道。

"我想让他给我一个脑子。"稻草人急切地说道。

"哦，这种事情奥兹可以轻易办到的，"这个人肯定地说，"他有许多脑子，用都用不完。"

"我想让他给我一颗心。"铁皮人说。

"那也难不倒他，"这个人继续说道，"奥兹有一大堆心，各种大小、各种形状的都有。"

"我想让他给我一点胆量。"胆小狮说。

"奥兹在他的王座室里藏着一大锅胆量呢，"这个男人说，"为了不让它们跑掉，他就用一个金色的盖子盖着。他会很乐意给你一点儿的。"

10. The Guardian of the Gate

"I don't know," replied Dorothy sorrowfully, "but it is my home, and I'm sure it's somewhere."

"Very likely. Well, Oz can do anything; so I suppose he will find Kansas for you. But first you must get to see him, and that will be a hard task; for the Great Wizard does not like to see anyone, and he usually has his own way. But what do you want?" he continued, speaking to Toto. Toto only wagged his tail; for, strange to say, he could not speak.

The woman now called to them that supper was ready, so they gathered around the table and Dorothy ate some delicious porridge and a dish of scrambled eggs and a plate of nice white bread, and enjoyed her meal. The Lion ate some of the porridge, but did not care for it, saying it was made from oats and oats were food for horses, not for lions. The Scarecrow and the Tin Woodman ate nothing at all. Toto ate a little of everything, and was glad to get a good supper again.

The woman now gave Dorothy a bed to sleep in, and Toto lay down beside her, while the Lion guarded the door of her room so she might not be disturbed. The Scarecrow and the Tin Woodman stood up in a corner and kept quiet all night, although of course they could not sleep.

The next morning, as soon as the sun was up, they started on their way, and soon saw a beautiful green glow in the sky just before them.

"That must be the Emerald City," said Dorothy.

"我想让他送我回堪萨斯州。"多萝茜说。

"堪萨斯州在什么地方？"男人惊讶地问道。

"我也不知道，"多萝茜伤心地回答说，"但那是我的家乡，我肯定有这么个地方。"

"可能是吧。奥兹是无所不能的，所以我想他会为你找到堪萨斯州的。但是，首先你们必须要见到他，那是一件非常困难的事情，因为这位伟大的魔法师不喜欢会见任何人，他总是我行我素的。可是你想要什么呢？"这个人又对着托托问道。托托只是摇了摇它的尾巴，因为，说来奇怪，托托竟然不会说话。

这时候，妇人招呼他们说晚饭准备好了，于是他们在桌子旁围坐下来，多萝茜吃了一些可口的燕麦粥，一碟炒蛋和一盘精致的白面包，尽情享受着她的晚餐。狮子也吃了一些燕麦粥，但是它并不喜欢，说这粥是用燕麦做的，而燕麦是给马吃的，而不是给狮子吃的。稻草人和铁皮人什么都没吃。托托把所有东西都吃了个遍，它很高兴又吃到了一顿美味的晚餐。

吃完晚饭，妇人就给多萝茜准备了一张床睡觉，托托睡在她的旁边，狮子就守着她的房门，这样她就不会被人打扰。稻草人和铁皮人一整夜都安静地站在角落里，当然他们用不着睡觉。

第二天早晨，太阳一出来，他们就出发上路了。不一会儿，他们就看见一道绿光闪耀在他们前面的天空中。

"那一定就是翡翠城了。"多萝茜说。

10. The Guardian of the Gate

As they walked on, the green glow became brighter and brighter, and it seemed that at last they were nearing the end of their travels. Yet it was afternoon before they came to the great wall that surrounded the City. It was high and thick and of a bright green color.

In front of them, and at the end of the road of yellow brick, was a big gate, all studded with emeralds that glittered so in the sun that even the painted eyes of the Scarecrow were dazzled by their brilliancy.

There was a bell beside the gate, and Dorothy pushed the button and heard a silvery tinkle sound within. Then the big gate swung slowly open, and they all passed through and found themselves in a high arched room, the walls of which glistened with countless emeralds.

Before them stood a little man about the same size as the Munchkins. He was clothed all in green, from his head to his feet, and even his skin was of a greenish tint. At his side was a large green box.

When he saw Dorothy and her companions the man asked, "What do you wish in the Emerald City?"

"We came here to see the Great Oz," said Dorothy.

The man was so surprised at this answer that he sat down to think it over.

"It has been many years since anyone asked me to see Oz," he said, shaking his head in perplexity. "He is powerful and terrible, and if you come on an idle or foolish errand to bother the wise reflections of

他们越往前走，那道绿光就变得越明亮，看来他们总算是走近旅行的目的地了。但是，直到下午他们才来到高大的城墙外面。那城墙又高又厚，漆着明亮的绿色。

在他们的前面，那条黄砖路的尽头，是一扇高大的城门，全都镶嵌着翡翠，在阳光的照耀下闪烁着光芒，即使是稻草人那双画出来的眼睛，也被这光照射得头晕目眩。

在城门旁边装着一个铃，多萝茜按了一下按钮，听到里面传来一阵清脆的叮当声。接着那扇高大的城门就慢慢打开了，他们全都走了进去，发现自己置身于一间拱形的房子之中，四周的墙上装饰着无数闪闪发光的翡翠。

在他们面前站着一个身材跟芒奇金人差不多的小矮人，他全身上下，从头到脚都穿着绿色，甚至连他的皮肤都透露着一种浅绿。在他的旁边是一只绿色的大箱子。

这个人看见了多萝茜和她的同伴，问道："你们来翡翠城有什么事情吗？"

"我们想拜见伟大的奥兹。"

听到这一回答，这个人感到非常惊讶，坐下来仔细地想了想。

"已经有很多年没有人跟我说要看奥兹大人了，"他疑惑不解地摇了摇头，说，"他的法力无边，令人生畏，如果你们只是因为一件无聊或愚蠢的事情而打扰这位伟大聪明的魔法师，他可能会发怒，立刻就会要了你们的命。"

the Great Wizard, he might be angry and destroy you all in an instant."

"But it is not a foolish errand, nor an idle one," replied the Scarecrow; "it is important. And we have been told that Oz is a good Wizard."

"So he is," said the green man, "and he rules the Emerald City wisely and well. But to those who are not honest, or who approach him from curiosity, he is most terrible, and few have ever dared ask to see his face. I am the Guardian of the Gates, and since you demand to see the Great Oz I must take you to his palace. But first you must put on the spectacles."

"Why?" asked Dorothy.

"Because if you did not wear spectacles the brightness and glory of the Emerald City would blind you. Even those who live in the City must wear spectacles night and day. They are all locked on, for Oz so ordered it when the City was first built, and I have the only key that will unlock them."

He opened the big box, and Dorothy saw that it was filled with spectacles of every size and shape. All of them had green glasses in them. The Guardian of the Gates found a pair that would just fit Dorothy and put them over her eyes. There were two golden bands fastened to them that passed around the back of her head, where they were locked together by a little key that was at the end of a chain the Guardian of the Gates wore around his neck. When they were on,

"但我们并不是为了愚蠢或是无聊的事情才来的，"稻草人回答说，"这件事情非常重要。而且我们听说奥兹是一位善良的魔法师。"

"确实是这样，"这个绿色的矮人说道，"他将翡翠城管理得有条不紊。但是对于那些不诚实的人，或因为好奇而想接近他的人，他就会变得极其恐怖，从来都没有人敢去请求看一看他的脸。我是守门人，既然你们要求拜见伟大的奥兹，我就必须把你们带去他的宫殿。但是首先你们必须得戴上眼镜。"

"这是为什么？"多萝茜问说。

"因为你们要是不戴眼镜，翡翠城灿烂的光芒就会让你们的眼睛失明。即便是住在这个城里的居民都得一天到晚戴着眼镜。眼镜全都被锁起来了，在这座城刚刚建成的时候，奥兹就下了这道命令，只有我一个人掌管着这把钥匙，可以打开这把锁。"

他打开了那只大箱子，多萝茜看到里面装满了各式各样大大小小的眼镜。每副眼镜都装着绿色的镜片。守门人给多萝茜找了一副适合她的眼镜给她戴上。眼镜上有两条金丝带，紧紧地系在她的后脑勺上，用一把小锁锁起来。那把钥匙就挂在守门人的脖子上。戴上眼镜之后，多萝茜就不能随意地把它摘下来了，不过，她当然也不想被翡翠城的光芒灼瞎了眼睛，因此她什么也没说。

然后，这个绿人就帮稻草人、铁皮人和狮子戴上了眼镜，甚至连小托托也不例外，所有眼镜都用一把小锁锁着。

10. The Guardian of the Gate

Dorothy could not take them off had she wished, but of course she did not wish to be blinded by the glare of the Emerald City, so she said nothing.

Then the green man fitted spectacles for the Scarecrow and the Tin Woodman and the Lion, and even on little Toto; and all were locked fast with the key.

Then the Guardian of the Gates put on his own glasses and told them he was ready to show them to the palace. Taking a big golden key from a peg on the wall, he opened another gate, and they all followed him through the portal into the streets of the Emerald City.

十.翡翠城的守门人

接着，守门人给自己也戴上了眼镜，告诉他们说他准备带他们进宫。他从墙上的挂钉上拿下一把巨大的金钥匙，打开了另外一扇门，他们都跟着这个人穿过那扇壮观的大门，走上了翡翠城的街道。

11. The Wonderful Emerald City of Oz

Even with eyes protected by the green spectacles, Dorothy and her friends were at first dazzled by the brilliancy of the wonderful City. The streets were lined with beautiful houses all built of green marble and studded everywhere with sparkling emeralds. They walked over a pavement of the same green marble, and where the blocks were joined together were rows of emeralds, set closely, and glittering in the brightness of the sun. The window panes were of green glass; even the sky above the City had a green tint, and the rays of the sun were green.

There were many people – men, women, and children – walking about, and these were all dressed in green clothes and had greenish skins. They looked at Dorothy and her strangely assorted company with wondering eyes, and the children all ran away and hid behind their mothers when they saw the Lion; but no one spoke to them. Many shops stood in the street, and Dorothy saw that everything in them was green. Green candy and green pop corn were offered for sale, as well as green shoes, green hats, and green clothes of all sorts. At one place a man was selling green lemonade, and when the children bought it Dorothy could see that they paid for it with green pennies.

十一.神奇的翡翠城

虽然多萝茜和她的朋友们都戴着绿色的眼镜,但是在一开始,这座奇妙城市的光芒还是让他们眼花缭乱。街道两旁全都是用绿色的大理石建成的漂亮房子,到处都镶嵌着闪闪发亮的翡翠。他们走在一条同样用绿色大理石铺砌而成的人行道上,每一块大理石都用一行行翡翠紧密地连接起来,在明亮的阳光下灿烂地闪烁着光芒。每一扇窗户上的玻璃都是绿色的,即便是这座城市的天空也散发着绿色,一道道太阳光也被染成了绿色。

在街上有许许多多行人:男人、女人和小孩,他们全都穿着绿色的衣服,连皮肤也是浅绿色的。他们都用好奇的目光打量着多萝茜和她带领的那群奇怪朋友,当他们看见狮子的时候,所有的小孩都跑开,躲到了他们妈妈的背后;但是谁都没有跟他们说一句话。街道上有许多琳琅满目的店铺,多萝茜发现店里的所有东西都是绿色的。有绿色的糖果,绿色的爆米花,以及各式各样的绿鞋子、绿帽子和绿衣服。在一个地方,有个人出售绿色的柠檬汽水,当有小孩买汽水的时候,她发现他们付的钱也是绿色的。

这里似乎没有马,也没有任何动物。人们推着绿色的小货车,运载货物。每个人看起来都非常快乐、满足、幸福。

守门人带领着他们穿街走巷,最后来到了正好位于城市中心的一座大厦面前,这就是伟大的魔法师奥兹的宫殿。门前站着一

11. The Wonderful Emerald City of Oz

There seemed to be no horses nor animals of any kind; the men carried things around in little green carts, which they pushed before them. Everyone seemed happy and contented and prosperous.

The Guardian of the Gates led them through the streets until they came to a big building, exactly in the middle of the City, which was the Palace of Oz, the Great Wizard. There was a soldier before the door, dressed in a green uniform and wearing a long green beard.

"Here are strangers," said the Guardian of the Gates to him, "and they demand to see the Great Oz."

"Step inside," answered the soldier, "and I will carry your message to him."

So they passed through the Palace Gates and were led into a big room with a green carpet and lovely green furniture set with emeralds. The soldier made them all wipe their feet upon a green mat before entering this room, and when they were seated he said politely:

"Please make yourselves comfortable while I go to the door of the Throne Room and tell Oz you are here."

They had to wait a long time before the soldier returned. When, at last, he came back, Dorothy asked:

"Have you seen Oz?"

"Oh, no," returned the soldier; "I have never seen him. But I spoke to him as he sat behind his screen and gave him your message. He said he will grant you an audience, if you so desire; but each one of

个士兵，穿着绿色的制服，留着一撮绿色的长胡子。

"这里有几位客人，"守门人对他说，"他们想要拜见伟大的奥兹。"

"进去吧，"士兵回答说，"我给你们通报一声。"

于是，他们走进宫殿的大门，被带到了一间大房子里，那里面铺着绿色的地毯，摆放着镶嵌着翡翠的可爱的绿色家具。在走进这间房子之前，士兵让他们在绿色的蹭鞋垫上擦干净鞋底。等他们全都坐下之后，他彬彬有礼地说道：

"你们先在这里随便休息一下，我去王座室门前向奥兹通报说你们来了。"

他们在这儿等了很长时间。最后当士兵回来时，多萝茜问道：

"你见到奥兹了吗？"

"哦，没有，"士兵回答说，"我从来都没有见过他。他坐在帷幔后面，我跟他说话，把你们的意思转告给他。他说，既然你们的欲望如此强烈，他允许你们去见他，但是，你们必须一个个进去会面，而且每天只能见一个。因此你们就得在这宫中待上好几天了，我带你们去看看房间，一路长途跋涉之后，你们可以舒舒服服地休息一下。"

"谢谢你，"小女孩回答说，"奥兹真是个大好人。"

这时候，士兵吹响了一只绿色的哨子，立刻就有一位穿着漂亮的绿色丝绸长袍的年轻姑娘走进房间。她长着可爱的绿头发和

you must enter his presence alone, and he will admit but one each day. Therefore, as you must remain in the Palace for several days, I will have you shown to rooms where you may rest in comfort after your journey."

"Thank you," replied the girl; "that is very kind of Oz."

The soldier now blew upon a green whistle, and at once a young girl, dressed in a pretty green silk gown, entered the room. She had lovely green hair and green eyes, and she bowed low before Dorothy as she said, "Follow me and I will show you your room."

So Dorothy said good-bye to all her friends except Toto, and taking the dog in her arms followed the green girl through seven passages and up three flights of stairs until they came to a room at the front of the Palace. It was the sweetest little room in the world, with a soft comfortable bed that had sheets of green silk and a green velvet counterpane. There was a tiny fountain in the middle of the room, that shot a spray of green perfume into the air, to fall back into a beautifully carved green marble basin. Beautiful green flowers stood in the windows, and there was a shelf with a row of little green books. When Dorothy had time to open these books she found them full of queer green pictures that made her laugh, they were so funny.

In a wardrobe were many green dresses, made of silk and satin and velvet; and all of them fitted Dorothy exactly.

"Make yourself perfectly at home," said the green girl, "and if you wish for anything ring the bell. Oz will send for you tomorrow morning."

绿眼睛，她一边向多萝茜深深地鞠了个躬，一边说道："请跟我来，我带你去看看你的房间。"

于是多萝茜跟她的朋友们告了别，除了托托，她把这只狗抱在怀里，跟着绿衣姑娘穿过7条走廊，爬上3座楼梯，最后来到了宫殿前部的一个房间里。这是世界上最可爱的小房间，里面摆放着一张柔软舒服的床，上面铺着绿色绸缎的床单，绿色天鹅绒的被褥。房间的中央有一个小型的喷水池，一股股绿色香水喷向空中，回落在一只雕刻精美的绿色大理石盆子里。窗户上摆放着一些娇艳的绿色花朵，窗户旁边还有一个书架，上面摆放着一排绿色小书。当多萝茜有空去打开这些书看时，发现里面都是些奇怪的绿色图片，这些图片非常有趣，令她发笑。

在一只衣橱里放着许多用丝绸、锦缎和天鹅绒做成的绿色衣服，而且这些衣服全都合多萝茜的身。

"就把这里当做自己家吧，不用拘谨，"绿衣姑娘说，"如果有什么需要，就按这个铃。明天早上，奥兹会派人来召见你的。"

她把多萝茜独自留在房里，然后回去找其他人。她也把他们领到各自的房里，每个人都发现自己住在这皇宫中非常惬意的房间里。当然，这样的礼貌周到，对稻草人来说完全是浪费了。因为当他发觉自己独自一个人待在房间里的时候，他就傻傻地站在门口，等待着天亮。他一躺下来就没办法休息，而且也不能闭眼睛，因此一整个晚上，他就凝视着房间角落的一只小蜘蛛织着它

11. The Wonderful Emerald City of Oz

She left Dorothy alone and went back to the others. These she also led to rooms, and each one of them found himself lodged in a very pleasant part of the Palace. Of course this politeness was wasted on the Scarecrow; for when he found himself alone in his room he stood stupidly in one spot, just within the doorway, to wait till morning. It would not rest him to lie down, and he could not close his eyes; so he remained all night staring at a little spider which was weaving its web in a corner of the room, just as if it were not one of the most wonderful rooms in the world. The Tin Woodman lay down on his bed from force of habit, for he remembered when he was made of flesh; but not being able to sleep, he passed the night moving his joints up and down to make sure they kept in good working order. The Lion would have preferred a bed of dried leaves in the forest, and did not like being shut up in a room; but he had too much sense to let this worry him, so he sprang upon the bed and rolled himself up like a cat and purred himself asleep in a minute.

The next morning, after breakfast, the green maiden came to fetch Dorothy, and she dressed her in one of the prettiest gowns, made of green brocaded satin. Dorothy put on a green silk apron and tied a green ribbon around Toto's neck, and they started for the Throne Room of the Great Oz.

First they came to a great hall in which were many ladies and gentlemen of the court, all dressed in rich costumes. These people had nothing to do but talk to each other, but they always came to wait

的网，好像这根本不是在这个世界上最舒适的房间里一样。铁皮人还记得自己血肉之躯时的情景，因此出于习惯，他就躺在了床上，不过就是睡不着，于是就整夜上上下下地运动关节，确保它们保持良好的状态。狮子宁愿睡在森林中用枯树叶铺成的床上，也不愿被关在房间里；不过它毕竟心智健全，不会让这种事情烦扰自己，因此它跳上床去，像一只猫似的蜷缩起来，不一会儿就睡着了。

第二天早晨，吃过早餐之后，绿衣姑娘就去叫多萝茜，给她穿上了一件用绿色锦缎做成的最最漂亮的衣裳。多萝茜又给自己穿了一条绿绸围裙，在托托的脖子上系了一条绿丝带。然后她们就动身前往伟大的奥兹的王座室。

一开始，她们来到了一个大厅，那里有许多宫廷中的贵妇和绅士，全都穿着华丽的衣服。这些人没什么事情可做，只是彼此闲聊着。每天早上，他们都会在王座室外面等候着，尽管他们从来都没有得到允许去拜见奥兹。当多萝茜走进去的时候，他们都好奇地注视着她，其中一个人轻声地问道：

"你真的要去拜见那可怕的奥兹吗？"

"当然，"小女孩回答说，"只要他愿意见我。"

"哦，他会见你的，"那个替她传信给魔法师的士兵说，"尽管他不喜欢有人去请求拜见他。起初他确实非常生气，还说你从哪儿来，就让我把你送回哪儿去。之后他又问我你长得什么样子。

outside the Throne Room every morning, although they were never permitted to see Oz. As Dorothy entered they looked at her curiously, and one of them whispered:

"Are you really going to look upon the face of Oz the Terrible?"

"Of course," answered the girl, "if he will see me."

"Oh, he will see you," said the soldier who had taken her message to the Wizard, "although he does not like to have people ask to see him. Indeed, at first he was angry and said I should send you back where you came from. Then he asked me what you looked like, and when I mentioned your silver shoes he was very much interested. At last I told him about the mark upon your forehead, and he decided he would admit you to his presence."

Just then a bell rang, and the green girl said to Dorothy, "That is the signal. You must go into the Throne Room alone."

She opened a little door and Dorothy walked boldly through and found herself in a wonderful place. It was a big, round room with a high arched roof, and the walls and ceiling and floor were covered with large emeralds set closely together. In the center of the roof was a great light, as bright as the sun, which made the emeralds sparkle in a wonderful manner.

But what interested Dorothy most was the big throne of green marble that stood in the middle of the room. It was shaped like a chair and sparkled with gems, as did everything else. In the center of the chair was an enormous Head, without a body to support it or any

当我提到你脚上的银鞋子时，他对此产生了极大的兴趣。最后，我又跟他说了你额角上那个记号，于是他就决定让你去见他的面了。"

就在这时候，响起了一阵铃声，绿衣姑娘对多萝茜说："来信号了，你必须一个人去王座室。"

绿意姑娘打开一扇小门，多萝茜大胆地走了进去，她发现自己来到了一个奇妙的地方。这是一间宽敞的圆形屋子，上面是高拱形的屋顶，四周的墙壁、天花板和地板全都用大块的翡翠紧密地接连着。屋顶的中间是一盏大灯，亮得像太阳一样，照得翡翠闪耀着神奇的光芒。

但是最让多萝茜感兴趣的是放在屋子中央的那把大理石的绿色宝座。它的形状像一把椅子，也跟其他的东西一样闪耀着光芒。椅子的正中是一个硕大的头颅，没有身体或是四肢支撑着它。这颗头上没有头发，不过有一双眼睛，一个鼻子和一张嘴巴，比世上最高大的巨人的头还要大很多。

正当多萝茜好奇而恐惧地凝视着这颗头时，那双眼睛慢慢转动起来，用尖锐而坚定的眼神注视着她。然后那张嘴巴也动了起来，多萝茜听到一个声音说道："我是奥兹，伟大而可怕的奥兹。你是谁？为什么要来找我？"

从这颗硕大的头颅中发出的声音并不像多萝茜预料的那么可怕，因此她就鼓起了勇气，回答道：

arms or legs whatever. There was no hair upon this head, but it had eyes and a nose and mouth, and was much bigger than the head of the biggest giant.

As Dorothy gazed upon this in wonder and fear, the eyes turned slowly and looked at her sharply and steadily. Then the mouth moved, and Dorothy heard a voice say:

"I am Oz, the Great and Terrible. Who are you, and why do you seek me?"

It was not such an awful voice as she had expected to come from the big Head; so she took courage and answered:

"I am Dorothy, the Small and Meek. I have come to you for help."

The eyes looked at her thoughtfully for a full minute. Then said the voice:

"Where did you get the silver shoes?"

"I got them from the Wicked Witch of the East, when my house fell on her and killed her," she replied.

"Where did you get the mark upon your forehead?" continued the voice.

"That is where the Good Witch of the North kissed me when she bade me good-bye and sent me to you," said the girl.

Again the eyes looked at her sharply, and they saw she was telling the truth. Then Oz asked, "What do you wish me to do?"

"Send me back to Kansas, where my Aunt Em and Uncle Henry are," she answered earnestly. "I don't like your country, although it is

"我是多萝茜，渺小而温顺的多萝茜。我找你是想请你帮个忙。"

那双眼睛若有所思地注视着她，足足过了一分钟，那声音才说道：

"你那双银鞋是从哪儿来的？"

"我的房子掉下来，压死了东方恶女巫，这双鞋就是从她那里拿来的。"多萝茜回答说。

"你额头上的印记又是从哪儿来的？"这个声音继续说道。

"这是北方善良女巫在跟我告别时吻我之后留下的，她让我来找你。"小女孩说。

那双眼睛再次用尖锐的眼神注视着她，它们看出这小女孩说的都是真话。于是奥兹问道："你想要让我做什么？"

"送我回堪萨斯州，我的艾姆婶婶和亨利叔叔就住在那里，"她诚恳地回答道，"尽管你的国土上风景如画，但是我并不喜欢。我想我离开家乡那么久，艾姆婶婶肯定在为我担心呢。"

这双眼睛眨了3下，然后又朝上望了望天花板，朝下看了看地面，它们奇怪地转动着，似乎把房间的角角落落都看了个遍。最后它们又看着多萝茜。

"我为什么要帮你呢？"奥兹问道。

"因为你是强者，而我是弱者；因为你是一个伟大的魔法师，而我只是一个无助的小女孩。"

so beautiful. And I am sure Aunt Em will be dreadfully worried over my being away so long."

The eyes winked three times, and then they turned up to the ceiling and down to the floor and rolled around so queerly that they seemed to see every part of the room. And at last they looked at Dorothy again.

"Why should I do this for you?" asked Oz.

"Because you are strong and I am weak; because you are a Great Wizard and I am only a helpless little girl."

"But you were strong enough to kill the Wicked Witch of the East," said Oz.

"That just happened," returned Dorothy simply; "I could not help it."

"Well," said the Head, "I will give you my answer. You have no right to expect me to send you back to Kansas unless you do something for me in return. In this country everyone must pay for everything he gets. If you wish me to use my magic power to send you home again you must do something for me first. Help me and I will help you."

"What must I do?" asked the girl.

"Kill the Wicked Witch of the West," answered Oz.

"But I cannot!" exclaimed Dorothy, greatly surprised.

"You killed the Witch of the East and you wear the silver shoes, which bear a powerful charm. There is now but one Wicked Witch

"但是，你却杀死了东方恶女巫，这已经非常强大了。"

"那只是碰巧发生的，"多萝茜单纯地回答道，"我并不是有意的。"

"那么，"这个头颅说，"我现在给你答复。你没有权利要求我送你回堪萨斯州，除非你也帮我做一件事以示回报。在这片国土中，每个人都要为自己得到的东西付出代价。如果你希望我用我的魔力送你回到你自己的家乡，那么首先你必须为我做点事情。你先帮我，然后我再帮你。"

"我要为你做什么事？"小女孩问说。

"杀死那西方恶女巫。"奥兹回答道。

"可是我办不到。"多萝茜大吃一惊，尖叫了起来。

"你杀死了东方女巫，穿上了这双带有巨大魔力的银鞋。如今在这片土地上就只剩下一个恶女巫了。只要你能告诉我说她已经死了，那我就送你回堪萨斯州。但是在此之前，我还不能帮你。"

小女孩开始哭泣起来，她失望极了。那双眼睛又眨了眨，焦急地看着她，这位伟大的奥兹似乎觉得只要她愿意，就能够帮助他的。

"我从来都不曾主动杀死过任何人，"她呜咽着说道，"就算我愿意，我又该如何杀死那恶女巫呢？像你这样伟大而可怕的人都无法亲自杀死她，你又怎么能指望我办到呢？"

"我不知道，"那颗头颅说，"但这就是我给你的答复，只

left in all this land, and when you can tell me she is dead I will send you back to Kansas – but not before."

The little girl began to weep, she was so much disappointed; and the eyes winked again and looked upon her anxiously, as if the Great Oz felt that she could help him if she would.

"I never killed anything, willingly," she sobbed. "Even if I wanted to, how could I kill the Wicked Witch? If you, who are Great and Terrible, cannot kill her yourself, how do you expect me to do it?"

"I do not know," said the Head; "but that is my answer, and until the Wicked Witch dies you will not see your uncle and aunt again. Remember that the Witch is Wicked – tremendously Wicked -and ought to be killed. Now go, and do not ask to see me again until you have done your task."

Sorrowfully Dorothy left the Throne Room and went back where the Lion and the Scarecrow and the Tin Woodman were waiting to hear what Oz had said to her. "There is no hope for me," she said sadly, "for Oz will not send me home until I have killed the Wicked Witch of the West; and that I can never do."

Her friends were sorry, but could do nothing to help her; so Dorothy went to her own room and lay down on the bed and cried herself to sleep.

The next morning the soldier with the green whiskers came to the Scarecrow and said:

"Come with me, for Oz has sent for you."

要恶女巫不死，你就再也见不到你的叔叔婶婶了。记住，那是个恶女巫——非常邪恶——她应该被杀死。你走吧，在你完成这一任务之前，不要再来见我。"

多萝茜满面忧伤地离开了王座室，回到狮子、稻草人和铁皮人那里，他们都等候着听听奥兹都对她说了些什么。

"我没希望了，"多萝茜伤心地说道，"在我杀死西方恶女巫之前，奥兹是不会送我回家的。可这件事我永远都做不到。"

她的朋友们也感到非常难过，但是也没有办法可以帮助她。于是多萝茜回到自己的房间，躺在床上，一个人哭泣着，不知不觉地睡着了。

第二天早晨，绿胡子士兵来找稻草人，他说：

"跟我来，奥兹要接见你。"

于是稻草人跟着他，走进了王座室，他在那里看见一位美丽动人的小姐坐在那翡翠宝座上，她穿着绿色的丝绸薄纱，飘逸的绿色长发上戴着一顶宝石皇冠。她的肩膀上长着一对翅膀，色彩艳丽，非常轻盈，即便是最轻微的气息拂动，也会使它们摆动起来。

稻草人极尽优雅地向这位美丽的小姐鞠了个躬。而这位小姐温柔地注视着他，说道：

"我是奥兹，伟大而可怕的奥兹。你是谁？为什么要来找我？"

So the Scarecrow followed him and was admitted into the great Throne Room, where he saw, sitting in the emerald throne, a most lovely Lady. She was dressed in green silk gauze and wore upon her flowing green locks a crown of jewels. Growing from her shoulders were wings, gorgeous in color and so light that they fluttered if the slightest breath of air reached them.

When the Scarecrow had bowed, as prettily as his straw stuffing would let him, before this beautiful creature, she looked upon him sweetly, and said:

"I am Oz, the Great and Terrible. Who are you, and why do you seek me?"

Now the Scarecrow, who had expected to see the great Head Dorothy had told him of, was much astonished; but he answered her bravely.

"I am only a Scarecrow, stuffed with straw. Therefore I have no brains, and I come to you praying that you will put brains in my head instead of straw, so that I may become as much a man as any other in your dominions."

"Why should I do this for you?" asked the Lady.

"Because you are wise and powerful, and no one else can help me," answered the Scarecrow.

"I never grant favors without some return," said Oz; "but this much I will promise. If you will kill for me the Wicked Witch of the West, I

此时此刻，稻草人惊讶不已，他原本以为会见到多萝茜所说的那个巨大的头颅。不过他非常勇敢地回答说：

"我只是个用稻草填塞而成的稻草人，因此我没有脑子。我来找你，是想求你把我脑袋中的人稻草换成一个脑子，这样我就能跟你国土上的任何人一样正常了。"

"我为什么要帮你做这件事呢？"这位小姐问道。

"因为你聪明而强大，除了你之外，任何人都帮不了我。"稻草人回答说。

"如果没有报酬，我是从来都不会给予恩惠的。"奥兹说，"但是最多我只能这么答应你，如果你能为我杀了西方恶女巫，我就赏赐你许许多多最最聪明的脑子，让你成为全奥兹国最最聪明的人。"

"我以为你已经让多萝茜去杀死那女巫了。"稻草人惊讶地说道。

"我是这么说过。我不在乎是谁杀死了女巫。但是只有等她死了，我才能满足你的愿望。你走吧，在你可以得到那个渴望已久的脑子之前，不要再来找我。"

稻草人满面忧伤地回到他朋友们的身边，把奥兹说过的话全都告诉了他们，多萝茜得知这位大魔法师不是她所看见的巨大头颅，而是一位美丽的小姐，这让她大吃了一惊。

稻草人说："不管怎样，她也跟铁皮人一样需要一颗心。"

will bestow upon you a great many brains, and such good brains that you will be the wisest man in all the Land of Oz."

"I thought you asked Dorothy to kill the Witch," said the Scarecrow, in surprise.

"So I did. I don't care who kills her. But until she is dead I will not grant your wish. Now go, and do not seek me again until you have earned the brains you so greatly desire."

The Scarecrow went sorrowfully back to his friends and told them what Oz had said; and Dorothy was surprised to find that the great Wizard was not a Head, as she had seen him, but a lovely Lady.

"All the same," said the Scarecrow, "she needs a heart as much as the Tin Woodman."

On the next morning the soldier with the green whiskers came to the Tin Woodman and said:

"Oz has sent for you. Follow me."

So the Tin Woodman followed him and came to the great Throne Room. He did not know whether he would find Oz a lovely Lady or a Head, but he hoped it would be the lovely Lady. "For," he said to himself, "if it is the Head, I am sure I shall not be given a heart, since a head has no heart of its own and therefore cannot feel for me. But if it is the lovely Lady I shall beg hard for a heart, for all ladies are themselves said to be kindly hearted."

But when the Woodman entered the great Throne Room he saw neither the Head nor the Lady, for Oz had taken the shape of a most

第二天早晨，绿胡子士兵来找铁皮人，他说：

"奥兹要召见你。跟我来。"

于是铁皮人跟着他来到了王座室。他不知道自己将要见到的奥兹是一位漂亮的小姐，还是一颗脑袋，不过他希望是一位漂亮小姐。"因为，"他自言自语道，"如果是一颗脑袋的话，我想我肯定得不到心，因为连脑袋自己都没有心，所以它肯定不会知道我的感受。但如果是一位漂亮的小姐，我就可以苦苦哀求她给我一颗心，因为据说小姐全都是慈悲为怀的。"

但是当铁皮人走进王座室的时候，他看到的既不是脑袋，也不是小姐，因为奥兹变成了一只最最可怕的野兽。它几乎有一只大象那么大，那把绿色的翡翠宝座似乎都无法承载它的重量了。这只野兽的头像犀牛，但是它的脸上却有 5 只眼睛，身上长出 5 条长臂，还有 5 条细长的腿。全身上下覆盖着羊毛状浓密的毛，再也想象不出比这更可怕的怪物了。在那一刻，幸好铁皮人还没有心，要不然，他的心就会因为恐惧而快速地怦怦直跳了。不过他只是个铁皮人，虽然非常失望，但是完全没有感到害怕。

"我是奥兹，伟大而可怕的奥兹！"野兽说道，那声音就像是在怒吼，"你是谁？为什么要来找我？"

"我是个樵夫，用铁皮做成的。因此我没有心，无法得到爱情。我请求你给我一颗心，可以让我像其他人一样。"

"我为什么要这么做呢？"野兽问道。

terrible Beast. It was nearly as big as an elephant, and the green throne seemed hardly strong enough to hold its weight. The Beast had a head like that of a rhinoceros, only there were five eyes in its face. There were five long arms growing out of its body, and it also had five long, slim legs. Thick, woolly hair covered every part of it, and a more dreadful-looking monster could not be imagined. It was fortunate the Tin Woodman had no heart at that moment, for it would have beat loud and fast from terror. But being only tin, the Woodman was not at all afraid, although he was much disappointed.

"I am Oz, the Great and Terrible," spoke the Beast, in a voice that was one great roar. "Who are you, and why do you seek me?"

"I am a Woodman, and made of tin. Therefore I have no heart, and cannot love. I pray you to give me a heart that I may be as other men are."

"Why should I do this?" demanded the Beast.

"Because I ask it, and you alone can grant my request," answered the Woodman.

Oz gave a low growl at this, but said, gruffly: "If you indeed desire a heart, you must earn it."

"How?" asked the Woodman.

"Help Dorothy to kill the Wicked Witch of the West," replied the Beast. "When the Witch is dead, come to me, and I will then give you the biggest and kindest and most loving heart in all the Land of Oz."

"因为我求你，只有你才能满足我的请求。"铁皮人说道。

奥兹听到这一回答，低沉地咆哮了一声，粗鲁地说道："如果你真的想要一颗心，你必须自己得到它。"

铁皮人问："怎么得到呢？"

"帮助多萝茜杀死西方恶女巫，"野兽回答说，"只要这个女巫一死，你就可以来找我，我会把全奥兹国中最大最仁慈最具爱的心给你。"

因此铁皮人只得愁眉苦脸地回到他朋友们那里，跟他们说起自己看到的那头可怕的野兽。他们全都对大魔法师可以让他自己变幻出那么多样子而感到万分惊讶。狮子说：

"如果我去拜见他时，他变成了一只野兽，我就发出最大的吼声，恐吓他，让他答应我所有的请求。如果他变成了漂亮的小姐，我就假装扑到她身上，强迫她答应我的请求。如果他变成了一个大头，他就会向我求饶，因为我满房间地滚动那颗头，直到他答应给我们想要的东西。所以，我的朋友们，乐观些，一切都会顺心如意的。"

第二天早晨，绿胡子士兵带着狮子来到王座室里，让它进去拜见奥兹。

狮子立刻就跳进那扇门，向四周看了一眼，它惊讶地发现在宝座前面的是一颗火球，熊熊燃烧着，火光四射，狮子几乎都无法盯着它看。刚开始它还以为奥兹遇上了火灾，被这颗火球烧死

161

So the Tin Woodman was forced to return sorrowfully to his friends and tell them of the terrible Beast he had seen. They all wondered greatly at the many forms the great Wizard could take upon himself, and the Lion said:

"If he is a Beast when I go to see him, I shall roar my loudest, and so frighten him that he will grant all I ask. And if he is the lovely Lady, I shall pretend to spring upon her, and so compel her to do my bidding. And if he is the great Head, he will be at my mercy; for I will roll this head all about the room until he promises to give us what we desire. So be of good cheer, my friends, for all will yet be well."

The next morning the soldier with the green whiskers led the Lion to the great Throne Room and bade him enter the presence of Oz.

The Lion at once passed through the door, and glancing around saw, to his surprise, that before the throne was a Ball of Fire, so fierce and glowing he could scarcely bear to gaze upon it. His first thought was that Oz had by accident caught on fire and was burning up; but when he tried to go nearer, the heat was so intense that it singed his whiskers, and he crept back tremblingly to a spot nearer the door.

Then a low, quiet voice came from the Ball of Fire, and these were the words it spoke:

"I am Oz, the Great and Terrible. Who are you, and why do you seek me?"

了。但是，当它试着靠近一点时，那火球酷热难当，烧焦了它的鬃毛，于是它就颤颤抖抖地爬回到靠近门口的地方。

这时候，从火球里传来一个低沉而平静的声音，说出这么一句话：

"我是奥兹，伟大而可怕的奥兹。你是谁？为什么要来找我？"

狮子回答说："我是一只胆小的狮子，什么东西都害怕。我来这里是想求你给我一些胆量，可以让我成为名副其实的百兽之王，就像人们称呼我的那样。"

"我为什么要给你胆量呢？"奥兹问道。

"因为在所有魔法师中，你是最最伟大的，只有你有能力实现我的请求。"

这时候，火球更加猛烈地燃烧了起来。那声音说："只要你能向我证明，那邪恶女巫已经死了，那么到时候，我就会给你胆量。但是，只要那恶女巫还活着，你就只能当一只胆小狮。"

对于这番话，狮子感到非常生气，但是它又无言以对。它默默地站在那里，盯着那火球。火球变得越来越热，因此它只能掉转身子，冲出了房间，它很高兴地看到朋友们都在等候着它，于是它把自己跟魔法师的可怕会面告诉了他们。

"现在我们该怎么办？"多萝茜遗憾地说道。

"我们就剩一条路可走了，"狮子回答说，"去温基人的故

And the Lion answered, "I am a Cowardly Lion, afraid of everything. I came to you to beg that you give me courage, so that in reality I may become the King of Beasts, as men call me."

"Why should I give you courage?" demanded Oz.

"Because of all Wizards you are the greatest, and alone have power to grant my request," answered the Lion.

The Ball of Fire burned fiercely for a time, and the voice said, "Bring me proof that the Wicked Witch is dead, and that moment I will give you courage. But as long as the Witch lives, you must remain a coward."

The Lion was angry at this speech, but could say nothing in reply, and while he stood silently gazing at the Ball of Fire it became so furiously hot that he turned tail and rushed from the room. He was glad to find his friends waiting for him, and told them of his terrible interview with the Wizard.

"What shall we do now?" asked Dorothy sadly.

"There is only one thing we can do," returned the Lion, "and that is to go to the land of the Winkies, seek out the Wicked Witch, and destroy her."

"But suppose we cannot?" said the girl.

"Then I shall never have courage," declared the Lion.

"And I shall never have brains," added the Scarecrow.

"And I shall never have a heart," spoke the Tin of Woodman.

乡，找到那个恶女巫，然后杀死她。"

"但是如果我们杀不死她呢？"小女孩说。

"那么，我就永远都不会有胆量。"狮子说。

"我就永远不会有脑子了。"稻草人接着说道。

"我就永远不会有心了。"铁皮人说。

"我也永远看不见艾姆婶婶和亨利叔叔了。"多萝茜说着，又哭了起来。

"小心！"绿衣姑娘叫喊道，"眼泪会掉在你那件绿缎长袍上，把衣服给弄脏的。"

于是多萝茜擦干了眼泪，说道："我想我们必须得尝试一下，但是我知道，即使是为了再次见到艾姆婶婶，我也不想杀任何人的。"

"我跟你一块儿去，可是我太胆小，不敢杀那个女巫！"狮子说。

"我也去，"稻草人郑重地说道，"可我是个笨蛋，肯定帮不上什么忙。"

"即便是一个女巫，我也无心去伤害她，"铁皮人说，"但是，如果你去，我当然会跟你一起去。"

因此他们决定第二天就出发开始旅程。铁皮人用一块绿色的磨石把他的斧头磨得锋利，还给自己身上的所有关节添了油。稻草人给自己塞了一些新鲜稻草，多萝茜给他重新画了眼睛，让他

165

"And I shall never see Aunt Em and Uncle Henry," said Dorothy, beginning to cry.

"Be careful!" cried the green girl. "The tears will fall on your green silk gown and spot it."

So Dorothy dried her eyes and said, "I suppose we must try it; but I am sure I do not want to kill anybody, even to see Aunt Em again."

"I will go with you; but I'm too much of a coward to kill the Witch," said the Lion.

"I will go too," declared the Scarecrow; "but I shall not be of much help to you, I am such a fool."

"I haven't the heart to harm even a Witch," replied the Tin Woodman; "but if you go I certainly shall go with you."

Therefore it was decided to start upon their journey the next morning, and the Woodman sharpened his axe on a green grindstone and had all his joints properly oiled. The Scarecrow stuffed himself with fresh straw and Dorothy put new paint on his eyes that he might see better. The green girl, who was very kind to them, filled Dorothy's basket with good things to eat, and fastened a little bell around Toto's neck with a green ribbon.

They went to bed quite early and slept soundly until daylight, when they were awakened by the crowing of a green cock that lived in the back yard of the palace, and the cackling of a hen that had laid a green egg.

可以看得更清楚一些。那位非常和善的绿衣姑娘将多萝茜的篮子装满了美味的食物，还在托托的脖子上系了一条绿色的丝带，上面绑着一个小铃铛。

他们很早就上了床，一直酣睡到天亮。皇宫后院的一只绿公鸡打着鸣，一只生下绿蛋的母鸡咯咯地叫着，把他们一群人给吵醒了。

12. The Search for the Wicked Witch

The soldier with the green whiskers led them through the streets of the Emerald City until they reached the room where the Guardian of the Gates lived. This officer unlocked their spectacles to put them back in his great box, and then he politely opened the gate for our friends.

"Which road leads to the Wicked Witch of the West?" asked Dorothy.

"There is no road," answered the Guardian of the Gates. "No one ever wishes to go that way."

"How, then, are we to find her?" inquired the girl.

"That will be easy," replied the man, "for when she knows you are in the country of the Winkies she will find you, and make you all her slaves."

"Perhaps not," said the Scarecrow, "for we mean to destroy her."

"Oh, that is different," said the Guardian of the Gates. "No one has ever destroyed her before, so I naturally thought she would make slaves of you, as she has of the rest. But take care; for she is wicked and fierce, and may not allow you to destroy her. Keep to the West, where the sun sets, and you cannot fail to find her."

They thanked him and bade him good-bye, and turned toward the West, walking over fields of soft grass dotted here and there with

十二.找寻恶女巫

那个绿胡子士兵带着他们穿街走巷，一直把他们送到守门人住的地方。守门人摘下了他们的眼镜，放回到那个大箱子里，然后，又彬彬有礼地为这几位朋友打开了城门。

"哪一条路可以到西方的恶女巫那里？"多萝茜问道。

"那里没有路，"守门人回答说，"没有一个人想要去那里。"

"那我们该如何找到她呢？"小女孩追问道。

"那倒容易得很，"这个人回答说，"因为只要恶女巫知道你们进入了温基国地界，她自己就会来找你们，把你们变成她的奴隶。"

"或许不会吧，"稻草人说，"我们准备去铲除她的。"

"哦，那可就大不一样了，"守门人说，"在此之前，从来没有人能铲除她，因此我自然而然就想到她会把你们变成她的奴隶，就像她对待其他人一样。不过你们可要小心了，这个女巫凶狠恶毒，不会这么轻而易举地让你们杀死她的。你们一直往西走，就是太阳下山的地方，肯定可以找到她的。"

他们对他说了声谢谢，跟他道了声再见，然后转向西方，走上柔软的草地，草地上到处都点缀着雏菊和毛茛。多萝茜仍旧穿

12. The Search for the Wicked Witch

daisies and buttercups. Dorothy still wore the pretty silk dress she had put on in the palace, but now, to her surprise, she found it was no longer green, but pure white. The ribbon around Toto's neck had also lost its green color and was as white as Dorothy's dress.

The Emerald City was soon left far behind. As they advanced the ground became rougher and hillier, for there were no farms nor houses in this country of the West, and the ground was untilled.

In the afternoon the sun shone hot in their faces, for there were no trees to offer them shade; so that before night Dorothy and Toto and the Lion were tired, and lay down upon the grass and fell asleep, with the Woodman and the Scarecrow keeping watch.

Now the Wicked Witch of the West had but one eye, yet that was as powerful as a telescope, and could see everywhere. So, as she sat in the door of her castle, she happened to look around and saw Dorothy lying asleep, with her friends all about her. They were a long distance off, but the Wicked Witch was angry to find them in her country; so she blew upon a silver whistle that hung around her neck.

At once there came running to her from all directions a pack of great wolves. They had long legs and fierce eyes and sharp teeth.

"Go to those people," said the Witch, "and tear them to pieces."

"Are you not going to make them your slaves?" asked the leader of the wolves.

着王宫里那件美丽的绸衣，可是这时候她惊讶地发现这件衣服不再是绿色的，而是变成了纯白色。系在托托脖子上的绿丝带也不再是绿色的，而是变成了跟多萝茜衣服一样的白色。

不一会儿，翡翠城就被他们远远地抛在了后面。随着他们不断前进，道路也变得越发崎岖陡峭起来了，在这西面区域，既没有农田，也没有房子，土地都没有开垦耕种过。

到了下午，太阳火辣辣地晒着他们的脸，没有树木可以为他们遮蔽阳光，因此，在天黑之前，多萝茜、托托以及狮子就已经筋疲力尽，躺在草地上睡着了，而铁皮人和稻草人都在旁边守护着。

那西方恶女巫虽然只有一只眼睛，但是那只眼睛却可以像望远镜一样看到任何地方。因此，当她坐在城堡的门口，偶然向四周眺望的时候，就看见多萝茜睡在草地上，她的朋友们全都围绕在她身边。虽然他们还离得非常遥远，但是邪恶女巫看见他们在自己的地盘就觉得非常愤怒，因此她吹响了那支挂在她脖子上的银笛。

一群恶狼立刻就从四面八方奔来。它们长着修长的腿，瞪着凶狠的眼睛，露出尖利的牙齿。

"去那边，"女巫命令道，"把他们全都撕成碎片。"

"你不把他们变成自己的奴隶吗？"恶狼头头问道。

12. The Search for the Wicked Witch

"No," she answered, "one is of tin, and one of straw; one is a girl and another a Lion. None of them is fit to work, so you may tear them into small pieces."

"Very well," said the wolf, and he dashed away at full speed, followed by the others.

It was lucky the Scarecrow and the Woodman were wide awake and heard the wolves coming.

"This is my fight," said the Woodman, "so get behind me and I will meet them as they come."

He seized his axe, which he had made very sharp, and as the leader of the wolves came on the Tin Woodman swung his arm and chopped the wolf's head from its body, so that it immediately died. As soon as he could raise his axe, another wolf came up, and he also fell under the sharp edge of the Tin Woodman's weapon. There were forty wolves, and forty times a wolf was killed, so that at last they all lay dead in a heap before the Woodman.

Then he put down his axe and sat beside the Scarecrow, who said, "It was a good fight, friend."

They waited until Dorothy awoke the next morning. The little girl was quite frightened when she saw the great pile of shaggy wolves, but the Tin Woodman told her all. She thanked him for saving them and sat down to breakfast, after which they started again upon their journey.

"不，"她回答道，"一个铁皮人，一个稻草人，一个小女孩，还有一只狮子。他们没一个可以干活的，因此就把他们撕成小碎片吧。"

"遵命！"这匹狼说着，用最快的速度跑开了，其他狼也紧随其后。

真是庆幸，铁皮人和稻草人没有睡觉，他们听见了恶狼的动静。

"让我来对付它们，"铁皮人说，"你们躲到我后面去，等它们来了，就让我来会一会。"

他拿起已经磨得锋利的斧头，当恶狼的头头奔过来时，铁皮人挥动着他的胳膊，砍掉了这匹狼的头，它立刻就断了气。他刚刚抡起斧头，就又有一匹狼冲上前来，而它也在铁皮人锋利的斧头下丢了性命。总共有 40 匹恶狼，挥动 40 次斧头之后，每一匹恶狼全都被砍死了。因此到了最后，在铁皮人的面前堆起了一大堆恶狼的尸体。

然后，他放下斧头，坐在稻草人旁边。稻草人说："朋友，这一仗打得漂亮。"

他们一直等到第二天早晨多萝茜醒来。看见这一大堆毛茸茸的恶狼，这小女孩着实吓了一跳，不过铁皮人把事情原原本本地告诉了她。她谢谢铁皮人救了他们，等坐下来吃完早餐之后，他

12. The Search for the Wicked Witch

Now this same morning the Wicked Witch came to the door of her castle and looked out with her one eye that could see far off. She saw all her wolves lying dead, and the strangers still traveling through her country. This made her angrier than before, and she blew her silver whistle twice.

Straightway a great flock of wild crows came flying toward her, enough to darken the sky.

And the Wicked Witch said to the King Crow, "Fly at once to the strangers; peck out their eyes and tear them to pieces."

The wild crows flew in one great flock toward Dorothy and her companions. When the little girl saw them coming she was afraid.

But the Scarecrow said, "This is my battle, so lie down beside me and you will not be harmed."

So they all lay upon the ground except the Scarecrow, and he stood up and stretched out his arms. And when the crows saw him they were frightened, as these birds always are by scarecrows, and did not dare to come any nearer. But the King Crow said:

"It is only a stuffed man. I will peck his eyes out."

The King Crow flew at the Scarecrow, who caught it by the head and twisted its neck until it died. And then another crow flew at him, and the Scarecrow twisted its neck also. There were forty crows, and forty times the Scarecrow twisted a neck, until at last all were lying dead beside him. Then he called to his companions to rise, and again they went upon their journey.

们又出发开始了旅程。

就在这天早晨，恶女巫来到城堡门口，用她那一只可以看得很远的眼睛向外眺望。她看见她那些恶狼全都死了，而那些陌生人却仍旧在她的领土上往前走。这就更加令她愤怒了，于是她又吹响了银笛。

一大群野乌鸦立刻向她飞了过来，数量多得都已经遮黑了天空。

恶女巫对乌鸦王说："立刻飞到那些陌生人身边，啄瞎他们的眼睛，把他们撕成碎片。"

一大群野乌鸦朝多萝茜和她的伙伴们飞去。小女孩看见这群乌鸦时，心里害怕极了。

但是稻草人说："这次就让我来对付它们。你们趴在我身边，就不会受到伤害了。"

于是他们全都趴在了地上，只有稻草人站在那里，伸出了手臂。当这些乌鸦看见了他时都变得慌里慌张的，这些鸟儿向来都害怕稻草人，都不敢再靠近。但是乌鸦王却叫道："那只是个稻草人而已。我去啄瞎他的眼睛。"

乌鸦王飞向稻草人，而稻草人一把抓住它的头，拧断了它的脖子，最后这只乌鸦断了气。接着又有一只乌鸦向他飞了过来，稻草人同样拧断了它的脖子。总共有 40 只乌鸦，稻草人拧了 40

12. The Search for the Wicked Witch

When the Wicked Witch looked out again and saw all her crows lying in a heap, she got into a terrible rage, and blew three times upon her silver whistle.

Forthwith there was heard a great buzzing in the air, and a swarm of black bees came flying toward her.

"Go to the strangers and sting them to death!" commanded the Witch, and the bees turned and flew rapidly until they came to where Dorothy and her friends were walking. But the Woodman had seen them coming, and the Scarecrow had decided what to do.

"Take out my straw and scatter it over the little girl and the dog and the Lion," he said to the Woodman, "and the bees cannot sting them." This the Woodman did, and as Dorothy lay close beside the Lion and held Toto in her arms, the straw covered them entirely.

The bees came and found no one but the Woodman to sting, so they flew at him and broke off all their stings against the tin, without hurting the Woodman at all. And as bees cannot live when their stings are broken that was the end of the black bees, and they lay scattered thick about the Woodman, like little heaps of fine coal.

Then Dorothy and the Lion got up, and the girl helped the Tin Woodman put the straw back into the Scarecrow again, until he was as good as ever. So they started upon their journey once more.

The Wicked Witch was so angry when she saw her black bees in little heaps like fine coal that she stamped her foot and tore her hair and gnashed her teeth. And then she called a dozen of her slaves, who

次脖子，到最后，乌鸦们全都死在了稻草人的身边。然后稻草人就叫他的同伴们起来，继续他们的旅程。

当恶女巫再次向外眺望时，看见自己的乌鸦全都死成了一堆，她大发雷霆，第三次吹响了她的银笛。

天空中立刻传来了一阵响亮的嗡嗡声，一群黑蜂向她飞了过来。

"去找那些陌生人，把他们全都螫死！"女巫下令道。于是黑蜂转过身，迅速飞往多萝茜和她朋友们赶路的地方。不过铁皮人已经看见了它们，而稻草人也已经想好了对付它们的方法。

"把我身上的稻草全都拿出来，撒在小女孩和小狗以及狮子的身上，"他对铁皮人说道，"这样黑蜂就螫不到他们了。"于是铁皮人照办了，多萝茜抱着托托，挨在狮子身旁躺了下来，稻草完全把他们给覆盖了。

黑蜂们赶到时，只看到铁皮人一个可以螫，因此它们全都飞到他的身上，它们的刺全都被铁皮给折断了，可是却没有对铁皮人造成丝毫的伤害。黑蜂的刺一断，它们就活不成了，全都散落在铁皮人的周围，就像一小堆上等煤块那么厚。

然后多萝茜和狮子站了起来，小女孩帮着铁皮人把稻草全都塞回到稻草人的身子里，让他恢复到以前那样完好。接着他们再次踏上了旅程。

were the Winkies, and gave them sharp spears, telling them to go to the strangers and destroy them.

The Winkies were not a brave people, but they had to do as they were told. So they marched away until they came near to Dorothy. Then the Lion gave a great roar and sprang toward them, and the poor Winkies were so frightened that they ran back as fast as they could.

When they returned to the castle the Wicked Witch beat them well with a strap, and sent them back to their work, after which she sat down to think what she should do next. She could not understand how all her plans to destroy these strangers had failed; but she was a powerful Witch, as well as a wicked one, and she soon made up her mind how to act.

There was, in her cupboard, a Golden Cap, with a circle of diamonds and rubies running round it. This Golden Cap had a charm. Whoever owned it could call three times upon the Winged Monkeys, who would obey any order they were given. But no person could command these strange creatures more than three times. Twice already the Wicked Witch had used the charm of the Cap. Once was when she had made the Winkies her slaves, and set herself to rule over their country. The Winged Monkeys had helped her do this. The second time was when she had fought against the Great Oz himself, and driven him out of the land of the West. The Winged Monkeys had also helped her in doing this. Only once more could she use this Golden Cap, for which reason she did not like to do so until all her

当恶女巫看见黑蜂像一小堆上等煤块一样死在那里时，她跺了跺脚，拉扯着自己的头发，气得咬牙切齿。于是她召集了 12 个来自温基的奴隶，分给他们锐利的长矛，命令他们去杀死那几个陌生人。

温基人并不勇敢，但是既然他们受到了命令，就只能去执行。因此他们出发向多萝茜靠近。这时候狮子发出一声怒吼，向他们扑了过去。可怜的温基人，他们害怕极了，撒了腿使劲往回逃。

当他们逃回城堡之后，恶女巫就用铁条鞭打他们，让他们回去干活。在这之后，女巫坐了下来，思考着接下来该如何行动。她不明白自己那些想要杀害陌生人的计划为什么都会失败，但是她是个法力高强的女巫，而且还是个恶女巫，很快，她又打定了主意。

在她的橱柜里放着一顶金帽子，四周镶嵌着钻石和宝玉。这顶金帽子有一种魔力，任何戴上它的人都可以召唤 3 次飞猴，不管是什么命令，这些飞猴都会服从。但是不管是谁都只能召唤这些奇怪的动物 3 次。这个恶女巫已经使用这顶金帽子的魔力两次了。第一次是让温基人变成她的奴隶，让她成为了这片领土的统治者。飞猴曾经帮助她完成了这一命令。第二次是她跟伟大的奥兹本人作战，把他驱逐出西方的时候，飞猴也曾在这件事上助她一臂之力。她只能再利用这顶金帽子的魔力一次了，因此在她的

other powers were exhausted. But now that her fierce wolves and her wild crows and her stinging bees were gone, and her slaves had been scared away by the Cowardly Lion, she saw there was only one way left to destroy Dorothy and her friends.

So the Wicked Witch took the Golden Cap from her cupboard and placed it upon her head. Then she stood upon her left foot and said slowly:

"Ep-pe, pep-pe, kak-ke!"

Next she stood upon her right foot and said:

"Hil-lo, hol-lo, hel-lo!"

After this she stood upon both feet and cried in a loud voice:

"Ziz-zy, zuz-zy, zik!"

Now the charm began to work. The sky was darkened, and a low rumbling sound was heard in the air. There was a rushing of many wings, a great chattering and laughing, and the sun came out of the dark sky to show the Wicked Witch surrounded by a crowd of monkeys, each with a pair of immense and powerful wings on his shoulder.

One, much bigger than the others, seemed to be their leader. He flew close to the Witch and said, "You have called us for the third and last time. What do you command?"

其他魔法没有用尽之前，她并不愿动用这顶金帽子。但是如今她那些恶狼、野乌鸦，还有螫人的黑蜂全都已经败下阵来，而她的奴隶们也被胆小的狮子吓退回来，她知道，只有一个方法可以杀死多萝茜和她的朋友们。

因此，恶女巫从她的衣柜里拿出了金冠，戴在头上。然后她用左脚站立着，慢慢地念道：

"波罗波罗蜜！"

接着她又用右脚站着念道：

"嘛哩嘛哩哄！"

之后她双脚站立，大声地喊道：

"咕噜咕噜叽！"

这时候，魔法开始起了作用。天色暗了下来，空中传来一阵低沉的隆隆声，只见许多飞猴快速地涌动而来，发出阵阵喧闹的叫喊声和嬉笑声。阳光从黑暗的天空中照射下来，照见了恶女巫身旁围绕着一群猴子，每一只猴子的肩膀上都长着一对宽大有力的翅膀。

其中有一只最大的猴子，它似乎是猴王，飞到女巫的面前说道："您这已经是第三次召唤我们，也是最后一次了。您有什么吩咐？"

"去找那些闯进我领土的陌生人，杀了他们，除了那只狮

12. The Search for the Wicked Witch

"Go to the strangers who are within my land and destroy them all except the Lion," said the Wicked Witch. "Bring that beast to me, for I have a mind to harness him like a horse, and make him work."

"Your commands shall be obeyed," said the leader. Then, with a great deal of chattering and noise, the Winged Monkeys flew away to the place where Dorothy and her friends were walking.

Some of the Monkeys seized the Tin Woodman and carried him through the air until they were over a country thickly covered with sharp rocks. Here they dropped the poor Woodman, who fell a great distance to the rocks, where he lay so battered and dented that he could neither move nor groan.

Others of the Monkeys caught the Scarecrow, and with their long fingers pulled all of the straw out of his clothes and head. They made his hat and boots and clothes into a small bundle and threw it into the top branches of a tall tree.

The remaining Monkeys threw pieces of stout rope around the Lion and wound many coils about his body and head and legs, until he was unable to bite or scratch or struggle in any way. Then they lifted him up and flew away with him to the Witch's castle, where he was placed in a small yard with a high iron fence around it, so that he could not escape.

But Dorothy they did not harm at all. She stood, with Toto in her arms, watching the sad fate of her comrades and thinking it would soon be her turn. The leader of the Winged Monkeys flew up to her,

子，"恶女巫说，"把那只野兽给我带回来，我要把它像马一样套上马具，让它干活。"

"我们会遵从您的命令的。"猴王说。然后，伴随着一阵嘈杂的叫声，这些飞猴向多萝茜和她朋友们赶路的地方飞了过去。

几只飞猴抓住了铁皮人，带着他飞在空中，来到一片堆满尖锐石头的地方。它们就从空中把这个可怜的樵夫扔了下去。铁皮人从那么高的地方跌落到石头上，结果摔得破烂不堪，满是凹陷，他躺在那里既不能动弹，也不能呻吟。

又有几只猴子抓住了稻草人，用它们长长的爪子把稻草人的衣服和脑袋里面的稻草全都拉了出来，把他的帽子、鞋子和衣服打成了一个小包，抛在一棵大树的树梢顶上。

剩下的猴子们甩出结实的绳子，团团围住狮子，在它身上、头上、腿上绕了好多圈绳子，使得它无论如何都没办法咬，没办法抓，也没办法挣扎。然后飞猴们抬起它，飞到女巫的城堡中去了。狮子被关在一个四周围着高大铁栅栏的小院子里，使得它根本无法逃脱。

但是，多萝茜一点儿都没有受到飞猴的伤害。她手里抱着托托，站在那里，眼睁睁地看着同伴们受罪，心里想着马上就要轮到自己了。猴王飞到了她面前，伸出它那双毛茸茸的手臂，面目可憎的脸上嘴巴咧开大笑着。但是它看到多萝茜额头上那个善良

his long, hairy arms stretched out and his ugly face grinning terribly; but he saw the mark of the Good Witch's kiss upon her forehead and stopped short, motioning the others not to touch her.

"We dare not harm this little girl," he said to them, "for she is protected by the Power of Good, and that is greater than the Power of Evil. All we can do is to carry her to the castle of the Wicked Witch and leave her there."

So, carefully and gently, they lifted Dorothy in their arms and carried her swiftly through the air until they came to the castle, where they set her down upon the front doorstep. Then the leader said to the Witch:

"We have obeyed you as far as we were able. The Tin Woodman and the Scarecrow are destroyed, and the Lion is tied up in your yard. The little girl we dare not harm, nor the dog she carries in her arms. Your power over our band is now ended, and you will never see us again."

Then all the Winged Monkeys, with much laughing and chattering and noise, flew into the air and were soon out of sight.

The Wicked Witch was both surprised and worried when she saw the mark on Dorothy's forehead, for she knew well that neither the Winged Monkeys nor she, herself, dare hurt the girl in any way. She looked down at Dorothy's feet, and seeing the Silver Shoes, began to tremble with fear, for she knew what a powerful charm belonged to them. At first the Witch was tempted to run away from Dorothy; but

女巫吻过之后留下的印记，便立刻停了下来，示意其他猴子不要去冒犯她。

"我们不能伤害这个小姑娘，"它对其他猴子说道，"因为她受到了善良女巫的保护，善良女巫的法力可比那邪恶女巫强大得多了。我们只能把她带到邪恶女巫的城堡里，把她丢在那里。"

因此，它们小心翼翼，斯斯文文地抬起多萝茜，带着她迅速飞到空中，来到了城堡。飞猴们把她放在城堡前门的石阶上。然后，那猴王对女巫说：

"我们已经尽量完成你的命令了。铁皮人和稻草人都已经完蛋了，狮子被绑在你的院子里。只是我们不敢伤害这个小女孩，也不敢伤害抱在她怀里的小狗。如今，你已经失去了召唤我们的权利，你永远都不会再见到我们了。"

说完之后，所有的飞猴伴随着嘈杂的笑声和叫声，飞到了空中，一眨眼工夫就消失在了眼前。

当这个恶女巫看见多萝茜额头上那个印记的时候，她这心里既觉得惊讶，又感到担忧，因为她非常清楚，不管是飞猴还是她自己都不敢伤害这个小女孩。她低下头看着多萝茜的脚，发现了那双银鞋，她害怕得哆嗦起来，因为她知道这双银鞋的魔力有多么强大。刚开始，这个恶女巫还想着溜之大吉，不过她偶然看见了小女孩的眼睛，发现这双眼睛背后的心灵是如此纯洁，小女孩

she happened to look into the child's eyes and saw how simple the soul behind them was, and that the little girl did not know of the wonderful power the Silver Shoes gave her. So the Wicked Witch laughed to herself, and thought, "I can still make her my slave, for she does not know how to use her power." Then she said to Dorothy, harshly and severely:

"Come with me; and see that you mind everything I tell you, for if you do not I will make an end of you, as I did of the Tin Woodman and the Scarecrow."

Dorothy followed her through many of the beautiful rooms in her castle until they came to the kitchen, where the Witch bade her clean the pots and kettles and sweep the floor and keep the fire fed with wood.

Dorothy went to work meekly, with her mind made up to work as hard as she could; for she was glad the Wicked Witch had decided not to kill her.

With Dorothy hard at work, the Witch thought she would go into the courtyard and harness the Cowardly Lion like a horse; it would amuse her, she was sure, to make him draw her chariot whenever she wished to go to drive. But as she opened the gate the Lion gave a loud roar and bounded at her so fiercely that the Witch was afraid, and ran out and shut the gate again.

根本不知道这双银鞋赋予她的神奇魔力。因此恶女巫暗地里笑着，心想："既然她不知道如何使用自己的魔法，那我仍旧可以让她变成我的奴隶。"于是，她粗鲁而严厉地对多萝茜命令道：

"跟我来，记住我跟你说的每一句话，要不然你的小命可就玩完了，就像我对待铁皮人和稻草人那样。"

多萝茜跟着女巫，走过了城堡中许多漂亮的房间，最后她们来到了厨房，恶女巫命令她把锅和水壶洗干净，打扫地板，给火堆添柴火。

多萝茜乖乖地干起活来。她下定决心一定要努力干活；因为她很高兴恶女巫没有决定要杀死她。

这边多萝茜辛勤地工作着，另一边恶女巫心想着该去院子里像马一样给那只胆小狮上挽具了。她想，如果能让这头狮子拉车，无论什么时候想去哪儿就去哪儿，那一定会非常有意思的。但是当她打开了门，狮子就对她怒吼了一声，凶狠地扑向她，把女巫吓得急急忙忙跑了出来，关上了门。

"如果我没办法让你套上挽具，"女巫透过门闩，对里面的狮子说，"我就让你挨饿。在你愿意给我做事之前，你就别想着吃东西了。"

从此以后，她真的没有给被囚的狮子吃过任何东西，可是每天中午，她都跑到门前问道："你愿意像马那样拉车了吗？"

12. The Search for the Wicked Witch

"If I cannot harness you," said the Witch to the Lion, speaking through the bars of the gate, "I can starve you. You shall have nothing to eat until you do as I wish."

So after that she took no food to the imprisoned Lion; but every day she came to the gate at noon and asked, "Are you ready to be harnessed like a horse?"

And the Lion would answer, "No. If you come in this yard, I will bite you."

The reason the Lion did not have to do as the Witch wished was that every night, while the woman was asleep, Dorothy carried him food from the cupboard. After he had eaten he would lie down on his bed of straw, and Dorothy would lie beside him and put her head on his soft, shaggy mane, while they talked of their troubles and tried to plan some way to escape. But they could find no way to get out of the castle, for it was constantly guarded by the yellow Winkies, who were the slaves of the Wicked Witch and too afraid of her not to do as she told them.

The girl had to work hard during the day, and often the Witch threatened to beat her with the same old umbrella she always carried in her hand. But, in truth, she did not dare to strike Dorothy, because of the mark upon her forehead. The child did not know this, and was full of fear for herself and Toto. Once the Witch struck Toto a blow with her umbrella and the brave little dog flew at her and bit her leg

而狮子回答说："不，如果你走进这院子，我就咬死你。"

狮子为什么不遂女巫的愿呢？原来每天夜里，当女巫睡着之后，多萝茜就从橱柜里给它带点食物过来。吃过东西之后，它就躺在用稻草铺成的床上，多萝茜则躺在它的身旁，把头枕在它那柔软而蓬松的鬃毛上，这时候他们谈论着各自的困难，计划着如何逃脱。但是他们想不出任何可以逃出城堡的方法，因为时时刻刻都有黄色的温基人看守着城堡，他们是恶女巫的奴隶，非常害怕她，不敢违抗她的命令。

白天，小女孩不得不努力干活，那个恶女巫手里总是拿着一柄旧雨伞，恐吓她说要用雨伞打她。但是，事实上，恶女巫并不敢打多萝茜，因为她额角上那个印记。可是小女孩并不知道这个原因，经常为了自己和托托而满心担忧。

有一次，女巫用她的雨伞打了托托一下，这只勇敢的小狗向她扑了过去，在她的腿上咬了一口。女巫被咬伤的地方并没有流血，因为她可恶至极，在好多年以前她的血就已经干枯了。

多萝茜的日子变得越来越困苦，她渐渐意识到自己要再回到堪萨斯州，回到艾姆婶婶的身边，已经是难上加难了。有时候，她会伤心地哭上好几个钟头，托托坐在她的脚边，看着她的脸，哀伤地呜咽着，表明自己为了小主人而伤心。托托一点儿都不介意自己是在堪萨斯州还是在奥兹国，只要它能和多萝茜在一起就

in return. The Witch did not bleed where she was bitten, for she was so wicked that the blood in her had dried up many years before.

Dorothy's life became very sad as she grew to understand that it would be harder than ever to get back to Kansas and Aunt Em again. Sometimes she would cry bitterly for hours, with Toto sitting at her feet and looking into her face, whining dismally to show how sorry he was for his little mistress. Toto did not really care whether he was in Kansas or the Land of Oz so long as Dorothy was with him; but he knew the little girl was unhappy, and that made him unhappy too.

Now the Wicked Witch had a great longing to have for her own the Silver Shoes which the girl always wore. Her bees and her crows and her wolves were lying in heaps and drying up, and she had used up all the power of the Golden Cap; but if she could only get hold of the Silver Shoes, they would give her more power than all the other things she had lost. She watched Dorothy carefully, to see if she ever took off her shoes, thinking she might steal them. But the child was so proud of her pretty shoes that she never took them off except at night and when she took her bath. The Witch was too much afraid of the dark to dare go in Dorothy's room at night to take the shoes, and her dread of water was greater than her fear of the dark, so she never came near when Dorothy was bathing. Indeed, the old Witch never touched water, nor ever let water touch her in any way.

But the wicked creature was very cunning, and she finally thought of a trick that would give her what she wanted. She placed a bar of

行。但是，它知道小女孩不快乐，这也让它没办法快乐起来。

这时候，恶女巫极其渴望地想要把小女孩一直穿着的银鞋占为己有。她的黑蜂、乌鸦和恶狼全都一堆堆地死光了，而金帽子的魔力也已被她用尽，但是，如果她能得到这双银鞋，那么她所失去的一切都会得到弥补，而且还会比以往的魔力更强大。她小心翼翼地监视着多萝茜，看她是否会脱掉鞋子，想着是不是可以把它们偷出来。但是小女孩非常宝贵她那双精美的鞋子，除了晚上或是洗澡的时候，她从来都不把鞋子脱下来。可是恶女巫非常怕黑，不敢在夜里溜进多萝茜的房间偷鞋子，而且，比起黑暗，她更加怕水，因此在多萝茜洗澡的时候，她从来都不敢靠近。这个老女巫确实从来都不碰水，也从来都不让水沾到自己身上。

但是，这个恶女巫诡计多端，最后她想到了一条妙计，可以让她得到自己想要得到的东西。她在厨房地板的中央放了一根铁棒，然后在上面施了魔法，让人的眼睛无法看见这根铁棒。因此，当多萝茜走过这地板上时，因为她看不见这根铁棒，便被它绊倒了。虽然她没受什么伤，但是在她摔倒的时候，一只银鞋掉了，而在她捡回来之前，却被女巫给抢了去，穿在她那瘦骨嶙峋的脚上。

那女巫为自己的诡计大获成功而沾沾自喜，只要有了这一只银鞋，就可以让她得到一半的魔力，即使将来多萝茜知道如何使

iron in the middle of the kitchen floor, and then by her magic arts made the iron invisible to human eyes. So that when Dorothy walked across the floor she stumbled over the bar, not being able to see it, and fell at full length. She was not much hurt, but in her fall one of the Silver Shoes came off; and before she could reach it, the Witch had snatched it away and put it on her own skinny foot.

The wicked woman was greatly pleased with the success of her trick, for as long as she had one of the shoes she owned half the power of their charm, and Dorothy could not use it against her, even had she known how to do so.

The little girl, seeing she had lost one of her pretty shoes, grew angry, and said to the Witch, "Give me back my shoe!"

"I will not," retorted the Witch, "for it is now my shoe, and not yours."

"You are a wicked creature!" cried Dorothy. "You have no right to take my shoe from me."

"I shall keep it, just the same," said the Witch, laughing at her, "and someday I shall get the other one from you, too."

This made Dorothy so very angry that she picked up the bucket of water that stood near and dashed it over the Witch, wetting her from head to foot.

Instantly the wicked woman gave a loud cry of fear, and then, as Dorothy looked at her in wonder, the Witch began to shrink and fall away.

用魔法，她也无法以此来与自己对抗了。

小女孩发现自己丢了一只美丽的鞋子，就生起气来，对着女巫说道："把鞋子还给我！"

"不还，"女巫回嘴道，"现在这只鞋子是我的了，不是你的。"

"你这个可恶的家伙！"多萝茜叫喊着，"你没有权利拿走我的鞋子。"

"可我也会像你这样保存着它，"女巫对着她哈哈大笑道，"总有一天，我还会从你那儿拿走另外一只鞋的。"

这话让多萝茜气急败坏，她提起身旁的一桶水，对着女巫泼了过去，把她从头到脚浇得湿透。

女巫立刻恐惧地大声尖叫起来，多萝茜惊讶地看着她，发现女巫的身体开始变小，然后摔倒在地上。

"看你干的好事！"女巫尖声叫道，"我马上就要被溶化了！"

"实在是非常抱歉。"多萝茜说，她看着这个女巫像红糖一样在自己面前溶化掉了，着实吓了一跳。

"你不知道水可以要了我的命吗？"女巫绝望地哭泣着问道。

"当然不知道，"多萝茜说，"我怎么会知道呢？"

"See what you have done!" she screamed. "In a minute I shall melt away."

"I'm very sorry, indeed," said Dorothy, who was truly frightened to see the Witch actually melting away like brown sugar before her very eyes.

"Didn't you know water would be the end of me?" asked the Witch, in a wailing, desperate voice.

"Of course not," answered Dorothy. "How should I?"

"Well, in a few minutes I shall be all melted, and you will have the castle to yourself. I have been wicked in my day, but I never thought a little girl like you would ever be able to melt me and end my wicked deeds. Look out – here I go!"

With these words the Witch fell down in a brown, melted, shapeless mass and began to spread over the clean boards of the kitchen floor. Seeing that she had really melted away to nothing, Dorothy drew another bucket of water and threw it over the mess. She then swept it all out the door. After picking out the silver shoe, which was all that was left of the old woman, she cleaned and dried it with a cloth, and put it on her foot again. Then, being at last free to do as she chose, she ran out to the courtyard to tell the Lion that the Wicked Witch of the West had come to an end, and that they were no longer prisoners in a strange land.

十二.找寻恶女巫

"好了，用不了几分钟我就会完全溶化了，你就可以拥有这座城堡了。我这辈子无恶不作，但是我万万没想到你这样一个小女孩竟会把我给溶化，结束我的恶行为。当心点——我去了！"

说完这番话，女巫就躺在地上，化成了一摊棕色的、溶化的、无形的东西，在整洁宽敞的厨房地板上蔓延开来。看着女巫果真化为了乌有，多萝茜又倒了一桶水，冲散了那一摊东西，然后把它们扫出了门。她捡起那只银鞋——这是老女巫留下的唯一一件东西——然后用布把它洗净擦干，穿在自己脚上。现在，她终于获得了自由，她跑出去，来到院子里，告诉狮子西方恶女巫已经完蛋了的消息，说他们已经不再是这个陌生地方的囚犯了。

13. The Rescue

The Cowardly Lion was much pleased to hear that the Wicked Witch had been melted by a bucket of water, and Dorothy at once unlocked the gate of his prison and set him free. They went in together to the castle, where Dorothy's first act was to call all the Winkies together and tell them that they were no longer slaves.

There was great rejoicing among the yellow Winkies, for they had been made to work hard during many years for the Wicked Witch, who had always treated them with great cruelty. They kept this day as a holiday, then and ever after, and spent the time in feasting and dancing.

"If our friends, the Scarecrow and the Tin Woodman, were only with us," said the Lion, "I should be quite happy."

"Don't you suppose we could rescue them?" asked the girl anxiously.

"We can try," answered the Lion.

So they called the yellow Winkies and asked them if they would help to rescue their friends, and the Winkies said that they would be delighted to do all in their power for Dorothy, who had set them free from bondage. So she chose a number of the Winkies who looked as if they knew the most, and they all started away. They traveled that day and part of the next until they came to the rocky plain where the

十三.营救

胆小狮听说恶女巫被一桶水给溶化了，真是满心欢喜，多萝茜立刻打开了关着它的牢门，把它放了出来。他们一起来到城堡，在那里，多萝茜做的第一件事就是把所有的温基人都召集在一起，告诉他们说，他们已经不再是奴隶了。

黄色的温基人发出阵阵欢呼，因为他们已经被恶女巫奴役了很多年，她经常残忍地对待他们，如今他们获得自由了。自此之后，他们就把这一天当成了节日，在盛宴与舞会中纪念这一天。

"如果我们的朋友，稻草人和铁皮人还跟我们在一起的话，"狮子说，"我就会更加开心了。"

"你觉得我们没办法救出他们了吗？"小女孩十分不安地问道。

"我们可以试试看。"狮子回答道。

于是，他们叫来了黄色的温基人，问他们是否愿意帮忙营救他们的朋友。温基人说他们非常乐意为多萝茜做些力所能及的事情，因为是她把他们从奴役中解放出来的。于是多萝茜挑选了好几个看起来非常聪明的温基人，然后一起出发了。他们走了一天多时间，最后来到了一片岩石密布的平原，铁皮人就躺在那里，全身上下扭曲凹陷。他的斧头落在他的身边，斧刃已经生锈了，斧柄也摔成了两半。

Tin Woodman lay, all battered and bent. His axe was near him, but the blade was rusted and the handle broken off short.

The Winkies lifted him tenderly in their arms, and carried him back to the Yellow Castle again, Dorothy shedding a few tears by the way at the sad plight of her old friend, and the Lion looking sober and sorry. When they reached the castle Dorothy said to the Winkies:

"Are any of your people tinsmiths?"

"Oh, yes. Some of us are very good tinsmiths," they told her.

"Then bring them to me," she said. And when the tinsmiths came, bringing with them all their tools in baskets, she inquired, "Can you straighten out those dents in the Tin Woodman, and bend him back into shape again, and solder him together where he is broken?"

The tinsmiths looked the Woodman over carefully and then answered that they thought they could mend him so he would be as good as ever. So they set to work in one of the big yellow rooms of the castle and worked for three days and four nights, hammering and twisting and bending and soldering and polishing and pounding at the legs and body and head of the Tin Woodman, until at last he was straightened out into his old form, and his joints worked as well as ever. To be sure, there were several patches on him, but the tinsmiths did a good job, and as the Woodman was not a vain man he did not mind the patches at all.

When, at last, he walked into Dorothy's room and thanked her for rescuing him, he was so pleased that he wept tears of joy, and

那些温基人轻手轻脚地把铁皮人抬起来，送回到了黄色的城堡中。多萝茜看到老朋友这种糟糕的状况，不禁流下了眼泪。狮子看了，也是心感悲恸。

当他们回到城堡之后，多萝茜对温基人说："你们这里可有铁皮匠？"

"哦，有啊，我们这里有好几个手艺精湛的铁皮匠呢。"他们告诉多萝茜说。

"那把他们带到我这儿来吧。"她说。之后铁皮匠来了，他们的篮子装着所有工具。多萝茜问他们说："你们能不能把这个铁皮人身上的凹陷敲平整，让他恢复原先的样子？他身上那些断裂的地方可以焊接回去吗？"

这些铁皮匠仔细地把铁皮人检查了一遍，然后回答说，他们觉得应该可以把他修复，让他变得跟从前一般完好。于是，他们就在这城堡中的一间宽敞的黄色屋子里工作起来，整整3天4夜，他们在铁皮人的腿上、身上和头上，又是锤打，又是扭动，又是弯曲，又是焊接，又是磨光，又是不断地敲打，最后终于让他恢复了老样子，所有关节也像从前一样活动自如了。当然，他的身上肯定会多出好几个补钉，不过这些铁皮匠已经出色地完成了任务，而且铁皮人也不是爱慕虚荣的人，根本不在乎。

最后，铁皮人来到多萝茜的房间里，感谢她对自己的救命之恩，开心地流下了喜悦的泪水，多萝茜用她的围裙仔细地替铁皮

13. The Rescue

Dorothy had to wipe every tear carefully from his face with her apron, so his joints would not be rusted. At the same time her own tears fell thick and fast at the joy of meeting her old friend again, and these tears did not need to be wiped away. As for the Lion, he wiped his eyes so often with the tip of his tail that it became quite wet, and he was obliged to go out into the courtyard and hold it in the sun till it dried.

"If we only had the Scarecrow with us again," said the Tin Woodman, when Dorothy had finished telling him everything that had happened, "I should be quite happy."

"We must try to find him," said the girl.

So she called the Winkies to help her, and they walked all that day and part of the next until they came to the tall tree in the branches of which the Winged Monkeys had tossed the Scarecrow's clothes.

It was a very tall tree, and the trunk was so smooth that no one could climb it; but the Woodman said at once, "I'll chop it down, and then we can get the Scarecrow's clothes."

Now while the tinsmiths had been at work mending the Woodman himself, another of the Winkies, who was a goldsmith, had made an axe-handle of solid gold and fitted it into the Woodman's axe, instead of the old broken handle. Others polished the blade until all the rust was removed and it glistened like burnished silver.

As soon as he had spoken, the Tin Woodman began to chop, and in a short time the tree fell over with a crash, whereupon the

人擦干脸上的每一滴眼泪，他的关节没有因此而生锈。与此同时，她自己也因为再次与老朋友重逢而开心得泪流满面，但是这些眼泪用不着擦掉。至于狮子呢，它也不停地用尾巴尖擦着眼睛，尾巴上那一簇毛都湿透了，它不得不走出房门，来到院子里，在太阳下晒干。

等多萝茜把发生的一切全都告诉铁皮人之后，他说："如果稻草人能跟我们重新在一起的话，那我就更加开心了。"

"我们一定要设法找到他。"小女孩说。

于是她又请来了温基人帮忙。他们走了一天多的路，最后来到了一棵大树面前，飞猴们把稻草人的衣服扔在了这棵大树的树枝上。

这是一棵参天大树，树干非常光滑，因此没有一个人可以爬得上去。不过铁皮人立刻说道："我可以把这棵树砍倒，到时候我们就能拿到稻草人的衣服了。"

之前，铁皮匠在修理铁皮人的时候，另一个温基人——他是个金匠——用纯金打了一把斧柄，装在铁皮人的斧头上，替代了原来那根摔断的斧柄。其他人打磨了斧刃，直到磨去了斧子上的锈，让它像磨光了的银器一样闪闪发亮。

铁皮人一说完这话，就开始动手砍了起来，不一会儿工夫，这棵树就砰然倒下了。稻草人的衣服从树枝上掉了下来，落到地上。

Scarecrow's clothes fell out of the branches and rolled off on the ground.

Dorothy picked them up and had the Winkies carry them back to the castle, where they were stuffed with nice, clean straw; and behold! here was the Scarecrow, as good as ever, thanking them over and over again for saving him.

Now that they were reunited, Dorothy and her friends spent a few happy days at the Yellow Castle, where they found everything they needed to make them comfortable.

But one day the girl thought of Aunt Em, and said, "We must go back to Oz, and claim his promise."

"Yes," said the Woodman, "at last I shall get my heart."

"And I shall get my brains," added the Scarecrow joyfully.

"And I shall get my courage," said the Lion thoughtfully.

"And I shall get back to Kansas," cried Dorothy, clapping her hands. "Oh, let us start for the Emerald City tomorrow!"

This they decided to do. The next day they called the Winkies together and bade them good-bye. The Winkies were sorry to have them go, and they had grown so fond of the Tin Woodman that they begged him to stay and rule over them and the Yellow Land of the West. Finding they were determined to go, the Winkies gave Toto and the Lion each a golden collar; and to Dorothy they presented a beautiful bracelet studded with diamonds; and to the Scarecrow they gave a gold-headed walking stick, to keep him from stumbling; and to

十三．营救

多萝茜捡起那件衣服，让温基人带回城堡去，他们在那里用干净的稻草塞满了这件衣服。看，稻草人复活了，就像原来一样神气活现的，他一遍遍地感谢着大伙儿对他的救命之恩。

此时，多萝茜和她的朋友们又重新欢聚在了一起。他们这一群人在黄色的城堡里快快乐乐地度过了好几天时光，在那里，他们可以得到任何能让他们过得舒服的东西。

但是有一天，小女孩忽然想到了艾姆婶婶，她说："我们得找奥兹去了，让他实践他的诺言。"

"是啊，"铁皮人说，"我终于可以得到我的心了。"

"我可以得到我的脑子了。"稻草人快活地接着说道。

"我可以得到我的胆量了。"狮子沉思地说道。

"我也可以回到堪萨斯州了，"多萝茜拍着手，叫了起来，"哦，明天我们就动身去翡翠城吧！"

他们就这么决定下来了。第二天，他们把温基人都召集在一起，跟他们告了别。

对于他们的告别，温基人感到非常不舍，因为他们非常喜欢铁皮人，恳求他能留下来，管理他们以及这片西方的黄色国土。但是看到他们去意已决，温基人就分别送给托托和狮子一条金色项圈，送给多萝茜一只镶嵌着钻石的美丽手镯，送给稻草人一根金头手杖，免得他走路时被绊倒，送给铁皮人一个银质油罐，上面镶嵌着金子和珍贵宝石。

13. The Rescue

the Tin Woodman they offered a silver oil-can, inlaid with gold and set with precious jewels.

Every one of the travelers made the Winkies a pretty speech in return, and all shook hands with them until their arms ached.

Dorothy went to the Witch's cupboard to fill her basket with food for the journey, and there she saw the Golden Cap. She tried it on her own head and found that it fitted her exactly. She did not know anything about the charm of the Golden Cap, but she saw that it was pretty, so she made up her mind to wear it and carry her sunbonnet in the basket.

Then, being prepared for the journey, they all started for the Emerald City; and the Winkies gave them three cheers and many good wishes to carry with them.

每一位旅行者都对这些温基人说了一番热情的言语，以示答谢，并且跟所有人握了手，最后连手臂都变得酸痛了。

多萝茜来到女巫的橱柜前，用篮子装满了食物，准备在路上的时候吃。她在那里看见了那顶金帽子。她戴在自己的头上试了试，正好合她的头。她一点儿都不知道有关这顶金帽子的魔力的事情，但是她发现这顶帽子非常美丽，就决定戴着它，把自己的无边遮阳帽放进篮子里。

在完成旅行的准备之后，他们一行人就动身前往翡翠城了。温基人向他们连呼3声，送上了许许多多美好的祝福。

14. The Winged Monkeys

You will remember there was no road — not even a pathway — between the castle of the Wicked Witch and the Emerald City. When the four travelers went in search of the Witch she had seen them coming, and so sent the Winged Monkeys to bring them to her. It was much harder to find their way back through the big fields of buttercups and yellow daisies than it was being carried. They knew, of course, they must go straight east, toward the rising sun; and they started off in the right way. But at noon, when the sun was over their heads, they did not know which was east and which was west, and that was the reason they were lost in the great fields. They kept on walking, however, and at night the moon came out and shone brightly. So they lay down among the sweet smelling yellow flowers and slept soundly until morning – all but the Scarecrow and the Tin Woodman.

The next morning the sun was behind a cloud, but they started on, as if they were quite sure which way they were going.

"If we walk far enough," said Dorothy, "I am sure we shall sometime come to some place."

But day by day passed away, and they still saw nothing before them but the scarlet fields. The Scarecrow began to grumble a bit.

"We have surely lost our way," he said, "and unless we find it again in time to reach the Emerald City, I shall never get my brains."

十四. 飞猴

你们应该记得，在恶女巫的城堡和翡翠城之间没有路相通，甚至连一条小路都没有。在这 4 位旅行者寻找恶女巫的时候，是恶女巫先发现了他们，于是就差遣飞猴去把他们给抓了过来。如果要穿过大片的毛茛和黄雏菊，寻找回去的路，那可比他们被抓时要困难得多。当然，他们知道必须得向着太阳升起的地方，一直往东边走。于是他们向着这个正确的方向动身了。到了中午时分，当太阳照在他们头顶上的时候，他们就无法分辨哪边是东，哪边是西了，就这样，他们在广袤无垠的田野中迷失了方向。不过他们仍旧不停地走着，一直走到了晚上，明月当空，闪耀着明亮的光芒。他们就在散发着芳香的黄色花丛中躺了下来，一直酣睡到天亮，当然，稻草人和铁皮人是不用睡觉的。

第二天早上，太阳躲到了乌云后面，不过他们依旧动身赶路，就像知道应该走哪条路似的。

"假使我们一直不断地走下去，"多萝茜说，"我想总有一天，我们肯定会走到那个地方的。"

但是日子一天天地过去了，在他们面前，除了一片深红色的田野之外，什么都看不见。于是稻草人起了一些怨言。

"我们肯定是迷路了，"他说，"除非我们能重新找到那条路，然后及时赶到翡翠城，要不然我就永远得不到我的脑子了。"

"Nor I my heart," declared the Tin Woodman. "It seems to me I can scarcely wait till I get to Oz, and you must admit this is a very long journey."

"You see," said the Cowardly Lion, with a whimper, "I haven't the courage to keep tramping forever, without getting anywhere at all."

Then Dorothy lost heart. She sat down on the grass and looked at her companions, and they sat down and looked at her, and Toto found that for the first time in his life he was too tired to chase a butterfly that flew past his head. So he put out his tongue and panted and looked at Dorothy as if to ask what they should do next.

"Suppose we call the field mice," she suggested. "They could probably tell us the way to the Emerald City."

"To be sure they could," cried the Scarecrow. "Why didn't we think of that before?"

Dorothy blew the little whistle she had always carried about her neck since the Queen of the Mice had given it to her. In a few minutes they heard the pattering of tiny feet, and many of the small gray mice came running up to her. Among them was the Queen herself, who asked, in her squeaky little voice:

"What can I do for my friends?"

"We have lost our way," said Dorothy. "Can you tell us where the Emerald City is?"

"Certainly," answered the Queen; "but it is a great way off, for you have had it at your backs all this time." Then she noticed Dorothy's Golden Cap, and said, "Why don't you use the charm of the Cap, and

"我也得不到我的心了，"铁皮人说，"我似乎已经没办法等到跟奥兹见面的那一天了，你们必须得承认，这趟旅程实在太漫长了。"

"你们看，"胆小狮呜咽地说道，"如果我们这样走下去而得不到丝毫结果的话，我就再也没胆量长途跋涉了。"

这时候，多萝茜也失去了信心。她坐在草地上，看着自己的伙伴们，他们也坐了下来看着她。托托生平第一次感到那么疲累，甚至都不想去追逐从它头顶上飞过的蝴蝶了。它吐着舌头，喘着粗气，看着多萝茜，就像是在问她，接下来他们该怎样办。

"如果我们叫来那些田鼠，"她提议说，"它们或许可以告诉我们该如何去翡翠城。"

"它们肯定知道的，"稻草人叫喊着，"之前我们怎么就没想到呢？"

多萝茜吹响了一只小哨子，那是田鼠女王送给她的，分别之后她就一直挂在脖子上。不一会儿，他们就听到了窸窸窣窣的脚步声，很多灰色的小田鼠向她跑了过来。田鼠女王也在其中，它用急促而尖细的声音询问道：

"朋友们，有什么需要帮忙的吗？"

"我们迷路了，"多萝茜说，"你能告诉我们翡翠城在哪里吗？"

"没问题，"女王回答说，"可是那地方距离这里可远着呢，

call the Winged Monkeys to you? They will carry you to the City of Oz in less than an hour."

"I didn't know there was a charm," answered Dorothy, in surprise. "What is it?"

"It is written inside the Golden Cap," replied the Queen of the Mice. "But if you are going to call the Winged Monkeys we must run away, for they are full of mischief and think it great fun to plague us."

"Won't they hurt me?" asked the girl anxiously.

"Oh, no. They must obey the wearer of the Cap. Good-bye!" And she scampered out of sight, with all the mice hurrying after her.

Dorothy looked inside the Golden Cap and saw some words written upon the lining. These, she thought, must be the charm, so she read the directions carefully and put the Cap upon her head.

"Ep-pe, pep-pe, kak-ke!" she said, standing on her left foot.

"What did you say?" asked the Scarecrow, who did not know what she was doing.

"Hil-lo, hol-lo, hel-lo!" Dorothy went on, standing this time on her right foot.

"Hello!" replied the Tin Woodman calmly.

"Ziz-zy, zuz-zy, zik!" said Dorothy, who was now standing on both feet. This ended the saying of the charm, and they heard a great chattering and flapping of wings, as the band of Winged Monkeys flew up to them. The King bowed low before Dorothy, and asked, "What is your command?"

因为你们一直都在朝相反的方向走。"这时候，田鼠女王注意到了多萝茜的金帽子，说，"你为什么不使用这顶金帽子的魔力，把飞猴们召唤过来呢？用不了一个钟头，它们就能把你们送到奥兹的翡翠城里了。"

"我都不知道这金帽子上面还有魔力，"多萝茜惊讶地说道，"那咒语是什么呢？"

"全都写在金帽子的里面呢，"田鼠女王回答说，"但是，如果你们准备叫那些飞猴来的话，我们就得先走了，它们满脑子都是恶作剧，以为捉弄我们可以得到极大的乐趣。"

"它们会伤害我吗？"小女孩不安地问道。

"哦，不会的。它们必须服从戴着这顶金帽子的人，再见了！"说完，田鼠女王一溜烟地跑开不见了，其他田鼠也都紧随其后离开了。

多萝茜看了看金帽子的里面，发现内衬上面写着一些字。她想，这些应该就是咒语了，于是她仔细地把这些说明看了一遍，然后又把金帽子戴在头上。

"波罗波罗蜜！"她一边用左脚站立着，一边念念有词。

稻草人不知道她在干什么，就问她说："你在说什么呀？"

"嘛哩嘛哩哄！"多萝茜继续念叨着，这一次，她用右脚单独站立着。

"喂！"铁皮人冷静地回答说。

211

14. The Winged Monkeys

"We wish to go to the Emerald City," said the child, "and we have lost our way."

"We will carry you," replied the King, and no sooner had he spoken than two of the Monkeys caught Dorothy in their arms and flew away with her. Others took the Scarecrow and the Woodman and the Lion, and one little Monkey seized Toto and flew after them, although the dog tried hard to bite him.

The Scarecrow and the Tin Woodman were rather frightened at first, for they remembered how badly the Winged Monkeys had treated them before; but they saw that no harm was intended, so they rode through the air quite cheerfully, and had a fine time looking at the pretty gardens and woods far below them.

Dorothy found herself riding easily between two of the biggest Monkeys, one of them the King himself. They had made a chair of their hands and were careful not to hurt her.

"Why do you have to obey the charm of the Golden Cap?" she asked.

"That is a long story," answered the King, with a Winged laugh; "but as we have a long journey before us, I will pass the time by telling you about it, if you wish."

"I shall be glad to hear it," she replied.

"Once," began the leader, "we were a free people, living happily in the great forest, flying from tree to tree, eating nuts and fruit, and doing just as we pleased without calling anybody master. Perhaps some of us were rather too full of mischief at times, flying down to

十四.飞猴

这时候多萝茜双脚站立着,念道:"咕噜咕噜叽!"咒语念完了,随后他们听到一阵嘈杂的叫声和翅膀拍动的声音,那群飞猴朝他们飞了过来。猴王向多萝茜深深地鞠了个躬,问道:

"您有什么需要?"

"我们想去翡翠城,"小女孩说,"可是我们迷了路。"

"那我们带你们去吧。"猴王回答道。这边话音刚落,两只猴子就抬起了多萝茜,带着她飞走了。另外几只猴子带上了稻草人、铁皮人和狮子,一只小猴子抓住托托,跟在他们后面,尽管这只小狗一直拼了命地想咬它。

刚开始,稻草人和铁皮人还吓得心惊胆战,因为他们还记得之前这些飞猴是如何残忍地对待他们的。不过后来他们看出这些飞猴并没有想要伤害他们,于是就快快活活地坐着飞在空中,俯瞰着远在他们底下的秀丽田园和树林,过得好不快活。

多萝茜坐在两只最大的猴子中间——其中一只就是猴王——觉得非常舒服自在。它们用手搭成椅子的形状,小心翼翼地不让自己伤到多萝茜。

她问道:"你们为什么要听从这顶金帽子的魔力呢?"

"这个故事说来话长了,"猴王大笑着回答说,"不过我们还有段路要赶,如果你想听的话,我就把这件事情告诉你听,让你消磨消磨时间。"

"我当然想听了。"她回答道。

pull the tails of the animals that had no wings, chasing birds, and throwing nuts at the people who walked in the forest. But we were careless and happy and full of fun, and enjoyed every minute of the day. This was many years ago, long before Oz came out of the clouds to rule over this land.

"There lived here then, away at the North, a beautiful princess, who was also a powerful sorceress. All her magic was used to help the people, and she was never known to hurt anyone who was good. Her name was Gayelette, and she lived in a handsome palace built from great blocks of ruby. Everyone loved her, but her greatest sorrow was that she could find no one to love in return, since all the men were much too stupid and ugly to mate with one so beautiful and wise. At last, however, she found a boy who was handsome and manly and wise beyond his years. Gayelette made up her mind that when he grew to be a man she would make him her husband, so she took him to her ruby palace and used all her magic powers to make him as strong and good and lovely as any woman could wish. When he grew to manhood, Quelala, as he was called, was said to be the best and wisest man in all the land, while his manly beauty was so great that Gayelette loved him dearly, and hastened to make everything ready for the wedding.

"My grandfather was at that time the King of the Winged Monkeys which lived in the forest near Gayelette's palace, and the old fellow loved a joke better than a good dinner. One day, just before the wedding, my grandfather was flying out with his band when he saw

十四. 飞猴

"从前，"猴王开始说道，"我们都是自由自在、无拘无束，幸福地生活在一片大森林中，在树上飞来飞去，吃着坚果和水果，自己高兴干什么就干什么，不听命于任何人。有时候，我们之中的某些弟兄会非常调皮，飞到地上拉扯那些没有翅膀的动物的尾巴，追逐小鸟，用坚果砸那些行走在森林中的人。但是我们生活得无忧无虑、幸福美满，充满着欢声笑语，享受着每一天每一分的乐趣。早在奥兹从云端下来统治这片地方之前，我们就已经这样生活了很多年。

"那时候，远在北方的土地上住着一位非常漂亮的公主，她也是一位法力无边的魔法师，她的所有魔法都是用来帮助人类的，从来都没有伤害过任何好人。她的名字叫做盖琳特，住在一座用巨大红宝石砌成的漂亮宫殿里。每个人都敬爱着她，然而让她最为伤心的是她找不到一个可以得到她爱情的男人，因为所有的男人都那么愚蠢丑陋，根本配不上这样一位美丽又聪明的公主。不过，最终她还是找到了一个男孩，他英俊潇洒、强壮勇敢、聪明伶俐，这些都超过了他的同龄人。盖琳特决定等他长大成人之后，就与他结为夫妇。于是她把这个人带到了红宝石宫殿中，用尽她所有的法术，把他变得像所有女性心目中的白马王子那样强壮、善良、可爱。等到长大成人之后，奎拉拉（这是他的名字）被尊为这片土地上最英俊最聪明的男人，他的男子气概如此强烈，使得盖琳特已经深深地爱上了他，忙着准备结婚所需的每一件东西。

Quelala walking beside the river. He was dressed in a rich costume of pink silk and purple velvet, and my grandfather thought he would see what he could do. At his word the band flew down and seized Quelala, carried him in their arms until they were over the middle of the river, and then dropped him into the water.

"'Swim out, my fine fellow,' cried my grandfather, 'and see if the water has spotted your clothes.' Quelala was much too wise not to swim, and he was not in the least spoiled by all his good fortune. He laughed, when he came to the top of the water, and swam in to shore. But when Gayelette came running out to him she found his silks and velvet all ruined by the river.

"The princess was angry, and she knew, of course, who did it. She had all the Winged Monkeys brought before her, and she said at first that their wings should be tied and they should be treated as they had treated Quelala, and dropped in the river. But my grandfather pleaded hard, for he knew the Monkeys would drown in the river with their wings tied, and Quelala said a kind word for them also; so that Gayelette finally spared them, on condition that the Winged Monkeys should ever after do three times the bidding of the owner of the Golden Cap. This Cap had been made for a wedding present to Quelala, and it is said to have cost the princess half her kingdom. Of course my grandfather and all the other Monkeys at once agreed to the condition, and that is how it happens that we are three times the slaves of the owner of the Golden Cap, whosoever he may be."

十四. 飞猴

　　"在那个时候，我的祖父是飞猴中的猴王，住在盖琳特宫殿附近的森林里。这个老家伙喜欢开玩笑，胜过吃上一顿美味佳肴。就在婚礼举行的前一天，我的祖父带着它的随从们飞了出去，看见奎拉拉在河边散步。他穿着一件用粉红色丝绸和紫色天鹅绒做的衣服，显得雍容华贵。我祖父想看看他到底有什么能耐，于是一声令下，随从们就飞了下去，抓住了奎拉拉，带着他飞到了河水的上空，然后把他丢进了河里。

　　"'年轻人，游上岸来吧，'我的祖父叫喊道，'看看河水会不会弄脏你的衣服。'不过奎拉拉那么聪明，当然不会不知道游泳，而他虽然享尽荣华，却也知道该怎样游泳，因此他哈哈大笑着浮上了水面，游到了岸边。然而，当盖琳特来到他身边的时候，却发现他的丝绸和天鹅绒衣服已经完全被河水弄脏了。

　　"这位公主大发雷霆，她当然知道这件事情是谁干的。她把所有飞猴都召集到她面前，直截了当地说，她要把它们的翅膀全都绑起来，然后像对待奎拉拉那样地惩罚它们，把它们丢进河水里。但是我的祖父竭力为它们求饶，因为它知道，如果绑着这些飞猴的翅膀，它们肯定会被河水给淹死的。奎拉拉也替它们说着好话。因此盖琳特最终还是赦免了它们，不过条件就是它们必须顺从这顶金帽子主人的 3 个命令。这顶金帽子是送给奎拉拉的结婚礼物，据说公主因此而花费了半个国家的财富。我的祖父和其他猴子当然是毫不迟疑地答应了这个条件。就这样，我们要被戴

"And what became of them?" asked Dorothy, who had been greatly interested in the story.

"Quelala being the first owner of the Golden Cap," replied the Monkey, "he was the first to lay his wishes upon us. As his bride could not bear the sight of us, he called us all to him in the forest after he had married her and ordered us always to keep where she could never again set eyes on a Winged Monkey, which we were glad to do, for we were all afraid of her.

"This was all we ever had to do until the Golden Cap fell into the hands of the Wicked Witch of the West, who made us enslave the Winkies, and afterward drive Oz himself out of the Land of the West. Now the Golden Cap is yours, and three times you have the right to lay your wishes upon us."

As the Monkey King finished his story Dorothy looked down and saw the green, shining walls of the Emerald City before them. She wondered at the rapid flight of the Monkeys, but was glad the journey was over. The strange creatures set the travelers down carefully before the gate of the City, the King bowed low to Dorothy, and then flew swiftly away, followed by all his band.

"That was a good ride," said the little girl.

"Yes, and a quick way out of our troubles," replied the Lion. "How lucky it was you brought away that wonderful Cap!"

这顶金帽子的人使唤 3 次了，不管这个人是谁都是如此。"

"那这些人都怎么样了呢？"多萝茜问道，她对这个故事表现出了极大的兴趣。

"奎拉拉是这顶金帽子的第一位主人，"飞猴回答说，"也是他第一个给我们提出了愿望。因为他的新娘不想再见到我们，所以在他们结婚之后，他就把我们全都召集到森林之中，让我们去一个永远都不会让公主看见我们的地方。我们当然非常乐意这么做，因为我们都非常害怕公主。

"我们就做了这么一件事情，直到后来这顶金帽子落到了西方恶女巫的手中，她命令我们把温基人变成她的奴隶，然后又命令我们把奥兹赶出这片西方国土。现在这顶金帽子是你的了，你有权利让我们实现你的 3 个愿望。"

当猴王说完这个故事，多萝茜向下眺望着，发现翡翠城那闪闪发光的绿色城墙已经出现在他们的面前。她为飞猴们的飞行速度感到惊讶，不过很高兴这段旅程终于结束了。这些奇怪的动物小心翼翼地把旅客们放在城门的前面，猴王深深地向多萝茜鞠了个躬，然后立刻带着它的随从们飞走了。

"这趟旅行真是愉快啊！"小女孩说。

"是啊，而且这么快就解决了我们的难题，"狮子回应说，"你把这顶奇妙的金帽子带在身边，还真是幸运呢！"

15. The Discovery of Oz, the Terrible

The four travelers walked up to the great gate of Emerald City and rang the bell. After ringing several times, it was opened by the same Guardian of the Gates they had met before.

"What! are you back again?" he asked, in surprise.

"Do you not see us?" answered the Scarecrow.

"But I thought you had gone to visit the Wicked Witch of the West."

"We did visit her," said the Scarecrow.

"And she let you go again?" asked the man, in wonder.

"She could not help it, for she is melted," explained the Scarecrow.

"Melted! Well, that is good news, indeed," said the man. "Who melted her?"

"It was Dorothy," said the Lion gravely.

"Good gracious!" exclaimed the man, and he bowed very low indeed before her.

Then he led them into his little room and locked the spectacles from the great box on all their eyes, just as he had done before. Afterward they passed on through the gate into the Emerald City. When the people heard from the Guardian of the Gates that Dorothy had melted the Wicked Witch of the West, they all gathered around the travelers and followed them in a great crowd to the Palace of Oz.

十五.可怕的奥兹穿帮了

这 4 位旅行者走到翡翠城的大门前,按响了门铃。响了好几声之后,门打开了,仍旧是他们之前见过的那个守门人开的门。

"哎呀,你们怎么回来了?"他惊讶地问道。

"你不是都看见我们了吗?"稻草人回答说。

"可我以为你们已经去找西方恶女巫了呢。"

"我们确实去找过她了啊。"稻草人说。

"她又放了你们?"守门人疑惑地问道。

"她不得不放啊,因为她溶化了。"稻草人解释道。

"溶化了!哦,那可真是个好消息,"守门人说,"是谁把她溶化的?"

"是多萝茜。"狮子勇敢地说道。

"这真是太好了!"守门人欢呼了起来,他深深地向多萝茜鞠了一躬。

接着,像上次一样,他带领着这帮人来到他的小屋,从大箱子里拿出眼镜给他们戴上,锁好。然后,他们穿过大门,走进翡翠城。人们听守门人说多萝茜把西方恶女巫给溶化了,这时候,他们纷纷跑过来围住了这几位旅行者,这一大堆人跟着他们来到了奥兹的王宫。

守在门前的仍旧是那个留着绿胡子的士兵,不过这一次他毫

221

15. The Discovery of Oz, the Terrible

The soldier with the green whiskers was still on guard before the door, but he let them in at once, and they were again met by the beautiful green girl, who showed each of them to their old rooms at once, so they might rest until the Great Oz was ready to receive them.

The soldier had the news carried straight to Oz that Dorothy and the other travelers had come back again, after destroying the Wicked Witch; but Oz made no reply. They thought the Great Wizard would send for them at once, but he did not. They had no word from him the next day, nor the next, nor the next. The waiting was tiresome and wearing, and at last they grew vexed that Oz should treat them in so poor a fashion, after sending them to undergo hardships and slavery. So the Scarecrow at last asked the green girl to take another message to Oz, saying if he did not let them in to see him at once they would call the Winged Monkeys to help them, and find out whether he kept his promises or not. When the Wizard was given this message he was so frightened that he sent word for them to come to the Throne Room at four minutes after nine o'clock the next morning. He had once met the Winged Monkeys in the Land of the West, and he did not wish to meet them again.

The four travelers passed a sleepless night, each thinking of the gift Oz had promised to bestow on him. Dorothy fell asleep only once, and then she dreamed she was in Kansas, where Aunt Em was telling her how glad she was to have her little girl at home again.

十五.可怕的奥兹穿帮了

不犹豫地就把他们带了进去。依旧是那位漂亮的绿衣姑娘招待了他们，把他们带到各自原先住过的房间，让他们好好休息，等待伟大的奥兹召见他们。

绿胡子士兵直接就把多萝茜和她的伙伴们杀死恶巫女，回到翡翠城的消息告诉了奥兹，但奥兹并没有回应什么。他们以为伟大的魔法师会即刻召见他们，但是这位魔法师并没有这么做。第二天他们也没有得到任何他的消息，第三天、第四天仍旧是杳无音信。这种等待显得无聊而令人厌倦，最后他们开始责怪起奥兹，埋怨他让他们遭受了那么多苦难，经历了那么多困苦，如今却如此冷漠地对待他们。稻草人请绿衣姑娘再给奥兹通报一声，说如果再不让他们立刻见到他，他们就要召唤飞猴来帮忙，看看他到底是不是个守信之人。这个魔法师一听到这条口信，心里害怕得不得了，于是下令让他们第二天早上9点零4分到王座室去见他。他曾经在西方跟飞猴们打过一次交道，这辈子都不想再见到它们了。

这4位旅行者度过了一个不眠之夜，每个人都想着奥兹答应给他们的礼物。多萝茜只睡了一小会儿，她梦见自己回到了堪萨斯州，艾姆婶婶告诉她说，看到小侄女平安回家，她真是高兴极了。

第二天早上刚到9点，绿胡子士兵就来找他们了，4分钟之后，他们全都走进了伟大的奥兹的王座室。

15. The Discovery of Oz, the Terrible

Promptly at nine o'clock the next morning the green-whiskered soldier came to them, and four minutes later they all went into the Throne Room of the Great Oz.

Of course each one of them expected to see the Wizard in the shape he had taken before, and all were greatly surprised when they looked about and saw no one at all in the room. They kept close to the door and closer to one another, for the stillness of the empty room was more dreadful than any of the forms they had seen Oz take.

Presently they heard a Voice, that seemed to come from somewhere near the top of the great dome, and it said solemnly:

"I am Oz, the Great and Terrible. Why do you seek me?"

They looked again in every part of the room, and then, seeing no one, Dorothy asked, "Where are you?"

"I am everywhere," answered the Voice, "but to the eyes of common mortals I am invisible. I will now seat myself upon my throne, that you may converse with me." Indeed, the Voice seemed just then to come straight from the throne itself; so they walked toward it and stood in a row while Dorothy said:

"We have come to claim our promise, O Oz."

"What promise?" asked Oz.

"You promised to send me back to Kansas when the Wicked Witch was destroyed," said the girl.

"And you promised to give me brains," said the Scarecrow.

"And you promised to give me a heart," said the Tin Woodman.

当然，他们每个人都以为自己将要见到的魔法师还是之前见过的样子，但是当他们看了看王座室，发现里面没一个人影的时候，他们全都惊讶不已。他们紧挨着彼此，站在门口附近，因为空荡荡的王座室里寂静无声，这比他们上次见到奥兹时的各种形象都更让他们觉得害怕。

这时候，他们听到了一个声音，似乎是从大圆顶附近传来的，那声音一本正经地说道：

"我是奥兹，伟大而可怕的奥兹。你们为什么来找我？"

他们看了看房间里的每一个角落，还是一个人都没有，多萝茜便问："你在哪里呀？"

"我无处不在，"那个声音说，"但是凡人的眼睛是看不到我的。现在我坐到宝座上去，你们可以跟我说话了。"真的，这时候，那个声音似乎直接从宝座那边传了过来。于是他们就向宝座走了过去，站成一排。多萝茜说：

"奥兹大人，我们是来找你兑现你对我们的承诺的。"

"什么承诺？"奥兹问。

"你答应过我们，只要杀死了恶女巫，你就送我回堪萨斯。"小姑娘说。

"你答应过我，要给我脑子的。"稻草人说。

"你答应过我，要给我一颗心的。"铁皮人说。

"你答应过我，要给我胆量的。"胆小狮说。

15. The Discovery of Oz, the Terrible

"And you promised to give me courage," said the Cowardly Lion.

"Is the Wicked Witch really destroyed?" asked the Voice, and Dorothy thought it trembled a little.

"Yes," she answered, "I melted her with a bucket of water."

"Dear me," said the Voice, "how sudden! Well, come to me tomorrow, for I must have time to think it over."

"You've had plenty of time already," said the Tin Woodman angrily.

"We shan't wait a day longer," said the Scarecrow.

"You must keep your promises to us!" exclaimed Dorothy.

The Lion thought it might be as well to frighten the Wizard, so he gave a large, loud roar, which was so fierce and dreadful that Toto jumped away from him in alarm and tipped over the screen that stood in a corner. As it fell with a crash they looked that way, and the next moment all of them were filled with wonder. For they saw, standing in just the spot the screen had hidden, a little old man, with a bald head and a wrinkled face, who seemed to be as much surprised as they were. The Tin Woodman, raising his axe, rushed toward the little man and cried out, "Who are you?"

"I am Oz, the Great and Terrible," said the little man, in a trembling voice. "But don't strike me – please don't – and I'll do anything you want me to."

Our friends looked at him in surprise and dismay.

"I thought Oz was a great Head," said Dorothy.

"恶女巫真的被你们杀了吗？"那个声音问道，多萝茜察觉到那个声音有点哆嗦。

"是啊，"她回答说，"我用一桶水把她给溶化了。"

"我的天哪，"那个声音叫道，"真是太突然了！好吧，明天再来找我，我得花点时间好好想一想。"

"你已经想很久了。"铁皮樵夫生气地说道。

"我们一天都不能再等了。"稻草人说。

"你必须信守对我们的承诺！"多萝茜叫道。

狮子心想吓唬吓唬这个魔法师也不错，于是它就大吼了一声，那吼声如此凶猛而可怕，托托惊慌失措地跳开它的身旁，撞到了一块放在墙角的屏风上面。屏风咣当一声倒在地上，他们都往那边看了过去，那一刻他们全都惊呆了。他们看见在屏风后面藏着一个小老头，脑袋光溜溜的没有头发，脸上布满了皱纹，看上去跟他们一样惊讶。铁皮人举起了斧头，朝着那个小老头冲了过去，叫道："你是谁？"

"我是奥兹，伟大而可怕的奥兹，"那小老头颤颤抖抖地说道，"但是别砍我——求你了！——你们让我干什么我都答应。"

我们这几位朋友看着他，心中满是惊讶与震惊。

"我以为奥兹是个巨大的头颅。"多萝茜说。

"我以为奥兹是个漂亮的小姐。"稻草人说。

"我以为奥兹是头可怕的野兽。"铁皮樵夫说。

"And I thought Oz was a lovely Lady," said the Scarecrow.

"And I thought Oz was a terrible Beast," said the Tin Woodman.

"And I thought Oz was a Ball of Fire," exclaimed the Lion.

"No, you are all wrong," said the little man meekly. "I have been making believe."

"Making believe!" cried Dorothy. "Are you not a Great Wizard?"

"Hush, my dear," he said. "Don't speak so loud, or you will be overheard – and I should be ruined. I'm supposed to be a Great Wizard."

"And aren't you?" she asked.

"Not a bit of it, my dear; I'm just a common man."

"You're more than that," said the Scarecrow, in a grieved tone; "you're a humbug."

"Exactly so!" declared the little man, rubbing his hands together as if it pleased him. "I am a humbug."

"But this is terrible," said the Tin Woodman. "How shall I ever get my heart?"

"Or I my courage?" asked the Lion.

"Or I my brains?" wailed the Scarecrow, wiping the tears from his eyes with his coat sleeve.

"My dear friends," said Oz, "I pray you not to speak of these little things. Think of me, and the terrible trouble I'm in at being found out."

"Doesn't anyone else know you're a humbug?" asked Dorothy.

"我以为奥兹是团燃烧的火球。"狮子叫道。

"不，你们都错了，"小老头温顺地说道，"那些都是我伪装的。"

"伪装的！"多萝茜大声叫道，"难道你不是伟大的魔法师吗？"

"嘘，亲爱的，"他说，"别叫得这么大声，会被人偷听去的——到时候我就完蛋了。别人都以为我是个伟大的魔法师。"

"所以你不是？"她问。

"完全不沾边，亲爱的，我只是个非常普通的人。"

"你可不只是个普通人，"稻草人伤心地说道，"你还是个大骗子。"

"没错！"小老头一边说着，一边揉搓着双手，似乎这样可以让他安定一些，"我是个骗子。"

"但是这真是糟糕透了，"铁皮人说，"我该如何得到我的心呢？"

"还有我的胆量？"狮子问。

"还有我的脑子？"稻草人一边用袖子擦着眼泪，一边哭着问道。

"我亲爱的朋友们，"奥兹说，"我求你们就别提这些小事情了。为我着想一下吧，现在我的事情穿帮了，这个麻烦真是可怕呀。"

15. The Discovery of Oz, the Terrible

"No one knows it but you four – and myself," replied Oz. "I have fooled everyone so long that I thought I should never be found out. It was a great mistake my ever letting you into the Throne Room. Usually I will not see even my subjects, and so they believe I am something terrible."

"But, I don't understand," said Dorothy, in bewilderment. "How was it that you appeared to me as a great Head?"

"That was one of my tricks," answered Oz. "Step this way, please, and I will tell you all about it."

He led the way to a small chamber in the rear of the Throne Room, and they all followed him. He pointed to one corner, in which lay the great Head, made out of many thicknesses of paper, and with a carefully painted face.

"This I hung from the ceiling by a wire," said Oz. "I stood behind the screen and pulled a thread, to make the eyes move and the mouth open."

"But how about the voice?" she inquired.

"Oh, I am a ventriloquist," said the little man. "I can throw the sound of my voice wherever I wish, so that you thought it was coming out of the Head. Here are the other things I used to deceive you." He showed the Scarecrow the dress and the mask he had worn when he seemed to be the lovely Lady. And the Tin Woodman saw that his terrible Beast was nothing but a lot of skins, sewn together, with slats to keep their sides out. As for the Ball of Fire, the false

"没有人知道你是个骗子吗？"多萝茜问。

"除了你们4个之外就没人知道了——当然还有我自己，"奥兹回答说，"那么久以来，我骗过了每一个人，还以为这件事永远都不会被人发现了。我让你们进我的王座室就已经铸成了大错。通常情况下我连自己的臣民都不会接见，因此他们都以为我非常可怕。"

"但是，我不明白，"多萝茜有些困惑地说道，"你接见我的时候为什么会变成一颗大脑袋呢？"

"那是我的一个诡计，"奥兹回答道，"请往这边来，我把所有事情都告诉你们。"

他带着路走进一间位于王座室后面的小房间里，其他人都跟在他后面。他指着其中一个角落，那里放着一个巨大的脑袋，是用很多厚纸板做成的，上面还仔细地画着一张脸。

"我用一根铅丝把这个脑袋从天花板上吊下来，"奥兹说，"我就站在屏风后面，拉着一根绳子，让眼睛和嘴巴活动起来。"

"可那个声音又是怎么回事呢？"多萝茜问。

"哦，我会口技，"小老头说，"我可以随心所欲地让我的声音从任何一个地方发出来，因此你会觉得那个声音是从脑袋里发出来的。这里还有另外一些用来欺骗你们的道具。"他给稻草人看了他装扮成漂亮小姐时穿的衣服以及戴的面具。铁皮人发现他装扮成可怕的野兽时用的道具只不过是把许多皮缝在一起，然后用

Wizard had hung that also from the ceiling. It was really a ball of cotton, but when oil was poured upon it the ball burned fiercely.

"Really," said the Scarecrow, "you ought to be ashamed of yourself for being such a humbug."

"I am – I certainly am," answered the little man sorrowfully; "but it was the only thing I could do. Sit down, please, there are plenty of chairs; and I will tell you my story."

So they sat down and listened while he told the following tale.

"I was born in Omaha – "

"Why, that isn't very far from Kansas!" cried Dorothy.

"No, but it's farther from here," he said, shaking his head at her sadly. "When I grew up I became a ventriloquist, and at that I was very well trained by a great master. I can imitate any kind of a bird or beast." Here he mewed so like a kitten that Toto pricked up his ears and looked everywhere to see where she was. "After a time," continued Oz, "I tired of that, and became a balloonist."

"What is that?" asked Dorothy.

"A man who goes up in a balloon on circus day, so as to draw a crowd of people together and get them to pay to see the circus," he explained.

"Oh," she said, "I know."

"Well, one day I went up in a balloon and the ropes got twisted, so that I couldn't come down again. It went way up above the clouds, so

一些木条把轮廓撑起来。至于那个燃烧的火球，那也是假魔法师从天花板上吊下来的，其实就是一只气球，但是在上面浇上汽油之后，它就熊熊地燃烧起来了。

稻草人说："你真该为自己这种骗人的行为而感到羞愧。"

"是的——我确实感到了羞愧，"小老头伤心地回答说，"但是我也只能这么做。坐下来吧，这里有很多椅子。我把我自己的故事告诉你们。"

于是他们坐了下来，听他讲讲起了他的故事：

"我出生在奥马哈——"

"哎呀，那地方离堪萨斯不远！"多萝茜叫道。

"是的，但是距离这儿就远得多了，"他一边朝她伤心地摇摇头，一边说道，"等我长大之后，我就成了一个口技师，接受一位大师的正规训练。我可以模仿任何鸟类和野兽的叫声。"说到这里他学了几声猫叫，托托竖起了耳朵，四处张望着，想看看这只猫在哪儿。"过了一段时间，"奥兹接着说道，"我就厌倦了口技，学会了气球驾驶。"

"那是干什么的？"多萝茜问。

"在马戏团表演节目前，有个人会坐在气球里，升到空中，吸引一帮人过来，让他们付钱看马戏表演。"他解释说。

"噢，"多萝茜说，"我明白了。"

"有一天，我坐在气球里，升到了空中，可是绳索缠在了一

far that a current of air struck it and carried it many, many miles away. For a day and a night I traveled through the air, and on the morning of the second day I awoke and found the balloon floating over a strange and beautiful country.

"It came down gradually, and I was not hurt a bit. But I found myself in the midst of a strange people, who, seeing me come from the clouds, thought I was a great Wizard. Of course I let them think so, because they were afraid of me, and promised to do anything I wished them to.

"Just to amuse myself, and keep the good people busy, I ordered them to build this City, and my Palace; and they did it all willingly and well. Then I thought, as the country was so green and beautiful, I would call it the Emerald City; and to make the name fit better I put green spectacles on all the people, so that everything they saw was green."

"But isn't everything here green?" asked Dorothy.

"No more than in any other city," replied Oz; "but when you wear green spectacles, why of course everything you see looks green to you. The Emerald City was built a great many years ago, for I was a young man when the balloon brought me here, and I am a very old man now. But my people have worn green glasses on their eyes so long that most of them think it really is an Emerald City, and it certainly is a beautiful place, abounding in jewels and precious metals, and every good thing that is needed to make one happy. I have been

起，我就没办法下去了。气球飞到了云层上端，遇到了一股气流，然后被带到了好多好多英里之外的地方。我在空中飞了整整一天一夜，到了第二天早晨，我醒过来，发现气球飞行在一个陌生而美丽的田野上空。

"气球慢慢地降到了地面上，我一点都没有受伤。但是我发现自己被一群陌生人团团围住了，他们见我从云层中而来，以为我是个伟大的魔法师。当然，我没有向他们表明自己的真实身份，因为他们都很怕我，我让他们干什么，他们都会完成。

"我只是为了消遣自己，也是为了让这些好心人有事可忙，我就命令他们建造了这座城市，以及我的宫殿。他们个个都心甘情愿、勤勤恳恳地干着活。之后，我想，既然这片田野这么绿意盎然，如此山清水秀，我就叫它翡翠城好了，为了让这座城市更加符合这个名字的意境，我就让每个人都戴上绿色眼镜，这样他们见到的每一件东西都是绿色的了。"

"但是，这里的东西不都是绿色的吗？"多萝茜问。

"跟其他城市一样，并非都是绿色的，"奥兹回答说，"但是，如果你们戴上了绿色眼镜，那么你们所见到的每一样东西当然都变成绿色的喽。很多年前，翡翠城就已经建成了，因为气球带我来这里时，我还是个年轻人，如今却已经是个老头子了。但是，这么多年来，我的子民们一直都戴着绿色眼镜，因此他们之中的大多数人都相信这真的是一座翡翠城，一个美丽的地方，有许多

good to the people, and they like me; but ever since this Palace was built, I have shut myself up and would not see any of them.

"One of my greatest fears was the Witches, for while I had no magical powers at all I soon found out that the Witches were really able to do wonderful things. There were four of them in this country, and they ruled the people who live in the North and South and East and West. Fortunately, the Witches of the North and South were good, and I knew they would do me no harm; but the Witches of the East and West were terribly wicked, and had they not thought I was more powerful than they themselves, they would surely have destroyed me. As it was, I lived in deadly fear of them for many years; so you can imagine how pleased I was when I heard your house had fallen on the Wicked Witch of the East. When you came to me, I was willing to promise anything if you would only do away with the other Witch; but, now that you have melted her, I am ashamed to say that I cannot keep my promises."

"I think you are a very bad man," said Dorothy.

"Oh, no, my dear; I'm really a very good man, but I'm a very bad Wizard, I must admit."

"Can't you give me brains?" asked the Scarecrow.

"You don't need them. You are learning something every day. A baby has brains, but it doesn't know much. Experience is the only thing that brings knowledge, and the longer you are on earth the more experience you are sure to get."

珠宝和稀有金属，以及所有可以让人们幸福的美好事物。我善待着这里的每个人，而他们也很喜欢我。但是自从这座宫殿建成之后，我就把自己关在里面，任何人都不接见。

　　"最让我感到害怕的就是那些女巫了，因为，我根本就没有魔力，而且很快我就发现，那些女巫真的可以做出一些令人称奇的事情来。在这片土地上共有 4 个女巫，她们统治着东南西北四方的人民。幸运的是，南北两方的女巫都是善良的，我知道她们不会对我造成伤害；但是东西两方的女巫都非常邪恶，只要让她们知道我的魔力不及她们，她们肯定就会加害于我。就这样，我战战兢兢地生活了好多年。因此，你可以想象得到，当我听说你家的房子掉下来压死了东方恶女巫时，我这心里有多高兴。当你们来找我时，我心想着只要你们能铲除另外一个恶女巫，我愿意答应你们的任何请求。但是，如今你已经把她溶化了，可我却要惭愧地对你们说我无法兑现自己的诺言。"

　　"我看你就是个十足大坏蛋！"多萝茜说。

　　"哦，不，亲爱的，我其实是个心地善良的好人。但是我必须承认，我是个非常糟糕的魔法师。"

　　"那你就没办法给我脑子了？"稻草人问说。

　　"你根本就不需要脑子，每天你都能学到新的东西。一个婴儿他虽然有脑子，但是却什么都不懂。只有经验才能给你带来知识，你在这个世上活的时间越长，你的经验肯定就越多。"

"That may all be true," said the Scarecrow, "but I shall be very unhappy unless you give me brains."

The false Wizard looked at him carefully.

"Well," he said with a sigh, "I'm not much of a magician, as I said; but if you will come to me tomorrow morning, I will stuff your head with brains. I cannot tell you how to use them, however; you must find that out for yourself."

"Oh, thank you – thank you!" cried the Scarecrow. "I'll find a way to use them, never fear!"

"But how about my courage?" asked the Lion anxiously.

"You have plenty of courage, I am sure," answered Oz. "All you need is confidence in yourself. There is no living thing that is not afraid when it faces danger. The True courage is in facing danger when you are afraid, and that kind of courage you have in plenty."

"Perhaps I have, but I'm scared just the same," said the Lion. "I shall really be very unhappy unless you give me the sort of courage that makes one forget he is afraid."

"Very well, I will give you that sort of courage tomorrow," replied Oz.

"How about my heart?" asked the Tin Woodman.

"Why, as for that," answered Oz, "I think you are wrong to want a heart. It makes most people unhappy. If you only knew it, you are in luck not to have a heart."

"这话也许说得不假，"稻草人说，"但是，除非你给我脑子，要不然我会非常生气的。"

这个伪装的魔法师仔细地看着他。

"好吧，"他叹了口气，说道，"我说过，我不是什么了不起的魔法师，但是，如果明天早晨你过来找我的话，我会用脑子塞进你脑袋里的。但是我不能告诉你该如何使用脑子，你必须得自己找到方法。"

"噢，谢谢你——谢谢你！"稻草人大声叫道，"不用怕，我会自己学会使用脑子的。"

"可是我的胆量呢？"狮子焦急地问道。

"我想你的胆量已经足够多了，"奥兹回答说，"你缺乏的就是自信。所有生物在面对危险时都会感到害怕，而真正的胆量就是在害怕的时候，你仍旧迎头面对危险，而你拥有许许多多这样的胆量。"

"或许我的确是有，但我还是害怕，"狮子说，"除非你能给我一种可以让人忘记害怕的胆量，要不然我会非常生气的。"

"好吧，明天我就会给你这种胆量的。"奥兹回答说。

"那我的心呢？"铁皮人问道。

"哦，这个嘛，"奥兹回答说，"我想你不应该要心的。心让很多人都过得不开心。如果你知道了这一点，就会觉得自己没有心是多么幸运了。"

15. The Discovery of Oz, the Terrible

"That must be a matter of opinion," said the Tin Woodman. "For my part, I will bear all the unhappiness without a murmur, if you will give me the heart."

"Very well," answered Oz meekly. "Come to me tomorrow and you shall have a heart. I have played Wizard for so many years that I may as well continue the part a little longer."

"And now," said Dorothy, "how am I to get back to Kansas?"

"We shall have to think about that," replied the little man. "Give me two or three days to consider the matter and I'll try to find a way to carry you over the desert. In the meantime you shall all be treated as my guests, and while you live in the Palace my people will wait upon you and obey your slightest wish. There is only one thing I ask in return for my help – such as it is. You must keep my secret and tell no one I am a humbug."

They agreed to say nothing of what they had learned, and went back to their rooms in high spirits. Even Dorothy had hope that "The Great and Terrible Humbug," as she called him, would find a way to send her back to Kansas, and if he did she was willing to forgive him everything.

"那应该只是人们的看法不同而已，"铁皮人说，"至于我，只要你能给我一颗心，我就愿意毫无怨言地承担所有的不幸。"

"好吧，"奥兹顺从地回答道，"明天你来找我，我会给你一颗心的。我已经假扮魔法师这么多年了，再多扮一会儿也并无大碍。"

"那么，"多萝茜说，"我该如何回到堪萨斯州呢？"

"至于这一点，我们应该好好想想，"小老头回答道，"给我两三天的时间考虑一下，我会尽量找出个办法让你穿过那片沙漠的。在这期间，我会像贵宾般款待你们，你们在我的王宫居住期间，我的仆人们会伺候你们，听从你们的任何吩咐。不过，作为我这些帮助的回报，我只求你们答应我一件事：必须保守这个秘密，不能告诉任何人说我是个骗子。"

他们答应对这件事情保持沉默，兴高采烈地回到了各自的房间。甚至连多萝茜都希望那个"伟大而可怕的骗子"——这是她对奥兹的称呼——可以找到一个送她回堪萨斯的办法，如果他能让此成真，她愿意原谅他的一切。

16. The Magic Art of the Great Humbug

Next morning the Scarecrow said to his friends: "Congratulate me. I am going to Oz to get my brains at last. When I return I shall be as other men are."

"I have always liked you as you were," said Dorothy simply.

"It is kind of you to like a Scarecrow," he replied. "But surely you will think more of me when you hear the splendid thoughts my new brain is going to turn out." Then he said good-bye to them all in a cheerful voice and went to the Throne Room, where he rapped upon the door.

"Come in," said Oz.

The Scarecrow went in and found the little man sitting down by the window, engaged in deep thought.

"I have come for my brains," remarked the Scarecrow, a little uneasily.

"Oh, yes; sit down in that chair, please," replied Oz. "You must excuse me for taking your head off, but I shall have to do it in order to put your brains in their proper place."

"That's all right," said the Scarecrow. "You are quite welcome to take my head off, as long as it will be a better one when you put it on again."

So the Wizard unfastened his head and emptied out the straw. Then he entered the back room and took up a measure of bran, which he

十六.大骗子的魔术

第二天早晨，稻草人对他的朋友们说："恭喜我吧。我终于要去奥兹那儿拿我的脑子了。等我回来的时候，我就会跟其他人一样健全了。"

"我一直都喜欢你原来的样子。"多萝茜天真地说道。

"你真善良，连稻草人的样子都喜欢，"他回答说，"不过，等你听到我那新脑子想出的那些绝妙想法之后，你肯定会更加看重我的。"说完之后，他就快快乐乐地跟所有人告别，走到了王座室，敲了敲门。

"进来。"奥兹说。

稻草人走了进去，看见这个小老头正坐在窗子旁边，沉思默想着。

"我来要我的脑子了。"稻草人有些局促不安地说。

"哦，是啊。请坐到那边的椅子上吧，"奥兹回答说，"不过，很抱歉，我得先把你的头拿下来。这样我才能把脑子放在一个正确的地方。"

"没关系，"稻草人说，"你尽管随意摘下我的头吧，只要等你把它装回去的时候，能比原来的好就行了。"

于是，魔法师摘下了他的脑袋，腾出里面的稻草。然后他跑进了里屋，拿出许多麦麸，里面混杂着大量的针，他把这些东西

243

mixed with a great many pins and needles. Having shaken them together thoroughly, he filled the top of the Scarecrow's head with the mixture and stuffed the rest of the space with straw, to hold it in place.

When he had fastened the Scarecrow's head on his body again he said to him, "Hereafter you will be a great man, for I have given you a lot of bran-new brains."

The Scarecrow was both pleased and proud at the fulfillment of his greatest wish, and having thanked Oz warmly he went back to his friends.

Dorothy looked at him curiously. His head was quite bulged out at the top with brains.

"How do you feel?" she asked.

"I feel wise indeed," he answered earnestly. "When I get used to my brains I shall know everything."

"Why are those needles and pins sticking out of your head?" asked the Tin Woodman.

"That is proof that he is sharp," remarked the Lion.

"Well, I must go to Oz and get my heart," said the Woodman. So he walked to the Throne Room and knocked at the door.

"Come in," called Oz, and the Woodman entered and said, "I have come for my heart."

"Very well," answered the little man. "But I shall have to cut a hole in your breast, so I can put your heart in the right place. I hope it won't

十六.大骗子的魔术

彻底搅匀之后，就把它们倒进稻草人的脑袋里，再用稻草塞满了空隙，把那些东西固定起来。

当他把稻草人的脑袋重新接回到他身上的时候，他对稻草人说："从此往后，你就是一个伟大的人物了，因为我给了你一个崭新的脑子。"

稻草人实现了他最大的愿望，既开心，又自豪，兴奋地感谢着奥兹，然后就回到他朋友们的身边。

多萝茜好奇地看着他。装了脑子之后，他的头顶就显得特别突出了。

"你觉得怎么样？"她问。

"我真觉得自己变聪明了，"他认真地回答道，"等我习惯了这个脑子之后，我就会知道所有事情了。"

"为什么这些针会戳到你脑袋外面了呢？"铁皮人问道。

"那就证明了他的脑袋非常敏捷。"狮子这么说道。

"好了，我要去奥兹那里拿我的心了。"铁皮人说。于是他来到了王座室，敲了敲门。

"进来。"奥兹说。铁皮人便走了进去，说道："我来拿我的心了。"

"很好，"小老头回答说，"但是我得先在你的胸膛上割出一个洞，这样我才能把你的心放在正确的地方。希望我不会因此而伤害到你。"

245

hurt you."

"Oh, no," answered the Woodman. "I shall not feel it at all."

So Oz brought a pair of tinsmith's shears and cut a small, square hole in the left side of the Tin Woodman's breast. Then, going to a chest of drawers, he took out a pretty heart, made entirely of silk and stuffed with sawdust.

"Isn't it a beauty?" he asked.

"It is, indeed!" replied the Woodman, who was greatly pleased. "But is it a kind heart?"

"Oh, very!" answered Oz. He put the heart in the Woodman's breast and then replaced the square of tin, soldering it neatly together where it had been cut.

"There," said he; "now you have a heart that any man might be proud of. I'm sorry I had to put a patch on your breast, but it really couldn't be helped."

"Never mind the patch," exclaimed the happy Woodman. "I am very grateful to you, and shall never forget your kindness."

"Don't speak of it," replied Oz.

Then the Tin Woodman went back to his friends, who wished him every joy on account of his good fortune.

The Lion now walked to the Throne Room and knocked at the door.

"Come in," said Oz.

"I have come for my courage," announced the Lion, entering the room.

"哦，不会，"铁皮人回答说，"我根本不会有感觉的。"

于是，奥兹拿来一把铁皮匠的大剪刀，在铁皮人胸膛的左边剪了一个方形的小洞。然后，他来到衣柜面前，拿出了一颗非常漂亮的心，完全是用丝绸织成的，里面塞满了锯末。

"这颗心是不是很漂亮？"他问。

"是，确实漂亮！"铁皮人满怀着兴奋回答道，"但这是一颗善良的心吗？"

"哦，非常善良！"奥兹回答说。他把这颗心放进铁皮人的胸膛，然后，在刚才割开的地方，用一块铁皮完美地焊接在一起。

"好了，"他说，"现在你有一颗任何人都会觉得自豪的心了。很抱歉，我不得不在你的胸膛上焊一个补钉，这的确是不可避免的。"

"用不着理会这个补钉，"铁皮人高兴地道，"我要大大地感激你，永远都不会忘记你为我做的好事。"

"不要这么客气。"奥兹回答说。

然后铁皮人就回到了他朋友们那里，他们都为他的好运而祝福着他。

这时候，狮子也走到了王座室，它敲了敲门。

"进来。"奥兹说。

狮子一走进去，就开门见山地说道："我来拿我的胆量了。"

"很好，"这个小老头回答说，"我会给你拿来的。"

他来到橱柜的旁边，伸手从高处的架子上拿来一个绿色的方

16. The Magic Art of the Great Humbug

"Very well," answered the little man; "I will get it for you."

He went to a cupboard and reaching up to a high shelf took down a square green bottle, the contents of which he poured into a green-gold dish, beautifully carved. Placing this before the Cowardly Lion, who sniffed at it as if he did not like it, the Wizard said:

"Drink."

"What is it?" asked the Lion.

"Well," answered Oz, "if it were inside of you, it would be courage. You know, of course, that courage is always inside one; so that this really cannot be called courage until you have swallowed it. Therefore I advise you to drink it as soon as possible."

The Lion hesitated no longer, but drank till the dish was empty.

"How do you feel now?" asked Oz.

"Full of courage," replied the Lion, who went joyfully back to his friends to tell them of his good fortune.

Oz, left to himself, smiled to think of his success in giving the Scarecrow and the Tin Woodman and the Lion exactly what they thought they wanted. "How can I help being a humbug," he said, "when all these people make me do things that everybody knows can't be done? It was easy to make the Scarecrow and the Lion and the Woodman happy, because they imagined I could do anything. But it will take more than imagination to carry Dorothy back to Kansas, and I'm sure I don't know how it can be done."

形瓶子，然后把里面的药水倒在一只雕刻精美的绿色金盘子里。他把这盘东西拿到胆小狮面前，狮子闻了一下，似乎并不喜欢这个味道。

"喝下去吧。"

"这是什么东西？"狮子问道。

奥兹回答说："这个嘛，如果这东西进到你的身体里面，它就会变成胆量。当然，你应该知道胆量通常都是在身体里面的，因此在你把这东西喝下去之前，它还不能被称为胆量。我建议你尽快把它喝下去。"

狮子没有再多作犹豫，把这盘子药水喝了个精光。

"现在你觉得怎么样？"奥兹问。

"充满了胆量！"狮子回答说，然后兴高采烈地回到了朋友们的身边，把自己的好运告诉了他们。

奥兹独自一个人留在王座室里，面带着笑容，心里默想着，他成功地把稻草人、铁皮人和胆小狮想要的东西给了他们。"这些人总是让我做一些明知是天方夜谭的事情，我又怎么能不再当一个骗子呢？"他说，"要满足稻草人、铁皮人和胆小狮，让他们开心，这是轻而易举的事情，因为他们以为我无所不能。但是要送多萝茜回堪萨斯州，那就不能仅仅是空想而已了，我还不知道该如何兑现这一诺言呢。"

17. How the Balloon Was Launched

For three days Dorothy heard nothing from Oz. These were sad days for the little girl, although her friends were all quite happy and contented. The Scarecrow told them there were wonderful thoughts in his head; but he would not say what they were because he knew no one could understand them but himself. When the Tin Woodman walked about he felt his heart rattling around in his breast; and he told Dorothy he had discovered it to be a kinder and more tender heart than the one he had owned when he was made of flesh. The Lion declared he was afraid of nothing on earth, and would gladly face an army or a dozen of the fierce Kalidahs.

Thus each of the little party was satisfied except Dorothy, who longed more than ever to get back to Kansas.

On the fourth day, to her great joy, Oz sent for her, and when she entered the Throne Room he greeted her pleasantly:

"Sit down, my dear; I think I have found the way to get you out of this country."

"And back to Kansas?" she asked eagerly.

"Well, I'm not sure about Kansas," said Oz, "for I haven't the faintest notion which way it lies. But the first thing to do is to cross the desert, and then it should be easy to find your way home."

"How can I cross the desert?" she inquired.

十七.乘热气球离去

3 天过去了，多萝茜没有从奥兹那里听到任何消息。虽然她的朋友们都非常开心与满足，可是这种日子对这个小女孩来说，实在是令人忧愁苦闷。稻草人告诉他们说，他的脑袋里满是奇妙的想法，可是又说不出来是什么，因为他知道除了自己之外，谁都无法理解这些想法。铁皮人走路的时候，会觉得自己的心在胸腔内跳动。而且他还告诉多萝茜说，他发现这颗心要比他还是肉身时拥有的那颗心更加善良，更加温柔。狮子说它已经不怕这个世界上的任何东西了，并且可以欣然地去迎战一大群人，或是十来只凶猛的卡利达斯。

在这几个人之中，除了多萝茜以外，个个都是心满意足的。因此，多萝茜就比以往更加渴望着回堪萨斯州去了。

到了第四天，奥兹召唤了她，这真是令她喜出望外。当她来到王座室时，奥兹高兴地对她说道：

"坐吧，我亲爱的孩子，我想我找到让你离开这片国度的方法了。"

"可以回到堪萨斯州吗？"她急切地问道。

"这个嘛，我无法肯定是否可以回到堪萨斯州，"奥兹说，"因为我根本不知道这个地方在哪里。但是首先要做的事情就是穿过这片大沙漠，到时候就可以轻而易举地找到你回家的路了。"

17. How the Balloon Was Launched

"Well, I'll tell you what I think," said the little man. "You see, when I came to this country it was in a balloon. You also came through the air, being carried by a cyclone. So I believe the best way to get across the desert will be through the air. Now, it is quite beyond my powers to make a cyclone; but I've been thinking the matter over, and I believe I can make a balloon."

"How?" asked Dorothy.

"A balloon," said Oz, "is made of silk, which is coated with glue to keep the gas in it. I have plenty of silk in the Palace, so it will be no trouble to make the balloon. But in all this country there is no gas to fill the balloon with, to make it float."

"If it won't float," remarked Dorothy, "it will be of no use to us."

"True," answered Oz. "But there is another way to make it float, which is to fill it with hot air. Hot air isn't as good as gas, for if the air should get cold the balloon would come down in the desert, and we should be lost."

"We!" exclaimed the girl. "Are you going with me?"

"Yes, of course," replied Oz. "I am tired of being such a humbug. If I should go out of this Palace my people would soon discover I am not a Wizard, and then they would be vexed with me for having deceived them. So I have to stay shut up in these rooms all day, and it gets tiresome. I'd much rather go back to Kansas with you and be in a circus again."

"I shall be glad to have your company," said Dorothy.

"我要如何才能穿过这沙漠呢？"她询问道。

"哦，我会把我的想法告诉你的，"小老头说，"你知道，我是乘坐着气球来到这个地方的。你也是被龙卷风带到这里来的，因此，我相信穿过这片沙漠最好的办法就是从天上飘过去。如今，我已经没这种魔力制造出一阵龙卷风了，不过我把这件事仔细思考一番，我想我可以做出一个气球来。"

"要怎么做？"多萝茜问道。

"气球是用丝绸做成的，"奥兹说，"上面涂了一层胶水，可以避免里面的气体跑出来。这宫殿之中有许多的丝绸，因此做出一个气球并不在话下。但是在这整个国家之中却没有可以用来填充气球，让它飘在空中的氢气。"

"如果气球飘不起来，那对我们来说就毫无用处了呀。"多萝茜说。

"是的，"奥兹回答说，"不过还有另外一个方法可以让它飘起来，那就是用热气灌到气球里，可是热气不如氢气有效，因为如果气体冷下来，气球就会掉落在沙漠中，我们也就迷失方向了。"

"我们!"女孩子大声叫道，"难道你要和我一块儿离开这里吗？"

"是啊，当然喽，"奥兹回答说，"我已经厌倦了这种骗子的生活。如果我走出这个宫殿，我的子民们就会马上发现我不是魔法师，然后他们会因为我欺骗了他们而感到生气。我就只能整

"Thank you," he answered. "Now, if you will help me sew the silk together, we will begin to work on our balloon."

So Dorothy took a needle and thread, and as fast as Oz cut the strips of silk into proper shape the girl sewed them neatly together. First there was a strip of light green silk, then a strip of dark green and then a strip of emerald green; for Oz had a fancy to make the balloon in different shades of the color about them. It took three days to sew all the strips together, but when it was finished they had a big bag of green silk more than twenty feet long.

Then Oz painted it on the inside with a coat of thin glue, to make it airtight, after which he announced that the balloon was ready.

"But we must have a basket to ride in," he said. So he sent the soldier with the green whiskers for a big clothes basket, which he fastened with many ropes to the bottom of the balloon.

When it was all ready, Oz sent word to his people that he was going to make a visit to a great brother Wizard who lived in the clouds. The news spread rapidly throughout the city and everyone came to see the wonderful sight.

Oz ordered the balloon carried out in front of the Palace, and the people gazed upon it with much curiosity. The Tin Woodman had chopped a big pile of wood, and now he made a fire of it, and Oz held the bottom of the balloon over the fire so that the hot air that arose from it would be caught in the silken bag. Gradually the balloon

天待在这些房间里，真是无聊透顶。我宁愿跟你一起回堪萨斯州，重新回到马戏团里。"

"我很高兴能有你这样的同伴。"多萝茜说。

"谢谢你，"他回答说，"那现在我们就开始做气球吧，你能帮我把这些丝绸缝在一起吗？"

于是多萝茜拿出针线，等奥兹把丝绸裁剪成合适大小之后，这个小女孩就把这些布块整齐地缝在一起。先是一块浅绿色的绸布，然后是深绿色的，接着是翡翠绿的。奥兹有一个奇妙的想法，他想用不同颜色的绸布做出一个五颜六色的气球。他们花了 3 天时间把所有的绸布都缝合在一起，完成之后，它就变成了一个二十多尺长的巨大的绿袋子。

接着奥兹就在这袋子里面涂上一层薄胶，让它密不透风，完成这一步之后，他就宣布气球已经做成了。

他说："不过我们还得找一个篮子来，可以让我们坐在里面。"于是他差遣那个绿胡子的士兵，找来了一只用来放衣服的大篮子。奥兹用许多绳子把这篮子紧紧地绑在气球的下面。

当一切准备就绪之后，奥兹就颁布通告，说他准备去拜访一位住在云端的大师兄。这一消息迅速地传遍了全城，每个人都跑来争相目睹这一神奇的景象。

奥兹下令把气球拿到宫殿的前面，人们全都好奇地看着它。铁皮人砍来了一大堆的木柴，这时候正在生火，奥兹把气球的底

swelled out and rose into the air, until finally the basket just touched the ground.

Then Oz got into the basket and said to all the people in a loud voice:

"I am now going away to make a visit. While I am gone the Scarecrow will rule over you. I command you to obey him as you would me."

The balloon was by this time tugging hard at the rope that held it to the ground, for the air within it was hot, and this made it so much lighter in weight than the air without that it pulled hard to rise into the sky.

"Come, Dorothy!" cried the Wizard. "Hurry up, or the balloon will fly away."

"I can't find Toto anywhere," replied Dorothy, who did not wish to leave her little dog behind. Toto had run into the crowd to bark at a kitten, and Dorothy at last found him. She picked him up and ran towards the balloon.

She was within a few steps of it, and Oz was holding out his hands to help her into the basket, when, crack! went the ropes, and the balloon rose into the air without her.

"Come back!" she screamed. "I want to go, too!"

"I can't come back, my dear," called Oz from the basket. "Good-bye!"

部放在火堆上面,使得火堆产生的热气全都跑进这个丝绸布袋中。气球渐渐地膨胀了起来,升到了空中,到后来那只篮子就只是轻轻地碰到地面而已。

然后奥兹就走进篮子里,用洪亮的声音对所有的百姓说道:

"现在,我要出门访问了。在我离开的这段日子里,就由稻草人掌管这个国家。我命令你们像服从我这样去服从他。"

这时候,气球用力地拉扯着把它固定在地上的绳子,因为里面的气体是热的,这就使得里面的气体比外面的轻很多,热气使劲地将气球升到了空中。

"快来,多萝茜!"魔法师叫道,"赶快上来,要不然这气球就要飞走了。"

"我找不到托托了,"多萝茜回答说,她不想丢下自己的小狗。托托跑到了人群之中,追着一只小猫乱吠,最后多萝茜终于找到了它。她一把抓住它,向气球跑去。

就在她距离气球不过几步路,奥兹伸出手来想要帮助她跨进篮子的时候,嘣的一声!绳子断了,气球升到了空中,却没有带上多萝茜。

"回来!"她大声叫道,"我也要去!"

"亲爱的,我回不去了,"奥兹从篮子里喊道,"再见!"

"再见!"所有人都叫喊着,每一双眼睛都注视着那位魔法师

17. How the Balloon Was Launched

"Good-bye!" shouted everyone, and all eyes were turned upward to where the Wizard was riding in the basket, rising every moment farther and farther into the sky.

And that was the last any of them ever saw of Oz, the Wonderful Wizard, though he may have reached Omaha safely, and be there now, for all we know. But the people remembered him lovingly, and said to one another:

"Oz was always our friend. When he was here he built for us this beautiful Emerald City, and now he is gone he has left the Wise Scarecrow to rule over us."

Still, for many days they grieved over the loss of the Wonderful Wizard, and would not be comforted.

乘坐的篮子，看着这只气球越飞越高，升到了空中。

这是所有人最后一次见到奥兹——这位神奇的魔法师，虽然我们都知道，他或许已经平安地到达了奥马哈，但是这里的每个人都亲切地思念着他，相互诉说着：

"奥兹永远都是我们的朋友。他在这里的时候，为我们建造了这座翡翠城，如今他去了，留下这位聪明的稻草人来领导我们。"

翡翠城的百姓失去了这位神奇的魔法师，他们为此而伤心了很多日子，久久无法得到安慰。

18. Away to the South

Dorothy wept bitterly at the passing of her hope to get home to Kansas again; but when she thought it all over she was glad she had not gone up in a balloon. And she also felt sorry at losing Oz, and so did her companions.

The Tin Woodman came to her and said:

"Truly I should be ungrateful if I failed to mourn for the man who gave me my lovely heart. I should like to cry a little because Oz is gone, if you will kindly wipe away my tears, so that I shall not rust."

"With pleasure," she answered, and brought a towel at once. Then the Tin Woodman wept for several minutes, and she watched the tears carefully and wiped them away with the towel. When he had finished, he thanked her kindly and oiled himself thoroughly with his jeweled oil-can, to guard against mishap.

The Scarecrow was now the ruler of the Emerald City, and although he was not a Wizard the people were proud of him. "For," they said, "there is not another city in all the world that is ruled by a stuffed man." And, so far as they knew, they were quite right.

The morning after the balloon had gone up with Oz, the four travelers met in the Throne Room and talked matters over. The Scarecrow sat in the big throne and the others stood respectfully before him.

十八.去南方

多萝茜再次错失了回到堪萨斯州的希望，伤心地哭泣起来。但是当她把这件事情全盘考虑之后，她反而庆幸自己没能乘上气球。她同样为奥兹的离开感到难过，她的同伴们亦是如此。

铁皮人来到她的身边，说："那个人给了我一颗心，如果我没有为他的离开而感到难过的话，那我实在是太忘恩负义了。奥兹走了，如果你愿意好心地帮我擦干眼泪的话（那样我就不怕生锈了），我真想大哭一场。"

"乐意至极。"多萝茜回答着，立刻拿出一块手帕。然后铁皮人就哭了好几分钟，多萝茜仔细地看着流出来的眼泪，用手帕擦干。等铁皮人哭完之后，他又非常亲切地感谢着多萝茜，然后用那只镶嵌着珠宝的油罐，给自己全身上下添了油，以防发生不测。

如今翡翠城由稻草人执政，虽然他不是魔法师，但是百姓们都以他为荣，他们说："因为在这个世界上，没有哪个城市是由一个稻草人掌管的。"就他们所知道的而言，这话倒是说得不假。

在奥兹乘坐热气球离开的第二天早晨，这4个旅行者聚集在王座室里，商量着事情。稻草人坐在伟大的王位上，其他几个则恭敬地站在他面前。

"其实我们也没那么不幸，"这位新国王说道，"因为这座宫殿和翡翠城全都是我们的了，我们喜欢干什么就干什么。我回想

18. Away to the South

"We are not so unlucky," said the new ruler, "for this Palace and the Emerald City belong to us, and we can do just as we please. When I remember that a short time ago I was up on a pole in a farmer's cornfield, and that now I am the ruler of this beautiful City, I am quite satisfied with my lot."

"I also," said the Tin Woodman, "am well-pleased with my new heart; and, really, that was the only thing I wished in all the world."

"For my part, I am content in knowing I am as brave as any beast that ever lived, if not braver," said the Lion modestly.

"If Dorothy would only be contented to live in the Emerald City," continued the Scarecrow, "we might all be happy together."

"But I don't want to live here," cried Dorothy. "I want to go to Kansas, and live with Aunt Em and Uncle Henry."

"Well, then, what can be done?" inquired the Woodman.

The Scarecrow decided to think, and he thought so hard that the pins and needles began to stick out of his brains. Finally he said:

"Why not call the Winged Monkeys, and ask them to carry you over the desert?"

"I never thought of that!" said Dorothy joyfully. "It's just the thing. I'll go at once for the Golden Cap."

When she brought it into the Throne Room she spoke the magic words, and soon the band of Winged Monkeys flew in through the open window and stood beside her.

起自己在不久之前，还被束缚在一根竹竿上面，插在农民的稻田里，可现在，我却成为了这个美丽城市的领导者，对于自己的命运，我感到非常满足。"

"我也非常满意自己这颗新心，"铁皮人说，"真的，这是我在这个世界上唯一需要的东西了。"

"至于我，虽然我不是最勇敢的，但是只要我知道自己比其他野兽更加勇敢，我就心满意足了。"狮子谦逊地说道。

"如果多萝茜愿意住在翡翠城的话，"稻草人接着说道，"我们就可以幸福地生活在一起了。"

"但是我不想住在这里，"多萝茜叫道，"我想回堪萨斯州，跟艾姆婶婶和亨利叔叔住在一起。"

"这样的话，我们该怎么办呢？"铁皮人问。

稻草人决定要好好想一想，他努力地思考着，连头上的针都戳到了脑袋的外面。最后他说：

"为什么不把飞猴们召唤过来呢，可以让它们把你带出沙漠？"

"我怎么从来都没想到呢！"多萝茜兴奋地说道，"就这么办。我现在就去拿金帽子。"

当她把金帽子拿到王座室，念完咒语之后，马上就有一大群飞猴从打开着的窗子飞了进来，站在她的身旁。

"这是你第二次召唤我们了，"猴王一边说着，一边对小女孩

18. Away to the South

"This is the second time you have called us," said the Monkey King, bowing before the little girl. "What do you wish?"

"I want you to fly with me to Kansas," said Dorothy.

But the Monkey King shook his head.

"That cannot be done," he said. "We belong to this country alone, and cannot leave it. There has never been a Winged Monkey in Kansas yet, and I suppose there never will be, for they don't belong there. We shall be glad to serve you in any way in our power, but we cannot cross the desert. Good-bye."

And with another bow, the Monkey King spread his wings and flew away through the window, followed by all his band.

Dorothy was ready to cry with disappointment.

"I have wasted the charm of the Golden Cap to no purpose," she said, "for the Winged Monkeys cannot help me."

"It is certainly too bad!" said the tender-hearted Woodman.

The Scarecrow was thinking again, and his head bulged out so horribly that Dorothy feared it would burst.

"Let us call in the soldier with the green whiskers," he said, "and ask his advice."

So the soldier was summoned and entered the Throne Room timidly, for while Oz was alive he never was allowed to come farther than the door.

"This little girl," said the Scarecrow to the soldier, "wishes to cross the desert. How can she do so?"

鞠了个躬，"您有什么吩咐呢？"

多萝茜说："我想让你们带我飞回堪萨斯州。"

但是猴王摇了摇头。

"那可办不到，"它说，"我们只属于这片国土，不能离开这里。在堪萨斯州一直都不存在飞猴，而且我想将来也肯定不会有，因为它们不属于那个地方。只要是我们力所能及的，不管用什么方法，我们都很乐意为你效劳。但是我们不能穿越沙漠。再见了！"

猴王又鞠了一个躬，张开翅膀，带领着它的一队人马从窗子飞了出去。

多萝茜失望得都快要哭出来了。

"飞猴们帮不了我，"她说，"我白白浪费了一次金帽子的魔力。"

"这实在是太糟糕了！"慈悲为怀的铁皮人说道。

稻草人又想了想，他的脑袋可怕地突了起来，多萝茜担心它要爆炸了。

"我们把那个绿胡子士兵找来，"他说，"问问他有什么建议。"

因此，那个士兵被召唤了过来，他胆怯地走进王座室，奥兹在这里的时候，从来都没让他踏进过这扇门。

"这个小女孩想要穿过沙漠，"稻草人对士兵说，"有什么办法可以办到呢？"

"我不敢肯定，"士兵回答说，"因为从来都没有人走出过这

18. Away to the South

"I cannot tell," answered the soldier, "for nobody has ever crossed the desert, unless it is Oz himself."

"Is there no one who can help me?" asked Dorothy earnestly.

"Glinda might," he suggested.

"Who is Glinda?" inquired the Scarecrow.

"The Witch of the South. She is the most powerful of all the Witches, and rules over the Quadlings. Besides, her castle stands on the edge of the desert, so she may know a way to cross it."

"Glinda is a Good Witch, isn't she?" asked the child.

"The Quadlings think she is good," said the soldier, "and she is kind to everyone. I have heard that Glinda is a beautiful woman, who knows how to keep young in spite of the many years she has lived."

"How can I get to her castle?" asked Dorothy.

"The road is straight to the South," he answered, "but it is said to be full of dangers to travelers. There are wild beasts in the woods, and a race of queer men who do not like strangers to cross their country. For this reason none of the Quadlings ever come to the Emerald City."

The soldier then left them and the Scarecrow said:

"It seems, in spite of dangers, that the best thing Dorothy can do is to travel to the Land of the South and ask Glinda to help her. For, of course, if Dorothy stays here she will never get back to Kansas."

"You must have been thinking again," remarked the Tin Woodman.

片沙漠，除非是奥兹本人。"

"难道这里就没有人可以帮到我了吗？"多萝茜真心诚意地问道。

"或许格琳达可以。"他建议说。

"谁是格琳达？"稻草人询问道。

"她是南方女巫，是所有女巫之中法力最最高强的，她统治着奎特林。而且，她的城堡就在沙漠旁边，因此她可能知道走出这片沙漠的办法。"

"格琳达是个善良女巫，对吗？"小女孩问道。

"奎特林人都说她心地善良，"士兵说，"她对每个人都非常和善。我还听说格琳达是个美若天仙的妇人，虽然她的年纪已经很大了，不过她懂得如何永葆青春。"

"我要怎样去她的城堡呢？"

"有一条路直接通向南方，"他回答说，"但是据说在这条路上危机四伏。森林里有野兽，还有一个奇怪的种族，他们不喜欢陌生人经过他们的领土。正是由于这个原因，奎特林人从来都没有来过翡翠城。"

士兵说完之后就退了下去，稻草人说："看来，最好的办法就只能是多萝茜不顾一切危险，前往南方，寻求格琳达的帮助。因为，当然啦，如果多萝茜住在这里，她就永远无法回到堪萨斯州了。"

18. Away to the South

"I have," said the Scarecrow.

"I shall go with Dorothy," declared the Lion, "for I am tired of your city and long for the woods and the country again. I am really a wild beast, you know. Besides, Dorothy will need someone to protect her."

"That is true," agreed the Woodman. "My axe may be of service to her; so I also will go with her to the Land of the South."

"When shall we start?" asked the Scarecrow.

"Are you going?" they asked, in surprise.

"Certainly. If it wasn't for Dorothy I should never have had brains. She lifted me from the pole in the cornfield and brought me to the Emerald City. So my good luck is all due to her, and I shall never leave her until she starts back to Kansas for good and all."

"Thank you," said Dorothy gratefully. "You are all very kind to me. But I should like to start as soon as possible."

"We shall go tomorrow morning," returned the Scarecrow. "So now let us all get ready, for it will be a long journey."

"你必须得再想个办法出来。"铁皮人说。

"我已经想过了。"稻草人说。

"我跟多萝茜一起去,"狮子说,"因为我已经厌倦了你的城市,渴望着回到森林,回到我的故乡。你知道,我是一只真正的野兽。况且,多萝茜也需要有人来保护她。"

"那倒没错,"铁皮人同意道,"或许我的斧头对她有用,所以,我也跟她一起去南方。"

"那我们什么时候出发?"稻草人问。

"你也去吗?"他们一脸惊讶地问道。

"当然啦。要不是多萝茜,我就永远得不到脑子了。她把我从稻田里的竹竿上拔了下来,带我来到了翡翠城,因此我的好运都应该归功于她,在她回到堪萨斯州之前,我永远都不会离开她的。"

"谢谢你们,"多萝茜感激地说道,"你们对我太好了,不过我想要尽快动身。"

"明天一早我们就出发,"稻草人回答说,"因此现在我们就去准备一下,这将是一趟漫长的旅行。"

19. Attacked by the Fighting Trees

The next morning Dorothy kissed the pretty green girl good-bye, and they all shook hands with the soldier with the green whiskers, who had walked with them as far as the gate. When the Guardian of the Gate saw them again he wondered greatly that they could leave the beautiful City to get into new trouble. But he at once unlocked their spectacles, which he put back into the green box, and gave them many good wishes to carry with them.

"You are now our ruler," he said to the Scarecrow; "so you must come back to us as soon as possible."

"I certainly shall if I am able," the Scarecrow replied; "but I must help Dorothy to get home, first."

As Dorothy bade the good-natured Guardian a last farewell she said:

"I have been very kindly treated in your lovely City, and everyone has been good to me. I cannot tell you how grateful I am."

"Don't try, my dear," he answered. "We should like to keep you with us, but if it is your wish to return to Kansas, I hope you will find a way." He then opened the gate of the outer wall, and they walked forth and started upon their journey.

The sun shone brightly as our friends turned their faces toward the Land of the South. They were all in the best of spirits, and laughed

十九.遭遇怪树的袭击

第二天早晨，多萝茜吻别了漂亮的绿衣姑娘，他们每个人都跟绿胡子士兵握了握手，士兵一直把他们送到了城门口。当守门人再次见到他们时，得知他们要离开这座美丽的城市，去招惹新的麻烦，这令他惊讶不已。不过他还是立刻摘下了他们的眼镜，放回绿箱子中，并且给他们送上了美好的祝福。

"你是我们的新国王，"他对稻草人说道，"因此你必须尽快回到这里。"

"如果可以的话，我肯定会尽快回来，"稻草人回答说，"但是，首先我必须帮助多萝茜回到她的故乡。"

至于多萝茜，她跟好脾气的守门人做着最后的告别，说：

"在你们这座美丽的城市中，我受到了友好的款待，所有人都对我很好。我说不出自己有多么感谢你们。"

"亲爱的，那就别说了，"他回答道，"我们应该让你留下来的，不过既然你想要回堪萨斯州，那我希望你能找到办法。"说完，他就打开外城墙的大门，他们走出城门，开始了新的旅程。

我们的朋友朝南方走去，明媚的阳光照耀着他们。他们个个都神采奕奕，一起欢笑，一起闲聊。多萝茜又一次燃烧起回家的希望，稻草人和铁皮人很乐意为她服务。至于狮子，它快活地呼

and chatted together. Dorothy was once more filled with the hope of getting home, and the Scarecrow and the Tin Woodman were glad to be of use to her. As for the Lion, he sniffed the fresh air with delight and whisked his tail from side to side in pure joy at being in the country again, while Toto ran around them and chased the moths and butterflies, barking merrily all the time.

"City life does not agree with me at all," remarked the Lion, as they walked along at a brisk pace. "I have lost much flesh since I lived there, and now I am anxious for a chance to show the other beasts how courageous I have grown."

They now turned and took a last look at the Emerald City. All they could see was a mass of towers and steeples behind the green walls, and high up above everything the spires and dome of the Palace of Oz.

"Oz was not such a bad Wizard, after all," said the Tin Woodman, as he felt his heart rattling around in his breast.

"He knew how to give me brains, and very good brains, too," said the Scarecrow.

"If Oz had taken a dose of the same courage he gave me," added the Lion, "he would have been a brave man."

Dorothy said nothing. Oz had not kept the promise he made her, but he had done his best, so she forgave him. As he said, he was a good man, even if he was a bad Wizard.

吸着新鲜空气，为自己重新回到田野之中而兴奋地摇晃着尾巴。而托托在他们的身边奔跑着，追赶着飞蛾和蝴蝶，欢快地吠着。

"我完全无法适应城市生活，"当他们以轻快的步伐向前走时，狮子说，"自从住在那座城里之后，我都瘦一圈了，现在我渴望着能有一个机会可以让我向别的野兽们展现一下我有多勇敢。"

这时候，他们转过身来，最后看了一眼翡翠城。他们只能望见绿色城墙后面那许许多多的塔楼和教堂尖顶，以及高出所有建筑的奥兹宫殿的塔尖和圆屋顶。

"其实奥兹也不算是个坏魔法师。"铁皮人说，他感觉到自己的心在胸膛里怦怦跳动。

"他知道该如何给我脑子，而且还是一个非常聪明的脑子。"稻草人说。

"如果奥兹的胆量如他给我的这般大，"狮子接着说道，"他就是一个勇敢的人了。"

多萝茜什么也没说，虽然奥兹没能兑现他所许下的承诺，但是他已经尽力了，因此她也就原谅了奥兹。正如奥兹所说的那样，即使他是个说谎的魔法师，但他仍旧是一个好人。

第一天的旅程穿过了从翡翠城四周延伸出来的绿色田野和鲜艳花丛，那天晚上，他们就睡在草地上，只有繁星闪烁在他们的上空，他们确实睡得相当安稳。

第二天早晨，他们继续赶路，来到了一片茂密的森林，都没

19. Attacked by the Fighting Trees

The first day's journey was through the green fields and bright flowers that stretched about the Emerald City on every side. They slept that night on the grass, with nothing but the stars over them; and they rested very well indeed.

In the morning they traveled on until they came to a thick wood. There was no way of going around it, for it seemed to extend to the right and left as far as they could see; and, besides, they did not dare change the direction of their journey for fear of getting lost. So they looked for the place where it would be easiest to get into the forest.

The Scarecrow, who was in the lead, finally discovered a big tree with such wide-spreading branches that there was room for the party to pass underneath. So he walked forward to the tree, but just as he came under the first branches they bent down and twined around him, and the next minute he was raised from the ground and flung headlong among his fellow travelers.

This did not hurt the Scarecrow, but it surprised him, and he looked rather dizzy when Dorothy picked him up.

"Here is another space between the trees," called the Lion.

"Let me try it first," said the Scarecrow, "for it doesn't hurt me to get thrown about." He walked up to another tree, as he spoke, but its branches immediately seized him and tossed him back again.

"This is strange," exclaimed Dorothy. "What shall we do?"

"The trees seem to have made up their minds to fight us, and stop our journey," remarked the Lion.

十九.遭遇怪树的袭击

有路可以绕过去，因为这片树林似乎是从左右两边延伸开来，一望无际。而且，他们担心自己迷了路，也都不敢改变行进的方向。因此他们就在这里寻找一个最容易进入森林的地方。

带头的稻草人终于发现了一棵大树，枝繁叶茂，树底下有足够的空间可以让这群人穿过去。于是他向那棵树走了过去，但是正当他走到最前面的树枝下时，它们都弯曲下来，缠住了他，接着，把他举到空中，倒栽葱似的丢回到了其他旅行者中间。

这样根本伤害不到稻草人，但是当多萝茜扶他起来的时候，他感觉到头晕目眩，这令他惊讶不已。

"这边树丛中有另外一个空隙。"狮子叫道。

"让我先去试试看，"稻草人说，"就算把我丢出来，我也不会受伤的。"他一边说着，一边走向另外一棵树，但是树枝们立刻抓住了他，又把他丢了回来。

"真奇怪啊，"多萝茜大声叫道，"我们该怎么办？"

"这些树似乎故意在跟我们作对，阻挡我们的去路。"狮子说道。

"我想应该让我去试试看。"铁皮人说着，举起他的斧头，走向第一棵粗暴对待过稻草人的树。当一根大树枝弯下来抓他时，铁皮人凶狠地将它砍成了两段。此时，那棵树像是感到了疼痛，摇动着所有树枝。铁皮人从树底下安全地走了过去。

"来吧，"他对同伴们叫喊道，"快一点儿！"

19. Attacked by the Fighting Trees

"I believe I will try it myself," said the Woodman, and shouldering his axe, he marched up to the first tree that had handled the Scarecrow so roughly. When a big branch bent down to seize him the Woodman chopped at it so fiercely that he cut it in two. At once the tree began shaking all its branches as if in pain, and the Tin Woodman passed safely under it.

"Come on!" he shouted to the others. "Be quick!"

They all ran forward and passed under the tree without injury, except Toto, who was caught by a small branch and shaken until he howled. But the Woodman promptly chopped off the branch and set the little dog free.

The other trees of the forest did nothing to keep them back, so they made up their minds that only the first row of trees could bend down their branches, and that probably these were the policemen of the forest, and given this wonderful power in order to keep strangers out of it.

The four travelers walked with ease through the trees until they came to the farther edge of the wood. Then, to their surprise, they found before them a high wall which seemed to be made of white china. It was smooth, like the surface of a dish, and higher than their heads.

"What shall we do now?" asked Dorothy.

"I will make a ladder," said the Tin Woodman, "for we certainly must climb over the wall."

十九.遭遇怪树的袭击

他们全都跑向前去，毫发无伤地从树下穿了过去，只有托托，它被一根小树枝抓住了，不停地吠着。不过铁皮人迅速砍下了那根树枝，救出了这只小狗。

森林中的其他树木都没有挡住他们的去路，因此他们确定只有第一排的树木才会弯下树枝，或许它们就是这片森林的警察，拥有这种神奇的本领，防止陌生人的进入。

4 个旅行者轻松自在地穿行在树林中，一直走到了树林的边界。这时候，他们惊讶地发现前面有一堵高墙，像是用白瓷堆砌而成的，墙面非常光滑，就像盘子的表面一样，而且比他们的头还要高出许多。

多萝茜问："现在我们该怎么办？"

"我来搭一个梯子，"铁皮人说，"我们肯定要从这墙上爬过去喽。"

20. The Dainty China Country

While the Woodman was making a ladder from wood which he found in the forest Dorothy lay down and slept, for she was tired by the long walk. The Lion also curled himself up to sleep and Toto lay beside him.

The Scarecrow watched the Woodman while he worked, and said to him:

"I cannot think why this wall is here, nor what it is made of."

"Rest your brains and do not worry about the wall," replied the Woodman. "When we have climbed over it, we shall know what is on the other side."

After a time the ladder was finished. It looked clumsy, but the Tin Woodman was sure it was strong and would answer their purpose. The Scarecrow waked Dorothy and the Lion and Toto, and told them that the ladder was ready. The Scarecrow climbed up the ladder first, but he was so awkward that Dorothy had to follow close behind and keep him from falling off. When he got his head over the top of the wall the Scarecrow said, "Oh, my!"

"Go on," exclaimed Dorothy.

So the Scarecrow climbed farther up and sat down on the top of the wall, and Dorothy put her head over and cried, "Oh, my!" just as the Scarecrow had done.

二十.美丽的瓷城

正当铁皮人从树林中砍来木材做木梯的时候，多萝茜躺在地上睡着了，因为经过长途跋涉之后，她已经疲倦了。狮子也蜷缩着身子睡了下来，托托则躺在它的身旁。

稻草人看着铁皮人工作，对他说：

"我不知道为什么这里会有一堵墙，建这么个东西有什么用呢？"

"让你的脑子休息休息吧，别再想这堵墙的事了，"铁皮人回答说，"等我们爬过去之后，就会知道对面有些什么东西了。"

过了一会儿，梯子完成了，虽然看上去有些笨拙，但是铁皮人相信它很牢固，肯定可以派上用场。稻草人唤醒了多萝茜、狮子和托托，告诉他们说梯子已经准备就绪了。稻草人第一个爬上了梯子，但是他的动作如此笨拙，使得多萝茜只好紧紧地跟在他后面，以防他掉下来。当稻草人把头探过墙顶的时候，他喊道："天哪！"

"快爬上去呀！"多萝茜大声叫道。

于是稻草人又往前爬过去，坐在墙顶上了。多萝茜把头探过墙顶，也像稻草人一样叫了起来："天哪！"

接着托托也爬了上去，它立刻就吠了起来，不过多萝茜让它安静了下来。

Then Toto came up, and immediately began to bark, but Dorothy made him be still.

The Lion climbed the ladder next, and the Tin Woodman came last; but both of them cried, "Oh, my!" as soon as they looked over the wall. When they were all sitting in a row on the top of the wall, they looked down and saw a strange sight.

Before them was a great stretch of country having a floor as smooth and shining and white as the bottom of a big platter. Scattered around were many houses made entirely of china and painted in the brightest colors. These houses were quite small, the biggest of them reaching only as high as Dorothy's waist. There were also pretty little barns, with china fences around them; and many cows and sheep and horses and pigs and chickens, all made of china, were standing about in groups.

But the strangest of all were the people who lived in this queer country. There were milkmaids and shepherdesses, with brightly colored bodices and golden spots all over their gowns; and princesses with most gorgeous frocks of silver and gold and purple; and shepherds dressed in knee breeches with pink and yellow and blue stripes down them, and golden buckles on their shoes; and princes with jeweled crowns upon their heads, wearing ermine robes and satin doublets; and funny clowns in ruffled gowns, with round red spots upon their cheeks and tall, pointed caps. And, strangest of all,

跟着狮子爬上了梯子，铁皮人最后上来，当他们俩从墙顶望过去的时候，都叫了一声"天哪"。此刻他们全都并排坐在城墙顶上，向下望去，看到了一片奇特的景象。

在他们面前出现了一片广阔的城市，那地面平滑、光亮、洁白，就像个大盘底一般。四周散布着许多房子，全都是用陶瓷筑成的，上面漆着鲜明的色彩。这些房子都非常小，其中最大一座也只有多萝茜的腰部这么高。那里还有许多漂亮的小马厩，四周围绕着瓷制的篱笆，里面站着一群群的牛、羊、马、猪和小鸡，这些全都是用陶瓷做成的。

但是最令人感到惊奇的是那些住在这个奇异国度里的百姓。挤奶女工和牧羊姑娘身穿着色彩明亮的背心，金黄色的斑点布满了衣服上下；公主们身穿着银色、金色和紫色的华丽长袍；牧羊人穿着粉色、黄色和蓝色条纹的短裤，他们的鞋子上有一颗金色的纽扣；王子们的头上戴着宝石镶嵌的皇冠，身上穿着貂皮长袍和锦缎上衣；滑稽的小丑们穿着皱巴巴的长袍，两边的脸颊上画着红色的圆点，头上戴着尖顶的高帽子。最最奇怪的是，这些人全都是用陶瓷做成的，甚至连他们的衣服也是如此。他们的个子都非常矮小，最高的都还不到多萝茜的膝盖。

刚开始，没有一个人注意到这几个旅行者，除了一只紫色的、脑袋特别大的小瓷狗，它跑到了城墙边上朝着他们吠了起来，声音非常细小。之后它又跑了回去。

these people were all made of china, even to their clothes, and were so small that the tallest of them was no higher than Dorothy's knee.

No one did so much as look at the travelers at first, except one little purple china dog with an extra-large head, which came to the wall and barked at them in a tiny voice, afterwards running away again.

"How shall we get down?" asked Dorothy.

They found the ladder so heavy they could not pull it up, so the Scarecrow fell off the wall and the others jumped down upon him so that the hard floor would not hurt their feet. Of course they took pains not to light on his head and get the pins in their feet. When all were safely down they picked up the Scarecrow, whose body was quite flattened out, and patted his straw into shape again.

"We must cross this strange place in order to get to the other side," said Dorothy, "for it would be unwise for us to go any other way except due South."

They began walking through the country of the china people, and the first thing they came to was a china milkmaid milking a china cow. As they drew near, the cow suddenly gave a kick and kicked over the stool, the pail, and even the milkmaid herself, and all fell on the china ground with a great clatter.

Dorothy was shocked to see that the cow had broken her leg off, and that the pail was lying in several small pieces, while the poor milkmaid had a nick in her left elbow.

"我们该怎么下去呢？"多萝茜问道。

他们发现梯子非常笨重，根本无法把它搬上来，于是稻草人就从墙上倒下去，其余人就跳到他的身上，如此一来，这坚硬的地面就不会伤到他们的脚了。当然，他们都尽量不往稻草人的头上跳，要不然他头上的针就会戳到他们的脚上。当所有人都安全跳下之后，他们扶起稻草人，他的身体已经被踩扁了，他们拍打着稻草人，使他恢复了原样。

"要想走到另外一边，我们就必须穿过这个奇怪的地方，"多萝茜说，"如果不向着南方，而改走其他路，那我们就太不明智了。"

他们开始穿过这个陶瓷之城。他们遇到的第一个人就是一个陶瓷的挤奶女工，挤着一头瓷牛的奶。当他们慢慢走近时，那头瓷牛突然蹬了一脚，踢翻了凳子和奶桶，甚至连挤奶女工也没能幸免，咣当一声摔倒在陶瓷地面上。

多萝茜惊讶地看到那头瓷牛断了一条腿，奶桶也摔成了许多碎片，而可怜的挤奶女工的左肘上也摔出了一道裂痕。

"喂！"挤奶女工生气地叫喊着，"看看你们都做了些什么！我的牛断了一条腿，我必须得带它去修理店，把这条腿粘回去。你们为什么要跑过来惊吓我的牛？"

"真是对不起，"多萝茜回答说，"请原谅我们。"

但是这位漂亮的挤奶女工非常生气，根本就不理他们。她生着闷气，捡起断腿，牵着牛走了，那头可怜的牛只能一瘸一拐地

"There!" cried the milkmaid angrily. "See what you have done! My cow has broken her leg, and I must take her to the mender's shop and have it glued on again. What do you mean by coming here and frightening my cow?"

"I'm very sorry," returned Dorothy. "Please forgive us."

But the pretty milkmaid was much too vexed to make any answer. She picked up the leg sulkily and led her cow away, the poor animal limping on three legs. As she left them the milkmaid cast many reproachful glances over her shoulder at the clumsy strangers, holding her nicked elbow close to her side.

Dorothy was quite grieved at this mishap.

"We must be very careful here," said the kind-hearted Woodman, "or we may hurt these pretty little people so they will never get over it."

A little farther on Dorothy met a most beautifully dressed young Princess, who stopped short as she saw the strangers and started to run away.

Dorothy wanted to see more of the Princess, so she ran after her. But the china girl cried out:

"Don't chase me! Don't chase me!"

She had such a frightened little voice that Dorothy stopped and said, "Why not?"

"Because," answered the Princess, also stopping, a safe distance away, "if I run I may fall down and break myself."

用 3 只脚走路。挤奶女工一边走着，一边转过头来，对这些愚蠢的陌生人投去很多责备的目光，她那条受伤的手臂紧靠在自己身边。

对于这次不幸，多萝茜感到非常懊恼。

"我们在这里必须要小心谨慎，"心地善良的铁皮人说，"要不然我们可能会伤害到这些可爱的小人，令他们永远都无法痊愈的。"

刚走了几步，多萝茜就遇见了一位衣着非常漂亮的年轻公主，当她看见这些陌生人之后，停顿了片刻，然后就跑开了。

多萝茜想要多看看这位公主，于是就追了上去，但是这位陶瓷公主叫喊道：

"别来追我！别来追我！"

她那细小的声音中流露出恐惧之情，使得多萝茜停下了脚步，问道："为什么呢？"

公主也停下脚步，跟多萝茜相隔着一段安全距离，回答说："因为我跑起来的时候可能会跌倒，我自己就会摔碎的。"

"可是你不能修补回去吗？"小女孩问道。

"哦，可以。但是你得知道，修补之后，这个人就永远不会那么漂亮了。"公主回答说。

"我想应该是这样吧。"多萝茜说。

"这里有一位乔克先生，他是我们的一个小丑，"陶瓷公主继

"But could you not be mended?" asked the girl.

"Oh, yes; but one is never so pretty after being mended, you know," replied the Princess.

"I suppose not," said Dorothy.

"Now there is Mr. Joker, one of our clowns," continued the china lady, "who is always trying to stand upon his head. He has broken himself so often that he is mended in a hundred places, and doesn't look at all pretty. Here he comes now, so you can see for yourself."

Indeed, a jolly little clown came walking toward them, and Dorothy could see that in spite of his pretty clothes of red and yellow and green he was completely covered with cracks, running every which way and showing plainly that he had been mended in many places.

The Clown put his hands in his pockets, and after puffing out his cheeks and nodding his head at them saucily, he said:

> "My lady fair,
> Why do you stare
> At poor old Mr. Joker?
> You're quite as stiff
> And prim as if
> You'd eaten up a poker!"

续说道，"他总是想用头站在地上，所以就会经常摔倒，他身上都已经修补一百多个地方了，变得一点都不好看。他过来了，你可以亲自看看他的样子。"

果然，一个滑稽的小丑正朝她们走了过来。尽管他穿着红色、黄色和绿色的漂亮衣服，多萝茜仍旧可以看出他身上满是裂缝，每走一步，就可以清楚地看到他修补过很多地方。

小丑的双手插在衣袋里，鼓起腮帮子，粗鲁莽撞地向她们点点头，唱道：

"漂亮的姑娘，

为什么盯着可怜的乔克老先生？

你如此呆板拘谨，

就像吞下了一根拨火棒！"

"先生，别唱了！"公主说，"你没看见这几位陌生朋友吗，你应该恭敬地对待他们！"

"哦，希望这样可以算有礼貌吧。"小丑说着，立刻用头倒立在地上。

"请别介意这位乔克先生，"公主对多萝茜说，"他的脑袋伤得很重，因此就变得愚蠢了。"

"哦，我一点儿都不介意，"多萝茜说，"不过你长得这么漂

"Be quiet, sir!" said the Princess. "Can't you see these are strangers, and should be treated with respect?"

"Well, that's respect, I expect," declared the Clown, and immediately stood upon his head.

"Don't mind Mr. Joker," said the Princess to Dorothy. "He is considerably cracked in his head, and that makes him foolish."

"Oh, I don't mind him a bit," said Dorothy. "But you are so beautiful," she continued, "that I am sure I could love you dearly. Won't you let me carry you back to Kansas, and stand you on Aunt Em's mantelshelf? I could carry you in my basket."

"That would make me very unhappy," answered the china Princess. "You see, here in our country we live contentedly, and can talk and move around as we please. But whenever any of us are taken away our joints at once stiffen, and we can only stand straight and look pretty. Of course that is all that is expected of us when we are on mantels and cabinets and drawing-room tables, but our lives are much pleasanter here in our own country."

"I would not make you unhappy for all the world!" exclaimed Dorothy. "So I'll just say good-bye."

"Good-bye," replied the Princess.

They walked carefully through the china country. The little animals and all the people scampered out of their way, fearing the strangers would break them, and after an hour or so the travelers reached the other side of the country and came to another china wall.

亮，"她接着说道，"我想我会非常喜欢你的，你愿意让我带你去堪萨斯州，把你放在艾姆婶婶的壁炉架上面吗？我可以把你放在篮子里带走。"

"那样一点儿都不会让我觉得开心，"陶瓷公主回答说，"你知道，我们在自己的国家里过得非常愉快、满足，只要自己开心，可以随便说什么，随便去哪里。但是不管什么时候，只要我们一被人带走，我们的关节就会立刻僵硬，只能笔直地站着，供人赏玩。当然，人们也希望我们可以站在壁炉台上、橱柜里，或是客厅的桌子上，但是我们在自己的国家过得更加快乐。"

"不管怎么样，我都不想让你不快乐！"多萝茜说，"因此我这就跟你告别了。"

"再见。"公主回答说。

他们小心翼翼地走过了这个陶瓷之国。所有的小动物和小人都跑着躲开他们，担心这几个陌生人把自己给打碎了。一个钟头之后，这些旅行者就来到了这个国度的另一边，遇到了另一堵瓷墙。

这堵墙没有之前那堵来得高，只要站在狮子的背上，他们就可以爬上墙头。然后狮子并拢四肢，跳上了瓷墙。但是在它起跳的时候，尾巴带到了一座陶瓷教堂，把它打得粉碎。

"这真是太糟糕了，"多萝茜说，"不过我想我们还算走运的，

It was not so high as the first, however, and by standing upon the Lion's back they all managed to scramble to the top. Then the Lion gathered his legs under him and jumped on the wall; but just as he jumped, he upset a china church with his tail and smashed it all to pieces.

"That was too bad," said Dorothy, "but really I think we were lucky in not doing these little people more harm than breaking a cow's leg and a church. They are all so brittle!"

"They are, indeed," said the Scarecrow, "and I am thankful I am made of straw and cannot be easily damaged. There are worse things in the world than being a Scarecrow."

除了弄断一头牛的腿，打碎一座教堂之外，没有对这些小人造成更多的伤害。他们全都那么脆弱！"

"是啊，"稻草人说，"我真是要谢天谢地了，我是个稻草人，不会这么轻易受伤。原来在这个世界上，还有比稻草人更加不如的东西。"

21. The Lion Becomes the King of the Beasts

After climbing down from the china wall the travelers found themselves in a disagreeable country, full of bogs and marshes and covered with tall, rank grass. It was difficult to walk without falling into muddy holes, for the grass was so thick that it hid them from sight. However, by carefully picking their way, they got safely along until they reached solid ground. But here the country seemed wilder than ever, and after a long and tiresome walk through the underbrush they entered another forest, where the trees were bigger and older than any they had ever seen.

"This forest is perfectly delightful," declared the Lion, looking around him with joy. "Never have I seen a more beautiful place."

"It seems gloomy," said the Scarecrow.

"Not a bit of it," answered the Lion. "I should like to live here all my life. See how soft the dried leaves are under your feet and how rich and green the moss is that clings to these old trees. Surely no wild beast could wish a pleasanter home."

"Perhaps there are wild beasts in the forest now," said Dorothy.

"I suppose there are," returned the Lion, "but I do not see any of them about."

二十一.狮子是万兽之王

翻过瓷墙之后，这几位旅行者发现自己来到了一个令人不快的地方，到处是沼泽与湿地，长满了长长的杂草。因为杂草浓密，挡住了他们的视线，所以没走几步路就会掉进泥泞的水潭里。不过，他们小心翼翼地选择行走路线，最后平平安安地走到了硬土地上。然而这个地方似乎比先前更加荒芜，他们疲惫不堪地走了很长一段时间，穿过了低矮的灌木林，来到了另一片森林中，那里的树木，比他们以前见过的都要来得高大、古老。

"这片森林真是让人赏心悦目，"狮子一边说着，一边兴奋地打量着四周，"我从没有见过比这更漂亮的地方了。"

"好像非常阴森恐怖。"稻草人说。

"一点儿都不阴森，"狮子回答说，"我真想永远都住在这里。看看你们脚下这些干草有多柔软，这些古树上的苔藓有多丰厚、碧绿。没有哪只野兽会渴望拥有比这里更合心意的家园了。"

"或许现在就已经有野兽住在这片森林里了吧。"多萝茜说。

"我想有吧，"狮子回答说，"不过我还没有在这附近看见过。"

他们行走在这片森林之中，直到天色太黑，无法继续前进时，他们才停下了脚步。多萝茜、托托和狮子躺下来睡觉，与此同时，铁皮人和稻草人像平常一样地守护着他们。

等天亮之后，他们继续上路。他们还没走多远，就听见一阵

21. The Lion Becomes the King of the Beasts

They walked through the forest until it became too dark to go any farther. Dorothy and Toto and the Lion lay down to sleep, while the Woodman and the Scarecrow kept watch over them as usual.

When morning came, they started again. Before they had gone far they heard a low rumble, as of the growling of many wild animals. Toto whimpered a little, but none of the others was frightened, and they kept along the well-trodden path until they came to an opening in the wood, in which were gathered hundreds of beasts of every variety. There were tigers and elephants and bears and wolves and foxes and all the others in the natural history, and for a moment Dorothy was afraid. But the Lion explained that the animals were holding a meeting, and he judged by their snarling and growling that they were in great trouble.

As he spoke several of the beasts caught sight of him, and at once the great assemblage hushed as if by magic. The biggest of the tigers came up to the Lion and bowed, saying:

"Welcome, O King of Beasts! You have come in good time to fight our enemy and bring peace to all the animals of the forest once more."

"What is your trouble?" asked the Lion quietly.

"We are all threatened," answered the tiger, "by a fierce enemy which has lately come into this forest. It is a most tremendous monster, like a great spider, with a body as big as an elephant and legs as long as a tree trunk. It has eight of these long legs, and as the

低沉的声音，好像有许多野兽在怒吼。托托小声地呜咽着，不过其他人都没有感到害怕，继续沿着小径往前走，最后来到了树林中的一片空地上，里面聚集着好几百只各种各样的野兽。有老虎、大象、熊、狼和狐狸，以及自然界中的所有兽类。多萝茜立刻就被吓坏了。不过狮子解释说这是动物们在举行会议，从它们的怒吼与咆哮声中，它判断出它们遇到了很大的麻烦。

正在狮子说话的当口，好几只野兽看见了它，一瞬间，这一大群野兽就像是着了魔似的，鸦雀无声。有一头最大的老虎走向狮子，鞠了个躬，说：

"欢迎回来，万兽之王！您来得正是时候，请您帮忙打败我们的敌人，还这森林中的野兽们一个和平吧。"

"你们遇上什么麻烦了？"狮子镇静地问道。

"最近在这片森林中来了一只极其凶猛的野兽，我们都受到了它的威胁，"老虎回答说，"它是一个极其可怕的怪物，长得像一只大蜘蛛，体形跟大象一样魁梧，腿脚跟树干一样修长。它长着 8 条这么长的腿，当这个怪物爬行在这片森林中时，它用一只脚抓住一只动物，然后塞进嘴里，吃下去，就像一只蜘蛛吃苍蝇一样。只要这头凶猛的怪物存在于世，我们就会永远不得安宁。你来到这里的时候，我们正在召开会议，商量该如何保卫自己。"

狮子沉思了片刻。

"这片森林里，还有其他狮子吗？"它问。

monster crawls through the forest he seizes an animal with a leg and drags it to his mouth, where he eats it as a spider does a fly. Not one of us is safe while this fierce creature is alive, and we had called a meeting to decide how to take care of ourselves when you came among us."

The Lion thought for a moment.

"Are there any other lions in this forest?" he asked.

"No; there were some, but the monster has eaten them all. And, besides, there were none of them nearly so large and brave as you."

"If I put an end to your enemy, will you bow down to me and obey me as King of the Forest?" inquired the Lion.

"We will do that gladly," returned the tiger; and all the other beasts roared with a mighty roar: "We will!"

"Where is this great spider of yours now?" asked the Lion.

"Yonder, among the oak trees," said the tiger, pointing with his forefoot.

"Take good care of these friends of mine," said the Lion, "and I will go at once to fight the monster."

He bade his comrades good-bye and marched proudly away to do battle with the enemy.

The great spider was lying asleep when the Lion found him, and it looked so ugly that its foe turned up his nose in disgust. Its legs were quite as long as the tiger had said, and its body covered with coarse black hair. It had a great mouth, with a row of sharp teeth a foot long;

"没有了，从前是有几只，可是这个怪物把它们全都吃掉了。况且，它们之中没有一个像你这么魁梧、这么勇敢。"

"如果我解决了你们的敌人，你们会不会服从我，像遵从森林之王那样地服从我？"狮子询问道。

"我们非常乐意服从你。"老虎回答说，其他的所有野兽也都发出震耳欲聋的吼声："我们愿意！"

"那个大蜘蛛现在在哪里？"狮子说。

"在那边的栎树林中，"老虎一边说，一边用前脚指点方向。

"替我小心照顾我的朋友们，"狮子说，"我立刻就去跟那个怪物会一会。"

他跟同伴们告了别，骄傲地向前走，去迎战那头怪物。

当狮子找到那个大蜘蛛时，它正躺着睡觉，那样子看上去丑恶至极，使得狮子厌恶地掩着自己的鼻子。它的脚长得跟老虎所说的一样长，身上覆盖着粗糙的黑色毛发。它长着一张大嘴，一排锋利的牙齿足有一尺长；但是连着它的头和矮胖身子的脖子却像黄蜂腰似的那么纤细。这就给了狮子一个提示，让他想出了一个攻击这头怪物的最好办法，它知道在它睡着时攻击它，要比它醒来时容易很多。因此狮子猛地跳了起来，直接扑到那个怪物的背上，然后举起一只沉重而长着利爪的脚掌打了下去，将那蜘蛛的头从它身上敲了下来。狮子看着它那些长脚不再抖动，知道它已经彻底完蛋之后，才跳了下来。

but its head was joined to the pudgy body by a neck as slender as a wasp's waist. This gave the Lion a hint of the best way to attack the creature, and as he knew it was easier to fight it asleep than awake, he gave a great spring and landed directly upon the monster's back. Then, with one blow of his heavy paw, all armed with sharp claws, he knocked the spider's head from its body. Jumping down, he watched it until the long legs stopped wiggling, when he knew it was quite dead.

The Lion went back to the opening where the beasts of the forest were waiting for him and said proudly:

"You need fear your enemy no longer."

Then the beasts bowed down to the Lion as their King, and he promised to come back and rule over them as soon as Dorothy was safely on her way to Kansas.

二十一.狮子是万兽之王

狮子回到空地，森林中的野兽们正在那里等候着它。狮子骄傲地说：

"你们再也不用害怕那个敌人了。"

于是野兽们尊狮子为万兽之王，膜拜着它。狮子答应它们，等多萝茜平安踏上回堪萨斯州的路之后，它就会回来统治它们。

22. The Country of the Quadlings

The four travelers passed through the rest of the forest in safety, and when they came out from its gloom saw before them a steep hill, covered from top to bottom with great pieces of rock.

"That will be a hard climb," said the Scarecrow, "but we must get over the hill, nevertheless."

So he led the way and the others followed. They had nearly reached the first rock when they heard a rough voice cry out, "Keep back!"

"Who are you?" asked the Scarecrow.

Then a head showed itself over the rock and the same voice said, "This hill belongs to us, and we don't allow anyone to cross it."

"But we must cross it," said the Scarecrow. "We're going to the country of the Quadlings."

"But you shall not!" replied the voice, and there stepped from behind the rock the strangest man the travelers had ever seen.

He was quite short and stout and had a big head, which was flat at the top and supported by a thick neck full of wrinkles. But he had no arms at all, and, seeing this, the Scarecrow did not fear that so helpless a creature could prevent them from climbing the hill. So he said, "I'm sorry not to do as you wish, but we must pass over your hill whether you like it or not," and he walked boldly forward.

二十二.奎特林国

4 位旅行者平安地走出了这片森林,当他们从阴森的树林中出来之后,就看见一座陡峭的山横在他们的面前,从山脚到山顶,全都堆着大块大块的岩石。

"要爬过这座山真是件困难的事情,"稻草人说,"尽管如此,我们还是得爬过去。"

于是他在前面带路,其他人紧随其后。在他们刚刚接近第一块岩石时,就听见一个粗厉的声音喊道:"滚回去!"

"你是谁?"稻草人问说。

这时,一颗脑袋从岩石后面探了出来,用同样的声音说道:"这座山是我们的,任何人都不许翻越这座山。"

"可是我们必须得爬过去,"稻草人说,"我们要去奎特林。"

"但是你们不能去!"那声音回答道,然后从岩石后面走出一个人来,这几位旅行者从来都没有见过这么奇怪的人。

他的身子非常矮小,却十分结实,粗壮而长满皱纹的脖子上支撑着一个平顶的大脑袋。但是他没有手臂。看到这一情景,稻草人根本不担心这样一个身体残障的东西可以阻止他们爬过山顶。于是他说:"很抱歉,我们无法让你如愿了,不管你喜不喜欢,我们都必须爬过你这座山。"说着,稻草人就大胆地往前走了过去。

就在这个时候,这个人的脑袋就像闪电似的射了出来,脖子

22. The Country of the Quadlings

As quick as lightning the man's head shot forward and his neck stretched out until the top of the head, where it was flat, struck the Scarecrow in the middle and sent him tumbling, over and over, down the hill. Almost as quickly as it came the head went back to the body, and the man laughed harshly as he said, "It isn't as easy as you think!"

A chorus of boisterous laughter came from the other rocks, and Dorothy saw hundreds of the armless Hammer-Heads upon the hillside, one behind every rock.

The Lion became quite angry at the laughter caused by the Scarecrow's mishap, and giving a loud roar that echoed like thunder, he dashed up the hill.

Again a head shot swiftly out, and the great Lion went rolling down the hill as if he had been struck by a cannon ball.

Dorothy ran down and helped the Scarecrow to his feet, and the Lion came up to her, feeling rather bruised and sore, and said, "It is useless to fight people with shooting heads; no one can withstand them."

"What can we do, then?" she asked.

"Call the Winged Monkeys," suggested the Tin Woodman. "You have still the right to command them once more."

"Very well," she answered, and putting on the Golden Cap she uttered the magic words. The Monkeys were as prompt as ever, and in a few moments the entire band stood before her.

向前伸长，直到平顶的脑袋把稻草人撞了个正着，稻草人摔倒在地上，滚啊滚，滚到了山脚下。那颗脑袋像伸出来时那般迅速地缩了回去，这个人发出刺耳的笑声，说道："这可不像你想象的那般容易！"

这时候，其他的岩石后面同时传出一阵喧闹的笑声，多萝茜看到山坡上有好几百个没有手臂的大头人，每块岩石后面都站着一个。

由于稻草人的不幸而引发的这种嘲笑声让狮子感到非常愤怒，它怒吼了一声，冲上山去，那回声像雷声一样在山间回荡。

又有一颗脑袋迅速地射了出来，大狮子就像是被炮弹打中了似的滚下了山。

多萝茜跑过去扶起稻草人，狮子也跑到她的身边，它摔得满身是伤，浑身疼痛，说道："跟这些脑袋可以出击的人斗了也是白斗，没人可以抵抗得住他们的攻击。"

"那我们该怎么办呢？"多萝茜问道。

"把飞猴们召唤过来，"铁皮人建议道，"你还有权利再命令它们一次。"

"是啊。"她回答说，于是就戴上金帽子，念起咒语。飞猴们像往常一样迅速，不一会儿就全都站在了她的面前。

"您有什么命令？"猴王深深地鞠了个躬，问道。

"带我们飞过这座山头，去奎特林。"小女孩回答说。

22. The Country of the Quadlings

"What are your commands?" inquired the King of the Monkeys, bowing low.

"Carry us over the hill to the country of the Quadlings," answered the girl.

"It shall be done," said the King, and at once the Winged Monkeys caught the four travelers and Toto up in their arms and flew away with them. As they passed over the hill the Hammer-Heads yelled with vexation, and shot their heads high in the air, but they could not reach the Winged Monkeys, which carried Dorothy and her comrades safely over the hill and set them down in the beautiful country of the Quadlings.

"This is the last time you can summon us," said the leader to Dorothy; "so good-bye and good luck to you."

"Good-bye, and thank you very much," returned the girl; and the Monkeys rose into the air and were out of sight in a twinkling.

The country of the Quadlings seemed rich and happy. There was field upon field of ripening grain, with well-paved roads running between, and pretty rippling brooks with strong bridges across them. The fences and houses and bridges were all painted bright red, just as they had been painted yellow in the country of the Winkies and blue in the country of the Munchkins. The Quadlings themselves, who were short and fat and looked chubby and good-natured, were dressed all in red, which showed bright against the green grass and the yellowing grain.

二十二.奎特林国

"没问题。"猴王说，然后飞猴们立刻抓住这4位旅行者和托托，带着他们飞上了天。当他们飞过山头的时候，这些大头人懊恼地叫喊着，脑袋高高地射到空中，但是他们怎么都没办法射到飞猴们。飞猴们带着多萝茜和她的同伴们平安地翻过了这座山，降落在美丽的奎特林。

"这是你最后一次召唤我们了，"猴王对多萝茜说，"那么就再见了，祝你好运。"

"再见，非常感谢你们的帮助。"女孩子回答道。飞猴们飞到空中，一眨眼工夫就消失在了眼前。

奎特林这个地方似乎非常富裕、幸福。这里有一片片成熟的稻田，平坦的道路横亘其中，潺潺流动的溪流上面架着坚固的桥梁。篱笆、房子和桥梁全都漆着鲜艳的红色，就像温基国漆成黄色，芒奇金国漆成蓝色一样。奎特林人长得矮小壮实，看起来胖乎乎的，脾气很好。他们全都穿着红色的衣服，在绿油油的青草和黄澄澄的谷物相衬之下，显得格外鲜明。

飞猴们把他们放在一间农舍附近，这4位旅行者走上前去，敲了敲门。开门的是农夫的妻子，当多萝茜向她要点东西填肚时，这个妇人给了他们一顿美味的午饭，有3种糕点，4种小饼，还给托托喝了一碗牛奶。

"这里距离格琳达的宫殿还有多远？"小女孩问。

"不是很远，"农夫的妻子回答说，"一直往南走，用不了多

22. The Country of the Quadlings

The Monkeys had set them down near a farmhouse, and the four travelers walked up to it and knocked at the door. It was opened by the farmer's wife, and when Dorothy asked for something to eat the woman gave them all a good dinner, with three kinds of cake and four kinds of cookies, and a bowl of milk for Toto.

"How far is it to the Castle of Glinda?" asked the child.

"It is not a great way," answered the farmer's wife. "Take the road to the South and you will soon reach it."

Thanking the good woman, they started afresh and walked by the fields and across the pretty bridges until they saw before them a very beautiful Castle. Before the gates were three young girls, dressed in handsome red uniforms trimmed with gold braid; and as Dorothy approached, one of them said to her:

"Why have you come to the South Country?"

"To see the Good Witch who rules here," she answered. "Will you take me to her?"

"Let me have your name, and I will ask Glinda if she will receive you." They told who they were, and the girl soldier went into the Castle. After a few moments she came back to say that Dorothy and the others were to be admitted at once.

少时间，你们就能到那里了。"

在向这位好心的妇人道谢之后，他们又重新出发，沿着田野，走过美丽的小桥，最后他们看见一座非常雄伟的城堡出现在了眼前。城门前站着3个年轻女子，穿着漂亮的装饰着金边的红色制服。当多萝茜走近时，其中的一个问道：

"你到南方国度里来干什么？"

"我来拜访统治这里的善良女巫，"她回答说，"你可以带我去见她吗？"

"告诉我你叫什么名字，我会通报格琳达，看她是否愿意接见。"于是他们报上了各自的名字，然后这位女士兵就走进城堡。几分钟之后，她回来了，说多萝茜和她的同伴们可以立刻去拜见格琳达。

23. Glinda Grants Dorothy's Wish

Before they went to see Glinda, however, they were taken to a room of the Castle, where Dorothy washed her face and combed her hair, and the Lion shook the dust out of his mane, and the Scarecrow patted himself into his best shape, and the Woodman polished his tin and oiled his joints.

When they were all quite presentable they followed the soldier girl into a big room where the Witch Glinda sat upon a throne of rubies.

She was both beautiful and young to their eyes. Her hair was a rich red in color and fell in flowing ringlets over her shoulders. Her dress was pure white but her eyes were blue, and they looked kindly upon the little girl.

"What can I do for you, my child?" she asked.

Dorothy told the Witch all her story: how the cyclone had brought her to the Land of Oz, how she had found her companions, and of the wonderful adventures they had met with.

"My greatest wish now," she added, "is to get back to Kansas, for Aunt Em will surely think something dreadful has happened to me, and that will make her put on mourning; and unless the crops are better this year than they were last, I am sure Uncle Henry cannot afford it."

Glinda leaned forward and kissed the sweet, upturned face of the loving little girl.

二十三.多萝茜如愿以偿

但是在他们见到格琳达之前,先被带到了城堡的一个房间里。多萝茜在那儿洗了把脸,整理了一下头发。狮子抖了抖鬃毛上的灰尘。稻草人拍了拍身子,让自己变得圆鼓鼓的。铁皮人擦了擦自己的铁皮,在关节上添了些油。

等他们全都准备完毕之后,女士兵就带着他们走进一个大房间里,格琳达女巫正坐在一把红宝石王座上。

在他们的眼中,这位女巫显得既漂亮又年轻,她的头发是深红色的,松软地垂在肩膀上。她穿着洁白的衣服,一双蓝色的眼睛和蔼地注视着这个小女孩。

"我的孩子,我能为你做些什么事呢?"她问道。

多萝茜把自己的故事全都告诉了女巫:龙卷风如何把她带到了奥兹国,她如何遇见了自己的同伴们,以及他们遇到的一件件奇妙的冒险故事。

"现在我最大的愿望就是回到堪萨斯州,"她接着说道,"因为艾姆婶婶肯定会以为我遇到了什么不测,她会因此而办理丧事。除非今年的收成比去年还要好,要不然,我想亨利叔叔肯定负担不了这笔费用的。"

格琳达俯身向前,亲吻着这个可爱小女孩向上仰起的脸颊。

"你的心地这么善良,"她说,"我想我一定会告诉你如何回

"Bless your dear heart," she said, "I am sure I can tell you of a way to get back to Kansas." Then she added,

"But, if I do, you must give me the Golden Cap."

"Willingly!" exclaimed Dorothy; "indeed, it is of no use to me now, and when you have it you can command the Winged Monkeys three times."

"And I think I shall need their service just those three times," answered Glinda, smiling.

Dorothy then gave her the Golden Cap, and the Witch said to the Scarecrow, "What will you do when Dorothy has left us?"

"I will return to the Emerald City," he replied, "for Oz has made me its ruler and the people like me. The only thing that worries me is how to cross the hill of the Hammer-Heads."

"By means of the Golden Cap I shall command the Winged Monkeys to carry you to the gates of the Emerald City," said Glinda, "for it would be a shame to deprive the people of so wonderful a ruler."

"Am I really wonderful?" asked the Scarecrow.

"You are unusual," replied Glinda.

Turning to the Tin Woodman, she asked, "What will become of you when Dorothy leaves this country?"

He leaned on his axe and thought a moment. Then he said,

"The Winkies were very kind to me, and wanted me to rule over them after the Wicked Witch died. I am fond of the Winkies, and if I

到堪萨斯州的。"然后，她又说道，"但是，如果我这么做了，你必须把这顶金帽子送给我。"

"我愿意！"多萝茜叫了起来，"其实这顶帽子对我来说已经没有用处了，不过你拥有它之后，就可以命令飞猴3次。"

"我想我正好需要它们替我服务 3 次。"格琳达微笑地回答道。

于是多萝茜把金帽子给了她，然后女巫对稻草人说："等多萝茜离开我们之后，你要去干什么？"

"我会回到翡翠城，"他回答说，"因为奥兹任命我来统治那个国家，而且百姓们也很爱戴我。唯一让我感到担忧的就是要如何越过那座由大头人占据着的山峰。"

"我会用这顶金帽子的魔力，命令飞猴们带你到翡翠城的大门前，"格琳达说，"如果那里的百姓失去了一位像你这样神奇的领袖就太可惜了。"

"我真有那么神奇吗？"稻草人问道。

"你非同寻常。"格琳达回答说。

然后她转向铁皮人，问道："等多萝茜离开这个国家之后，你会怎么样呢？"

铁皮人靠在他的斧头上，沉思了一会儿，然后他说：

"温基人对我非常亲切，恶女巫死了之后，他们就想让我去领导他们。我也喜欢温基人，如果我能够回到西方，我想我会永

could get back again to the Country of the West, I should like nothing better than to rule over them forever."

"My second command to the Winged Monkeys," said Glinda "will be that they carry you safely to the land of the Winkies. Your brain may not be so large to look at as those of the Scarecrow, but you are really brighter than he is – when you are well polished – and I am sure you will rule the Winkies wisely and well."

Then the Witch looked at the big, shaggy Lion and asked,

"When Dorothy has returned to her own home, what will become of you?"

"Over the hill of the Hammer-Heads," he answered, "lies a grand old forest, and all the beasts that live there have made me their King. If I could only get back to this forest, I would pass my life very happily there."

"My third command to the Winged Monkeys," said Glinda, "shall be to carry you to your forest. Then, having used up the powers of the Golden Cap, I shall give it to the King of the Monkeys, that he and his band may thereafter be free for evermore."

The Scarecrow and the Tin Woodman and the Lion now thanked the Good Witch earnestly for her kindness; and Dorothy exclaimed:

"You are certainly as good as you are beautiful! But you have not yet told me how to get back to Kansas."

"Your Silver Shoes will carry you over the desert," replied Glinda. "If you had known their power you could have gone back to your Aunt Em the very first day you came to this country."

远领导他们的。"

"那我对飞猴的第二个命令就是让它们把你安全地带到温基国去。"格琳达说,"你的脑袋看起来可能没有稻草人那么大,但是只要你把自己擦亮了,你就会比他聪明了,我想你肯定会英明地领导温基人的。"

然后,女巫又看着那只庞大、多毛的狮子,问道:

"等多萝茜回到她自己的家乡之后,你会怎么样?"

"在大头人占领的山坡的另一边,"它回答说,"有一片非常古老的森林,住在那里的所有野兽都尊我为大王。如果我能回到那片森林,我会在那里非常幸福地度过我的一生。"

"那我对飞猴们的第三个命令就是把你带回到森林里去。"格琳达说,"在用完这顶金帽子的魔力之后,我会把它还给猴王,从此之后,它和它的随从们就永远自由了。"

这时候,稻草人、铁皮人和狮子真诚地感谢着善良女巫的仁慈。多萝茜喊道:

"你的心就像你的容颜那么漂亮善良!可是你还没告诉我要如何回到堪萨斯州呢。"

"你脚上那双银鞋可以带你穿过沙漠,"格琳达回答说,"如果你知道它们的魔力,在你来到这片国度的第一天,你就可以回到你艾姆婶婶的身边了。"

"可这样我就不会有这神奇的脑子了!"稻草人叫喊道,"我

"But then I should not have had my wonderful brains!" cried the Scarecrow. "I might have passed my whole life in the farmer's cornfield."

"And I should not have had my lovely heart," said the Tin Woodman. "I might have stood and rusted in the forest till the end of the world."

"And I should have lived a coward forever," declared the Lion, "and no beast in all the forest would have had a good word to say to me."

"This is all true," said Dorothy, "and I am glad I was of use to these good friends. But now that each of them has had what he most desired, and each is happy in having a kingdom to rule besides, I think I should like to go back to Kansas."

"The Silver Shoes," said the Good Witch, "have wonderful powers. And one of the most curious things about them is that they can carry you to any place in the world in three steps, and each step will be made in the wink of an eye. All you have to do is to knock the heels together three times and command the shoes to carry you wherever you wish to go."

"If that is so," said the child joyfully, "I will ask them to carry me back to Kansas at once."

She threw her arms around the Lion's neck and kissed him, patting his big head tenderly. Then she kissed the Tin Woodman, who was weeping in a way most dangerous to his joints. But she hugged the soft, stuffed body of the Scarecrow in her arms instead of kissing his

可能要在农民的稻田里度过我的一生。"

"我也不会有我这颗可爱的心了，"铁皮人说，"我可能会生锈地站在森林中，直到世界末日。"

"而我就要永远胆小地生活了，"狮子说，"在所有的森林中，没有一只野兽会对我说一句好话。"

"你们说的这些都没错，"多萝茜说，"我很高兴能对这些好朋友产生点作用。但是现在，他们每个人都实现了自己最大的愿望，领导着一个国家，幸福地生活着，我想我应该回堪萨斯州了。"

"这双银鞋具有神奇的魔力。"善良的女巫说道，"其中一个最最神奇的魔力就是可以在 3 步之内，带你去这个世界上的任何地方，每一步都只需一眨眼的工夫。你只需要碰 3 次后脚跟，然后就能命令这双鞋子带你去你想要去的任何地方了。"

"如果这是真的，"小女孩兴高采烈地说道，"我立刻就让它们带我回到堪萨斯州。"

她伸出双手，抱住狮子的脖子，亲了它一下，温柔地拍了拍它那硕大的脑袋，然后她又亲吻了一下铁皮人，他流着眼泪，这对他的关节来说太危险了。不过，她没有亲吻稻草人那张画出来的脸，而是拥抱着他那塞着稻草的柔软的身子。跟自己亲爱的朋友们告别，这让多萝茜伤心地哭了起来。

格琳达从她那红宝石王座上走了下来，亲吻着这个小女孩，跟她告别。多萝茜感谢着她的善心，多谢她接见了自己以及这些

painted face, and found she was crying herself at this sorrowful parting from her loving comrades.

Glinda the Good stepped down from her ruby throne to give the little girl a good-bye kiss, and Dorothy thanked her for all the kindness she had shown to her friends and herself.

Dorothy now took Toto up solemnly in her arms, and having said one last good-bye she clapped the heels of her shoes together three times, saying:

"Take me home to Aunt Em!"

Instantly she was whirling through the air, so swiftly that all she could see or feel was the wind whistling past her ears.

The Silver Shoes took but three steps, and then she stopped so suddenly that she rolled over upon the grass several times before she knew where she was.

At length, however, she sat up and looked about her.

"Good gracious!" she cried.

For she was sitting on the broad Kansas prairie, and just before her was the new farmhouse Uncle Henry built after the cyclone had carried away the old one. Uncle Henry was milking the cows in the barnyard, and Toto had jumped out of her arms and was running toward the barn, barking joyously.

Dorothy stood up and found she was in her stocking-feet. For the Silver Shoes had fallen off in her flight through the air, and were lost forever in the desert.

朋友们。

这时候，多萝茜郑重其事地抱起托托，最后说了一声再会，然后连续敲了3次鞋跟，说：

"带我回家，回到艾姆婶婶的身边！"

瞬间，她就被卷到了空中，速度如此之快，她所能看到或感受到的就只有大风吹过耳畔的呼啸声。

这双银鞋只不过走了3步，多萝茜就突然停了下来，她在草地上打了好几个滚之后，才知道自己落在了什么地方。

最后，她终于坐了起来，看了看自己的周围。

"天哪！"她叫喊了起来。

因为她已经坐在了堪萨斯州的大草原上，在她面前的就是一座新农舍，在龙卷风刮走那座旧农舍之后，亨利叔叔就造了一座新的。亨利叔叔正在农场谷仓周围的空地上挤着牛奶。托托已经从她的怀抱中跳了出去，欢快地吠着，跑向了那个谷仓。

多萝茜站了起来，发现自己的脚上只穿了一双袜子。因为当她在空中飞行时，那双银鞋就掉了，永远遗失在了沙漠之中。

24. Home Again

Aunt Em had just come out of the house to water the cabbages when she looked up and saw Dorothy running toward her.

"My darling child!" she cried, folding the little girl in her arms and covering her face with kisses. "Where in the world did you come from?"

"From the Land of Oz," said Dorothy gravely. "And here is Toto, too. And oh, Aunt Em! I'm so glad to be at home again!"

(THE END)

二十四.回家了

艾姆婶婶刚好从屋子里走出来，给卷心菜浇水，她抬起头来，却看见多萝茜正朝她跑来。

"我亲爱的孩子！"艾姆婶婶一边叫着，一边把这个小女孩抱在怀里，亲吻着她的脸蛋，"你究竟去哪儿了！"

"我去奥兹国了，还有托托也是，啊，艾姆婶婶，我又在家里了，真高兴呀！"

（完）

欢迎来到奥兹世界

奥兹国（Land of Oz）又称为奥兹仙境，是弗兰克·鲍姆在他的小说《绿野仙踪》（*The Wonderful Wizard of Oz*）中描述的一个国度——他一共写了 14 本书讲述奥兹国的故事。鲍姆去世后，Ruth Plumly Thompson 接着写了很多奥兹国系列故事，再加上其他作家的 7 本奥兹国的故事，形成著名的"Famous Forty"，这些都被视为 Oz 的经典原版。

那么，奥兹国到底在哪里呢？

据鲍姆说，奥兹国在一个很大很大的沙漠里，那里的人与外界隔绝——所以奥兹国像桃花源一样难以找到。奥兹国有一位君主，他统治着一个首都和四个主要国家。

奥兹国的国土大致为长方形，以对角线切割成四个主要国家。东边是 Munchkin Country，西边是 Winkie Country，北边 Gillikin Country，南边是 Quadling Country，中央交界处是奥兹的首都翡翠城（Emerald City）。

1914 年出版的《奥兹国的嘀嗒机器人》（*Tik-Tok of Oz*）中，奥兹地图将西方画在右边，东方在左边，北方仍在上，南方在下。瞧，这就是奥兹国的地图：

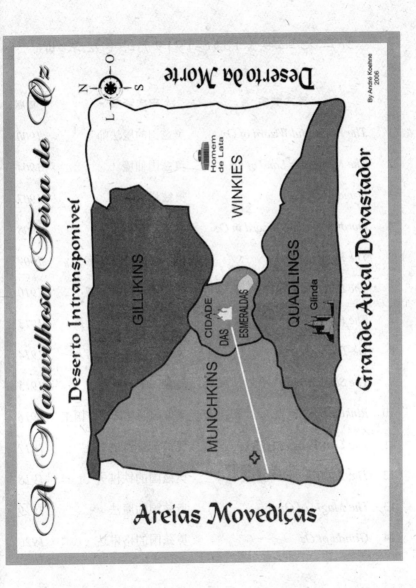

弗兰克·鲍姆（1856~1919）的 Oz 系列

英文书名	中文译名	首版
1 *The Wonderful Wizard of Oz*	奥兹国的魔法师	*1900*
2 *The Marvelous Land of Oz*	奥兹国仙境	*1904*
3 *Ozma of Oz*	奥兹玛女王	*1907*
4 *Dorothy and the Wizard in Oz*	桃乐丝与巫师	*1908*
5 *The Road to Oz*	桃乐丝的奇幻之旅	*1909*
6 *The Emerald City of Oz*	矮人王攻打翡翠城	*1910*
7 *The Patchwork Girl of Oz*	奥兹国的拼布偶女孩	*1913*
8 *Tik-Tok of Oz*	奥兹国的嘀嗒机器人	*1914*
9 *The Scarecrow of Oz*	奥兹国的稻草人	*1915*
10 *Rinkitink in Oz*	奥兹国的林奇汀奇国王	*1916*
11 *The Lost Princess of Oz*	奥兹国失踪的公主	*1917*
12 *The Tin Woodman of Oz*	奥兹国的铁樵夫	*1918*
13 *The Magic of Oz*	奥兹国的魔法	*1919*
14 *Glinda of Oz*	奥兹国的格琳达	*1920*